DECLAN - HEART OF A TIGER

ROYAL TAIGA STREAK BOOK ONE

J.R. LOVELESS

1

SEAN

The sound of the basement door opening caused Sean to stiffen and his breath to catch at the sound of a small voice crying out to be, "Let go!"

"Shut up!" His father's harsh voice snapped and then the wooden stairs shook with his heavy boots as he clamored down, carrying a boy of about six over his shoulders who struggled and beat his fists at his broad back.

The boy landed in a heap in front of Sean, but he didn't stay there long. He jumped to his feet and attempted to rush to the stairs, desperate to escape. Sean's father backhanded him, sending him flying into Sean, who caught him with thin arms and a rattle of chains. Sean winced at the hard impact of fist against flesh and hoped nothing had been broken, but knew it wouldn't take long for any injuries to heal at least. The boy whimpered, but remained there in Sean's arms this time instead of attempting to get up again.

When Sean saw his father looking around the basement and heard the sound of Tara's and Samantha's sobs, Sean wanted to cry along with them, knowing his father would be relentless in his passions that night. He always was after a successful kidnapping. Dark brown eyes settled on Sam, the least pregnant of the two girls at five months along, and the hulking figure of a man unsnapped the keys from his belt, opened her cage, and grabbed hold of her arm, wrenching her out and dragging her, screaming, up the stairs. Sean flinched as the door slammed shut and was locked from the outside. The only thing any of them downstairs could do was listen to Sam's screams as Sean's father brutalized her, a sound Sean had heard more than once over the years, one which would haunt him for the rest of his life, however long that may be.

The younger children whimpered in their cages while Tara sobbed in relief and yet agony for her best friend and companion. They all knew it would be at least an hour or more of pain for Sam before their father would drag her unconscious body back to the basement. Sean couldn't help but wonder if this time would be when she lost the baby. It wouldn't be the first time. This was Sam's third pregnancy, having miscarried the previous two in their first trimester. Though it was a blessing in the disguise of death for the babies, as terrible as the thought may sound, because an innocent didn't deserve to be born in the hell they called life. Sean worried about Sam's mental health after the second one, but even more so now that she was pregnant with the third one and so far along this time.

Sean brushed the hair out of the face of the young boy he held and gave him a tremulous, but hopefully encouraging smile. "Are you all right?"

The boy glared, a bruise growing on his cheek. "Where am I? Who are you?"

Sean could see the spirit in the young shifter he held, eyes glowing bright in the dull lighting. Yes, every single one of the seven occupants of the dingy, dark basement were shapeshifters of some kind or another. Tara, a white wolf, sixteen, had been taken from her family at the age of eight. Samantha, shortened to Sam, a beautiful lynx, now fifteen had joined both Sean and Tara in their nightmare when she was seven. They'd been there the longest. The twins, Fredrick and Tomas, both liger shifters, were nine. The other female, Vicky, another lynx, was eight. His father had blessedly left her alone so far, but he knew it wouldn't be for long. He'd started eyeing Vicky already. Sean hoped to find some way to get her out before it could happen, although how, he didn't know. She never spoke a word to anyone, too frightened since the day his father beat her so badly for shifting when expressly forbidden.

Sean... he was the oldest at twenty-one. He had no idea what kind of shifter he was. His father had never allowed him to shift and never told him what he was. Since he could remember, he'd worn a collar, something enchanted by some form of magic. It was locked in place by a spell which grew with age and size as Sean did, preventing him from shifting. The thing wouldn't budge, no matter what he tried to remove it with. A few times Carl had placed a similar collar on a couple of the cubs he'd abducted, but something happened to them over the course of several months and they wasted away to nothing. Eventually, Carl stopped trying to prevent the others from shifting with a collar and just used threats and beatings to prevent them.

He'd once made the mistake of asking what he was, one he'd paid for dearly with fresh bruises, broken bones, and a scar over his left eye, a wound which had nearly taken his eyesight. Since then, he'd never broached the subject. The only things he knew of his mother were the awful words his father called her when drunk. Sean had no memory of her and knew she'd either died or left before he could remember. He liked to fantasize that she'd been a beautiful woman, a woman with a kind heart who'd passed away, because there was no way she'd have left him behind to remain with a man the likes of Carl McNeely.

There'd been others, ones who'd disappeared over the years, ones who hadn't been "good little boys and girls". Sean shuddered as he remembered the ones who hadn't made it through his father's beatings and sexual assaults. He'd been the unlucky one to bury their bodies out behind the house whenever one didn't make it. He tried to help the others, to keep them from angering his father, taught them how to stay out of Carl's way, to do the right things and complete their chores without mishap. The ones who struggled the most were the youngest cubs. They didn't tend to have the coordination of the older shifters. Whenever one of them made a mistake, Sean took the heat, claiming the mess as his own. On the days he could walk, he walked with a limp, a bone never set properly after a particularly bad beating. Oh, he healed faster than a human, but being unable to shift, he couldn't draw on his inner animal to heal himself and it still took days to heal something which would only take minutes or hours if he were able to take on his animal form. Thankfully, the bruise on the newest addition's cheek would heal quickly once the boy shifted.

"My name is Sean and... this... this..." How did he answer where they were? They were in his father's house, prison, hell. Gods, what did he call it? "What's your name?" he asked instead of answering the other question.

"Ronnie." Ronnie stood and looked around, shivering at the cages, and he scented the air. "You're all shifters, too. What does he want with us?"

"My father-"

"Your father!" Ronnie squawked, spinning around to gape at Sean. "That bastard's your father?"

Sean couldn't quite keep the corner of his mouth from curving up. Somehow he figured Ronnie's parents wouldn't approve of the boy's language. "My father doesn't like shifters."

Ronnie raised a brow, crossing his slender arms over his chest. Sean tried to guess what kind of shifter Ronnie was. He'd learned no two kinds of shifters smelled alike and Ronnie didn't smell the same as any of the others who'd come through the house before. Dark brown hair with light eyes, Ronnie didn't stand but around waist high on Sean, who was five foot eleven. "Where did you come from then?"

Sean shrugged a slender shoulder. "I've never really known the answer to that."

"How long have you all been down here? I can smell the forest outside, we're still in my streak's area. I know it."

None of the others spoke, fearful Sean's father would return, and they always allowed Sean to explain the way of their world to the new arrivals. Sean sighed into the waning light and drew his knees to his chest, the clothing he wore was dirty and tattered, the jeans barely enough to be called that while the shirt, several sizes too big or perhaps just from his being half-starved, hung off his shoulders, moth-eaten in multiple places. "Some of us a couple of years, others longer."

"You've never tried to escape?" Ronnie demanded, mouth turned down at the corners, eyes roaming the room for possible exits.

Sean didn't really know how to answer the question without scaring the boy. Others had tried. The ones who'd been semi-successful were buried in the backyard. "The house... it's in a place where there are no neighbors. No one to hear anything or see anything. Father... Father chose this place on purpose. He doesn't allow any of us out of the house. Those of us he allows upstairs are always kept on chains."

"You still should have tried! There has to be a way to get out."

Sean shook his head. "If one of us escaped, the others would be punished for it. Besides, where would we go?"

"The police! Or my streak!"

"Would they believe us? How would we survive?" Sean asked.

"My Alpha would believe you! He'd care for you. I know he would!" Ronnie jammed his hands on his hips. "He's my uncle."

Sean didn't really know too much about packs or prides or streaks having grown up in the basement for most of his life. He'd learned a little about the hierarchy system and some of their rules from the older cubs taken over the years and knew Alphas were tough, could be mean when necessary, and they were usually strong. They protected their own when threatened. Sean wondered if Carl knew he'd taken an Alpha's nephew. The man would be looking for Ronnie. It gave Sean some hope. Maybe the others could get out finally, could be rescued. He glanced up at the bars on the small window. Maybe... before his father could put Ronnie in a cage... "Ronnie, what kind of shifter are you?"

"Can't you tell?" Ronnie asked, frowning.

"No," Sean replied.

Ronnie rolled his eyes, snorting as though Sean were stupid. "I'm a tiger," he said proudly.

A strange tightness spread across Sean's chest and he rubbed at the skin over his heart, wondering at the odd reaction. "See those bars? Do you think in your tiger form you can fit through them?" Sean asked after a few moments, standing, his chains rattling.

None of the others were allowed freedom, in the loosest sense of the word, of course. They were all kept in various sized cages. Sean was the only one allowed to remain in chains, to provide and care for the others when they needed something or after one of his father's "treatments". He figured his father felt safe enough leaving him in chains since Sean really had nowhere else to go even if he did get loose. Plus Carl knew Sean would never leave without the others.

Ronnie studied the bars for a moment and then nodded. "I think so."

"If you can get out, you can get help for the others. Bring some of your streak to help them. Do you think you can remember your way back here?"

"Yes, I can do it," Ronnie said, nodding his head with purpose. He removed his clothing, closed his eyes, and shifted.

Sean smiled and reached down to scratch behind the small tiger cub's ears. The bright orange with black striped fur left his chest tight with some undefined emotion. The sight of those stripes left a niggling feeling at the back of his mind, like a memory dying to be set free, but not quite there, as though it couldn't get out of the chains in his mind, much like the chains around his wrists and ankles. He pulled up the window, propping it open, and then bent down to pick up Ronnie, lifting him to the bars. At first, he didn't think Ronnie would fit, but the boy managed to squirm through, a small yowl of triumph making Sean smile. Ronnie butted his head against the hand Sean stuck through the bars. "Please, hurry," Sean whispered.

Ronnie yowled quietly in answer and turned, loping into the trees. Sean watched for a moment before closing the window and sinking back to the floor, waiting for his father to return, knowing he wouldn't survive the night. Helping Ronnie escape was most likely the last thing he'd ever do, but it would be worth his life if it would set the others free from the horror known as Carl McNeely.

"You shouldn't have done that," Tomas told him the moment he'd closed the window.

Sean smiled sadly and lifted one shoulder in a small shrug.

"He'll kill you this time for sure!" Fredrick whispered frantically.

"Maybe," Sean replied, uncaring. "But at least you'll all be free, and I'll no longer have to live like this."

"Sean, no!" Tara gasped, pressing close to the bars. Most of them were clothed in the barest of items, things Sean had managed to sew together from scraps his father had thrown away. He'd been beaten on more than one occasion for daring to steal, even from the garbage, but they needed something to try and keep out the cold. "We need you!" she cried.

Sean reached out and gripped her hand, rubbing his cheek with it. "You'll be fine. Ronnie's alpha will take care of you. You won't need me anymore."

"We'll always need you," Tara sniffled. "You're family."

Fredrick and Tomas agreed. Vicky nodded fiercely to which Sean smiled, humbled and heart hurting. "What matters is getting you all out of here, back to your real families. I have no family to go home to. Carl... I have nothing outside of these walls."

"You can stay with us," Tara growled. "Besides, who knows what any of us have to go home to. After all, we have no idea how our families have changed or if they'll even want us anymore."

"They'll want you," Sean said quietly, reaching up to stroke her dirty cheek. "They've missed you. I'm sure of it."

Sean knew his father would be beyond furious the moment he discovered Ronnie's disappearance, but he remained hopeful it wouldn't be until Ronnie had gotten far enough way to not be recaptured. The gods must have been listening because it wasn't for at least another two hours before Carl dragged Sam back downstairs and shoved her, almost unconscious back into her cage. Sean winced at the sight of the blood on her face and inner thighs, wondering what they'd done to deserve the hell they'd all been living through for so long.

"Where's the runt?" Carl barked, dragging his gaze around the room, eyes narrowing as he realized the newest shifter was gone.

Steeling his nerves, Sean raised his head and calmly replied, "I let him go."

Carl swung around. "You did what?" he snarled, stomping toward Sean and backhanding him.

Sean's head hit the wall, hard, and his ears started to ring, covering whatever else his father began spewing as the fists began flying. The sound of his own bones breaking were loud in his head, but the most painful part wasn't his wrist snapping or his clavicle fracturing, it was the jagged edge of a rib bone, caused by another brutal kick from his father's boot, piercing his heart. Sean screamed in agony, blackness, blessed darkness, loomed before him as he fell swiftly toward unconsciousness. The last thing he heard before it swallowed him whole was a roar thunderous enough to rock the foundation of the place he'd called home his entire life.

2

DECLAN

Alpha Declan Page paced his living room floor, running a hand through his dark blond hair. "We need to find him," he growled.

"We are looking everywhere, Alpha," Victor, his beta, soothed from the doorway, knowing better than to get in his alpha's way.

Declan looked at his sister Rose. She stood near the window, face wet with tears, eyes haunted. They and other surrounding packs had suffered through similar disappearances over the years. None of the children had ever been recovered. He prayed they would find Ronnie. His sister wouldn't survive losing her child, not after having lost her mate only a year ago in a car accident. He crossed to the window and dragged her into his arms, holding her tightly. A sob broke free and she shuddered. "I can't lose him, too, Dec."

"I know, Rose. We'll find him. I know we will. Is there anything else you can remember?"

"No. One minute he was there and the next gone. I turned my back for two seconds, Dec. Two seconds! I'm a horrible mother."

"Stop it, Rose. You are not." Declan stroked her hair and pressed a kiss to her forehead. "Did you notice anyone watching you? Following you?"

"No. I stopped to talk to Brigette from the flower shop for a second. He'd been playing a game on his handheld computer thingy."

Declan couldn't help but smile. She'd never been very good with technology. Declan remembered buying Ronnie the Nintendo DS as a gift a couple of Christmases ago. "Okay. What else?"

"When I looked back, the game was on the ground and he was gone!" she wailed, crying even harder into his broad chest.

He rubbed his hands in circles on her back, teeth clenched so hard they could have shattered. He would gut whoever had taken his nephew. "Shh, shh. It's going to be okay, honey. Michael is asking the businesses in the area for security video footage to see if we can find anything that way. I'm sure they must have picked up something."

Rose sniffled and nodded, but her shoulders still shook. Ronnie had been missing for eight hours, seemingly a life time to a distraught mother, Declan knew. One of the streak enforcers, Michael, had tried to locate a scent, but the trail went cold in an alley, meaning the son of a bitch had taken Ronnie to some form of vehicle and driven from there. Ronnie was smart. If the boy had a chance to get away, he would, but the knowledge of just how many shifter children had gone missing in the last so many years caused sweat to break out over Declan's brow and a chill to race down his spine. None of those children had ever been found again.

The thought didn't have the chance to become a litany of nightmarish ideas of the boy being hurt or worse when a cry went up outside, far into the forest, and another, alerting the nearby streak members something, or someone, had been found. The cacophony of sounds were good, noises of joy getting closer to the house, meaning Ronnie had been found. Rose started crying again, tears of happiness this time, and Declan couldn't stop a smile from breaking across his tanned features, grateful the gods had been listening this time. Rose raced to open the front door, meeting Ronnie at the top of the porch steps with open arms, Declan just behind her.

"Mama, Mama!" Ronnie cried, shifting midstride, throwing his skinny arms around her neck. "Uncle Declan!"

Declan caught a whiff of Ronnie's scent mingled with another and suddenly froze, eyes dilating and fangs dropping. "Mine!" he snarled. Fur sprouted along his forearms and his hands half-shifted, fingers becoming claws. Mint and fresh earth tantalized his tiger, sending spirals of lust straight to his cock. Declan growled, his entire body vibrating with the sound.

Rose startled, cradling Ronnie close. "What the hell, Dec?"

It took all of Declan's alpha strength to rein in his instincts to tear through the forest to find the source of the scent clinging to Ronnie. He knew without a single shred of doubt the smell on Ronnie's skin belonged to his mate, the one person he'd been waiting for his entire life, the one person he wanted more than anything. His blood sang with joy while his body rose to the occasion.

"Uncle Declan, you have to help them! Please! You have to help Sean and the others!" Ronnie tore free from his mother and rushed to Declan's side, grabbing his uncle's hand and tugging. "Please, hurry!"

Declan dropped to one knee in front of Ronnie, ignoring his tiger spirit demanding he forget all reason and listen to the boy. "Slow down, Ronnie. What happened to you? Tell me, who is Sean?"

Ronnie scowled, his usual spunk showing through the panic and fear. "Some bastard-"

"Ronnie!" Rose admonished.

"-grabbed me while I was playing my game. He took me to this really creepy place out in the forest where there's all these shifter kids in cages. Sean helped me get away. He's really nice, Uncle Dec. We have to help them. Please."

Declan's heart beat fiercely against his ribcage. His mate was in trouble. "Do you think you can show me where?"

Ronnie furiously nodded his head. "I marked the trees on the way, Uncle Dec. Like you showed me. We have to go right now though! I think-I think he's going to do something bad to Sean for helping me. He-he was hurting one of the girls when I got out."

Declan wanted to race off into the forest, to find the son of a bitch hurting his mate and grind the fucker into the ground, but he knew he couldn't handle the situation alone. "We need to get a few members of the streak, Ronnie."

"We have to go right now. It may already be too late. It took me a lot longer to get here than I thought it would," Ronnie muttered ashamed. "The sun wasn't all the way down when I left."

Heart stuttering, Declan calculated the two or three hours the sun had been down and clenched his jaw. "All right. Rose, tell Michael to gather some of the enforcers and follow after us. I'll take Victor with us."

"Do you really need Ronnie to go if he marked the path?" Rose asked, clinging to her son's shoulders.

"Mom!" Ronnie protested, twisting around to glare up at her. "I'm not a baby anymore. I need to go. They know me. They won't know Uncle Dec or the others!"

"He's right, Rose. I promise to bring him back in one piece." Declan glanced down at Ronnie. "Why don't you go inside and grab Victor?"

Ronnie gave a serious nod and went into the house.

Declan pinned Rose in place with a serious stare. "My mate is one of them, Rose."

Rose gasped, her eyes going wide. "Are you sure?"

"Yes. I can smell him all over Ronnie. I'm fairly certain it's the one who helped him escape, the one named Sean." The knowledge that his mate was kind and cared for others caused his heart to swell, but it only made sense of course. The fates wouldn't pair him, an alpha, with anyone other than a suitable match, someone to compliment who he was and what he stood for. Declan smiled slightly. "I finally found him."

Rose gripped his forearm. "Then go. Hurry, Dec. But be safe."

"I will. Don't worry. I'll bring Ronnie home, sis."

"You better," she growled at him.

Declan kissed her temple, shed his clothing, and shifted the moment his nephew and Victor exited the front door. He impatiently waited as they followed suit and then the three of them were off, running into the forest. The scent of Ronnie on the trees leading south of the streak's grounds was strong and Declan outran the other two, his large paws eating up the distance between him and his mate. When a house appeared, where the smell of his mate slammed into his entire being, Declan almost growled to the heavens, but it was the muffled sound of screams coming from somewhere within the house that wrenched an earth-shaking roar from him.

Racing up the stairs of the porch, he broke through the front door as if it were made of toothpicks, wooden splinters raining down around him. The precious seconds it took for him to follow the noises of fists connecting with flesh and bones snapping under a boot felt like hours. Declan found the basement and practically flew down the stairs. A man, hulking and muscular, stood over the prone form of Declan's young mate, screaming at him. "You stupid, good for nothing, excuse for a son! You're nothing but a whore's cast off. You hear me!"

Declan could barely hear his mate's heart. With a mighty roar, one which shook the house on its very foundation, sending plaster and loose dirt raining down on top of the occupants of that sad little room, he launched himself at the son of a bitch. He aimed for the man's jugular, intending on ending it quickly. The man swung around, eyes widening in horror at the sight of a full grown tiger coming at him, too frightened to move out of the way in time, or too drunk from what Declan could smell. Declan hit the man going full speed, slamming him into the wall and bringing him down with deadly accuracy, his powerful teeth sinking in and wrenching away the meaty part of the fucker's throat.

He didn't take the time to savor watching the bastard die, instead shifting and rushing to his mate's side. Sean was barely breathing. Declan gingerly lifted him into his arms, wincing when Sean moaned. "Don't you dare die on me," Declan begged, soft and broken, eyes tearing up. There was too much blood saturating Sean's hair for Declan to tell the true color, and his fingers were immediately coated with it, bright red against the pale white of his mate's skin. "Not after I just found you, damn it!"

Victor and Ronnie clamored down the stairs right then, coming to a halt when they saw what lay before them. Victor shifted and crouched beside him, placing one hand on Declan's shoulders. "I'm so sorry, Alpha."

Declan growled, fangs flashing at Victor, who immediately backed away. "No. NO! He will not die! Not now!"

The last came out almost unintelligible, a part of his animal breaking through. Declan rocked Sean, holding him as close to his chest as possible, his heart breaking as Sean's arms hung limply, one at an odd angle, clearly broken. If the bastard wasn't already dead, he'd kill him all over again for daring to hurt such a fragile being. Sean's lungs were laboring and Declan could hear Sean's heart stuttering, a broken rib bone most likely having pierced it. There were others crying nearby, a female sobbed Sean's name, but Declan didn't pay attention to any of it. His entire focus remained on the man in his arms, praying for a way to save his mate. He barely registered the sounds of the other shifters being released and urged upstairs by his beta.

"Alpha," Victor began hesitantly, clearly reluctant to face Declan's wrath once more, "there ma-may be a way."

"How?" Declan demanded, swinging a deadly glare around at Victor.

"It's risky, Alpha."

"I don't care!" Declan roared.

Victor visibly swallowed. "If you were to share your life force with him, Alpha..."

Declan knew sharing his life force with Sean would tie them together irrevocably. If one of them died, the other would, too. It wasn't the same as being mated. It would mean if something were to happen to Declan, if some other alpha were to ever challenge him and he were to lose, Sean would die, too. Declan hesitated, but only for a breath of a second, and then he struck, sinking his teeth into the junction of Sean's shoulder and neck, drinking only long enough to get the taste of his mate's blood, one which set his body on fire and his cock swelling beneath the gentle curve of Sean's backside. He broke free, gasping, and allowed one claw free to slice at the same juncture on his own body.

Lifting Sean, he forced Sean's mouth against the cut. "Drink, baby," he murmured, "drink."

At first, he worried Sean would not be able to do so in his unconscious state, but his animal side must have sensed the importance of the moment for Sean's mouth latched onto his shoulder and began sucking, drawing weakly, but enough to imbibe the necessary blood. Under the guidance of his long dead ancestors, Declan closed his eyes and chanted the words to bind their life force as one. "Hear my words, hear my cry, take my soul and split asunder. Half remains, half be gone, two halves as one, until one is no longer."

Declan felt something rip inside of himself and bit back a cry, hands tightening momentarily on his mate's broken body. He slumped over Sean slightly and breathed, deep and even, trying to get a hold of himself. He could never regret what he'd just done, but something felt different, and he didn't feel right inside his skin, his tiger prowled beneath his human form, yowling unhappily. One thing he did notice, Sean's heartbeat had grown stronger and his lungs were no longer labored. Declan smiled, sweat running down his face. He brushed the blood-soaked hair back from Sean's face and pressed a kiss to Sean's forehead. His mate would survive.

Victor sighed. "Alpha."

Declan shook his head. "It's done."

"You know you can never tell anyone. Not even him."

"I know."

"Alpha-"

"Enough. It's done, Victor. Now please... go back upstairs and wait for the others to arrive. We'll transport the cubs back to the compound and decide what to do about them there."

Victor bowed his head. "As you wish, Alpha."

When Declan lifted Sean's still laboring, but recovering, body from the floor and ascended the stairs, Ronnie approached him cautiously. "I-is Sean going to be okay, Uncle Dec?"

"Yes, Ronnie, Sean is going to be okay," Declan replied, smiling at his nephew and holding his mate as gently as he could.

3

SEAN

Sean felt like he was floating, enveloped in warmth and softness, as though on a giant cloud. Death had claimed him and he rode along on a fog of happiness. Until he moved and pain slid along his nerves. Sean's good eye flew open, the other swollen shut from the severe beating, and he gasped, loud and sharp into the stillness. When he could breathe again, he found himself lying in the middle of a huge four poster bed surrounded by plush white pillows and covered by a stark white down comforter. Panic set in. Where was he? Where were the others? Sean struggled to sit up, sweat popping out along his forehead and upper lip as his body protested the movements.

Shh, lay still, love. Everyone is fine. If you keep moving around like that, you'll hurt yourself further. Shock held Sean immobile. What the hell... no... *who* the hell was that? The door of the bedroom Sean lay in opened and Sean's eyes widened, his breath catching. At first, he couldn't make out the features of the man standing there, but the sheer size reminded him of his father and he thought Carl had returned to finish the job.

Sean bit back a whimper and once more attempted to get away.

A whispered oath came from the doorway and then warm, strong hands gripped Sean's shoulders. "Stay still, Sean. No one here will hurt you. I promise."

The voice, the hands, they didn't belong to his father. Sean stilled and blinked up into the face, the gorgeous face, of a man who definitely wasn't Carl. Golden blond hair hung down around the man's features, jagged, but neatly so. Sean's fingers itched to stroke them and he gripped the sheets to keep from doing so. Strong, high cheekbones gave the stranger a regal, almost royal look, and reminded Sean of a prince he'd once caught a glimpse of on television in the rare times he'd been allowed upstairs while his father had been watching the news. Full lips were firm above a slightly cleft chin and as Sean's gaze dipped lower, he realized the man wore only a white tank top which barely covered the man's very tan, very muscular body. He noted an image of a tiger on the man's bicep before jerking his stare back to the man's face once more.

Heat trickled through Sean, along his nerve endings and deep down into his groin, causing a surprising and embarrassing reaction, one Sean knew what it meant, but he'd never had such a reaction to another person. A blush spread over his cheeks and he thought he saw mirth dance through light hazel eyes flecked with gold before being buried beneath concern and sympathy. "Wh-Who are you?" Sean whispered.

The stranger released him and stepped back, flexing his fingers slightly. "I am Declan Page, alpha of the Royal Taiga Streak. I believe you are the one who saved my nephew Ronnie."

Sean immediately became more alert and fired off several

questions. "Is he all right? Where are the others? Tara? Sam? Vicky? Fredrick and Tomas?"

Declan chuckled and hooked his foot around the leg of a chair nearby, dragging it closer to sit. "Ronnie is perfectly fine. He's resilient, my nephew. The others are as okay as can be expected. Samantha, Tara, and Vicky are downstairs with my sister Rose. Fredrick and Tomas are actually with their family now. Their parents are part of my streak. They want to thank you for taking care of them as soon as you are well."

Sean couldn't believe it. They'd found Fredrick and Tomas's home, too. Tears stung Sean's eyes and he rubbed at them with one hand, the one not with the wrist in a cast. That was when he noticed he wasn't as badly broken as he'd anticipated. Frowning, he looked at Declan. "What happened? How am I still alive?"

Declan glanced away, not meeting Sean's gaze.

"Please tell me, sir. What happened to my-my father?" He stumbled over the words. He figured he already knew the answer, but needed to hear it out loud.

Declan's mouth firmed and Sean noticed the way Declan's fingers tightened on the handles of the chair until they were white. "He's dead."

Sean figured his father had to be. It was the only way he'd have let any of them get away. A ghost of a sad smile flitted over Sean's lips. "I see."

The world would not mourn the loss of a man like Carl McNeely. Sean couldn't bring himself to feel anything about the death of his father other than numbness. "May I see Sam and the others? Please?"

"Of course. You don't need to ask, but don't move from this bed. Your injuries were quite severe and you are still healing. I think it would be a good idea for you to shift as soon as you are able." Declan stood. "Then we will see about removing that collar. I attempted to remove it, but there is no clasp and nothing would cut through it. I've never seen such a device before."

Sean reached up to touch the collar, not bothering to tell Declan he didn't even know if he could shift. He'd never done it, and wasn't even sure if his animal half could be called on after never having shifted. Over the years, he'd dreamt of running through tall grasses, forests, and trees, but always through the eyes of his beast, never able to see what his spirit half was. "I don't know if that is possible, sir."

Declan surprised him when he suddenly pressed close to him, mouth so close to his own, both hands shoved deep into the pillow on either side of his head. "Declan."

"I'm sorry?" Sean pulled back a bit, mouth parted on a sharp intake of air. His heart beat fast and furious at his ribcage, a nervous fluttering of wings.

"My name is Declan, never sir. Not to you. Declan or Dec."

The man's breath whispered over Sean's lips, sending the same spiraling heat down to Sean's belly and he swallowed hard. "O-Okay."

"Say it," Declan growled.

"D-Declan," Sean murmured, licking his suddenly dry lips.

Declan rumbled low in his throat, muttered something too low for Sean to understand, and wrenched away, storming out of the room. Sean stared after him wide-eyed. What had he done to upset the man? Had he gone from one bad situation to another? Was this Alpha Declan as unpredictable as his father had been? The idea left a sour taste in his mouth and Sean's stomach twisted in his belly. Sean rubbed at the area with his uninjured arm.

He wondered how long he'd been unconscious as he took stock of his body. A cast encased his wrist while he was bruised in many other places and a swathing of bandages around his chest, but he could have sworn his father had broken his arm and at least one leg. He'd never healed so fast before. How was it possible he wasn't in an entire body cast practically? For that matter, he shouldn't even have been alive. His bladder chose that moment to protest, badly, distracting him from thinking about his health condition. Sean spotted an open door leading into an adjoined bathroom and moved gingerly, wincing as his body objected, but his bladder didn't give him the choice of remaining in bed as Declan wanted him to. When his foot met carpeting so soft, so amazingly plush, Sean sighed, envious of anyone living with such luxury after lying on the cold damp cement for almost two decades, then berated himself for having any such thoughts.

Rolling his eyes, he clung to one of the wooden four posters and eyed the distance to the doorway, wondering if he could make it without falling. When his stomach cramped again, Sean knew he had to try or he'd make an even bigger fool of himself. So, taking a deep breath, he let go of the bed and took a tentative step. He let out said breath when, though wobbly, his legs seemed to hold him. Of course, luck wasn't on his side though because he'd only made it half way when Declan returned, scaring the crap out of him, thankfully not literally!

4

DECLAN

"What the hell do you think you're doing?" Declan raged the moment he opened the door and spied Sean on his feet. He'd left to go downstairs to retrieve the girls for his mate, knowing Sean required the familiarity and to assure himself they were indeed all right. But Declan had also needed to put some space between them before he'd done something stupid himself, like kissing Sean before the man was ready to accept him. Declan scowled and stomped into the room, sweeping Sean up into his arms.

Sean squeaked in surprise, gripping Declan's shoulders. Declan ignored the two girls behind him standing in the hallway staring. He started toward the bed with his mate only to stop when Sean shook his head. "I-I need to use the bathroom," Sean mumbled, clearly embarrassed.

Declan grunted. "You should have told me."

Red dusted the thin ridges of Sean's cheekbones, causing tenderness to soften the set line of Declan's mouth, and he turned back toward the bathroom, carefully setting Sean on the top of the toilet seat. "Do you need me to help you?" Declan asked.

"No! Uh... no. I can manage on my own," Sean muttered, not meeting Declan's gaze.

"I'll be right outside if you need me. Call me when you're done."

Sean nodded, still not looking at Declan. Declan exited the bathroom, closing the door, but leaned against the wall just to the left, and waited for Sean to finish. The moment he'd seen the bright sapphire blue of his mate's good eye he'd been fascinated with the color. He could only imagine how beautiful they'd be sparkling with happiness. It was hard to tell just how exquisite Sean was with all the bruising, but Declan just knew Sean would be breathtaking underneath the purples and blues covering his skin. After Declan had managed to rinse the blood from Sean's almost shoulder-length hair the other night, he'd found the strands were a rich mahogany brown, so deep and gorgeous Declan had been unable to keep from running his fingers through the softness every chance he'd gotten. It was crudely cut, as though done with a blunt knife, and considering the state of the basement and the living conditions Sean had been found in, Declan had no doubt they'd had to resort to using one of the kitchen knives to do it.

He heard the toilet flush and the sink run, itching to be the one to help Sean with everything. When he'd seen the condition of Sean's body after they'd arrived back at the pack compound, he'd almost dropped to his knees, his stomach heaving, ready to lose what little content it held. Once removed, the tattered clothing Sean wore revealed countless scars from old beatings and cuts along with fresh bruises, including one the shape of a boot print along the delicate line of Sean's ribcage. The pack doctor had told Declan he was surprised Sean had even survived all these years with how severe most of the beatings appeared to have been. Declan's ears rang with those words, at how close he'd come to never having found his mate, and he swore he'd never allow another being on this earth to cause Sean pain of any kind.

When the door opened, Declan gave Sean a chiding look, but didn't say anything, just picked him up again and brought him to the bed. Sam and Tara edged into the room, obviously eager to see their friend. Sean held out his arms and their gazes flicked to Declan who gave a barely perceptible nod before they rushed over to him, climbing onto the bed. Declan bit back his jealousy when Sean accepted their ginger hugs and kisses with obvious eagerness, Sean smiling widely at seeing them.

"We were so worried, Sean," the one called Sam cried, nuzzling at his neck. Declan clenched his hands into fists, forcing himself to fight the urge to rip her away from his mate.

Sean stroked her hair. "I didn't matter, Sam. All that mattered was getting you guys away from there and safe."

Declan didn't realize the growl he let out at Sean's words until the three of them turned to look at him in surprise. He cleared his throat. "I'll let you three talk. Rose will bring Vicky up in a few moments."

Abruptly departing, Declan stopped outside the room, leaning his head back against the wall and tried to get hold of himself. Hearing Sean dismiss his own life so easily angered Declan. "We like it here, Sean," he heard Tara say.

"Are they treating everyone okay?" Sean asked.

"Yes. It's nice here," Sam replied.

"Is Vicky doing all right?"

"She's as well as can be expected. Rose doesn't understand why she won't talk," Tara murmured.

Sean sighed and Declan heard him move amongst the sheets. "I need to explain to them about Carl. Maybe if they knew how far he's traveled, they could identify your homes. Find your families."

"We don't want to leave you, Sean!" Tara exclaimed.

"You should be with your people," Sean insisted.

"You are our people. We aren't leaving you," Sam snarled.

Declan smiled, hearing the feisty tone in her voice. She seemed to be the fighter of the two girls. How any of the cubs had survived to be anything except a broken shell amazed him, humbled him even. It spoke of their inner strength and made him more determined than ever to help them. For the last two days while Sean had remained unconscious, Declan had attempted to uncover what he could about their situation. The girls hadn't really revealed too many of the details, but they had all been held captive at the hands of Sean's father in the basement, beaten and made into slaves, sexual and otherwise from what Declan could tell. He would have loved to bring the fucker back from the dead just to kill the son of a bitch all over again for what he'd done to innocent children.

Declan learned everything he could from Sam and Tara about his mate. Thankfully, Sean was indeed over eighteen despite how small he appeared beside Declan. He'd wondered if he would have to control his libido longer, but it seemed as soon as he could convince Sean to accept their mating bond, he could claim Sean as his.

"Alpha Declan says we can stay here as long as we need," Tara said quietly.

Tensing, Declan waited for Sean's response.

"He seems like a good man," Sean replied gently. "I will have to thank him for saving you."

"I know how you can thank him," Sam piped up.

"Sam!" Tara admonished.

Declan smiled, lips tilting at the corners as he pictured the pretty blonde, blue-eyed wolf with a scandalized expression. She seemed rather more reserved out of the two girls as well. Sam, a dark-haired, brown-eyed lynx shifter had been more demanding during their initial conversation the day before. She'd wanted to know what Declan intended on doing with them, insisted on seeing Sean, and never let the others out of her sight. Declan could still scent her fear, but she'd buried it behind the need to protect what she saw as her pack. Sean's pack. It made him proud to see so many willing to stand up for his mate when the others had gathered close to Sam, had her back, and wanted the same thing.

"What are you talking about, Sam?" Sean asked, the obvious confusion in his voice.

"Oh, please, Sean. As if you didn't notice the way he was looking at you."

"I don't understand. What do you mean about the way he was looking at me?"

Sam sighed. Declan could almost picture her rolling her eyes at Sean. "I forgot. You weren't raised by shifters. Sean, do you remember what I told you about mates?"

Declan tensed and decided it was time to stop the topic of conversation, not wanting Sam to tell Sean about them being mates. Somehow she'd figured out what Sean was to him. He didn't want to risk scaring Sean off before he had the chance to claim him. Thankfully, Rose chose that very moment to appear at the top of the stairs with Vicky. He shoved away from the wall and made sure their approach couldn't be missed. "Well hello, Miss Vicky," he said loudly, but not loud enough to scare the little girl.

Vicky gave him a solemn look and Declan's heart ached for the adorably sweet lynx shifter. She'd been taken at a young age, he could tell. Holding out his hand, he waited for her to accept it. She took it into her own, but slow, as though still not sure she could trust him. He smiled at her, kind and gentle. "It's okay, sweetheart. No one here will ever hurt you. I promise. You want to see, Sean?"

She nodded. Declan led her into the bedroom. Sean turned his head to be able to see Vicky with his good eye. "Vicky," he smiled, but Declan could see the struggle Sean had at not crying.

Vicky didn't run to the bed as the others had. She approached carefully, still holding onto Declan's hand. Declan looked down at her. "Would you like me to lift you up?"

She shook her head.

"Are you sure, sweetie?"

Sean glanced at Declan. "Please, sir, I mean, Declan. If you wouldn't mind helping her, that is."

Declan couldn't even begin to imagine the horrors these poor children had suffered through as he knelt beside Vicky and carefully slid his hands under Vicky's arms, lifting her onto the edge of the bed. Sean gave him a grateful look as Vicky instantly curled into Sean's side, Tara having moved to allow Vicky room. Running the fingers of his good hand through the golden locks of Vicky's hair, Sean pressed a kiss to Vicky's head. "How's my little Vicky? Did you shift yet today?"

Vicky shook her head.

"You know you get testy if you don't shift," Sean teased, fondness buried in his voice.

Vicky pouted and slid her thin arms around Sean's waist causing Sean to grimace in pain, but Sean never made a sound. Declan felt a hand on his wrist and glanced over to see his sister beside him, her eyes watering at the sight before them. They still didn't know the extent of everything the four in front of them had suffered or what truly happened in the dingy basement where they'd been found. Declan couldn't believe this had been on the edge of his pack lands and he hadn't been aware, especially considering his mate's proximity. It set his teeth on edge, and he couldn't stop the fury at himself and at the monster who'd caused such pain.

"Just for a little while, Vicky, then you need to shift, okay?" Sean murmured.

The little girl nodded against Sean's ribcage and Declan could see sweat bead along Sean's forehead. He stepped forward to intervene and Sean's gaze whipped to his. Sean gave him a shake of his head, telling him silently to stay back. Declan stopped, but it wasn't easy, his mouth firming into a thin line. After several breaths, Vicky finally lightened her grip and pulled back, her face scrunched up. She released Sean and moved to the end of the bed, crawling into Tara's lap. Sean smiled wearily and wiped at his forehead, giving Declan another look of thanks.

"I think Sean has had enough excitement for now," Declan said. "He needs his rest."

There was no protest from anyone, not even Sean, as the three girls climbed off the bed. Sean sank back amongst the pillows, his breathing a bit thready. Declan frowned, ignoring the others exit, and he helped Sean straighten out the sheets. "Are you all right?"

"I'm fine," Sean said, smiling tiredly.

Declan pursed his lips. "I should have the streak's doctor come back and look at you again."

"I just need to rest. That's all." Sean yawned, covering his mouth with his good hand.

Reaching out, Declan brushed away a strand of hair from Sean's forehead, still worried. "If you're sure..."

Sean hummed at him, eyes closed. "'M used to it."

Declan's heart froze and his stomach clenched. God, to hear something said so casually, it annihilated him, left him breathless and fighting the desire to tear something apart with his bare hands. "You shouldn't be," he murmured.

"'S okay," Sean sighed, slipping into sleep.

Declan wanted to rage at the heavens, but kept his mouth shut and settled his long length beside his mate, back against the headboard, arm resting on the pillow above Sean's head and just watched over Sean. Never again, he vowed, never again.

5

SEAN

When Sean woke again, the first thing he noticed was the twilight bathing the room. The second thing he noticed was a heavy warmth next to him. He didn't react to the strange sensation of someone beside him immediately, merely yawned and blinked, burrowing closer to the warm body. Had Sam crawled onto his mattress with him? Wait, he frowned. That wasn't right. Events came back to him slowly. They were no longer in the basement. Sean opened his eyes wide, a small gasp escaping him as heat flooded his cheeks. He scrambled backward a bit, almost falling off the bed, and causing his body to protest the harsh movements. He couldn't quite contain a cry of agony which disturbed the sleeping giant beside him.

Declan moved with a preternatural speed Sean could only hope to have. "What's wrong?" Declan demanded, eyes searching every corner of the room for a hidden enemy, claws extended and body tensed to fight.

Sean clutched his ribs with one arm, sweat beading along his forehead as he clenched his jaw. His body throbbed with the intensity of the torture pouring through him. "I'm so-sorry. I didn't mean to wake you," Sean managed.

Declan seemed to understand what had happened because he sheathed his claws and the dangerous look softened. He flicked on the lamp on the nightstand and then came around to Sean's side of the bed. "Are you all right?" Declan asked, sliding a couple of pillows behind Sean's back to help support him.

"Ye-yeah, ju-just moved too fast," Sean gasped.

A frown marred Declan's handsome face. "Did something scare you?"

Sean almost snorted, but held it back. He wondered if Declan would think him pathetic if he admitted the truth of just how surprised he'd been to find himself cuddling with a huge alpha such as Declan. "N-no. I tried to sit up too quick is all."

Declan hummed, but didn't press. "Do you need the restroom again? Are you hungry? Is there anything you need?"

It baffled Sean why Declan seemed so focused on him. He knew he'd saved Declan's nephew, but it surely didn't warrant the personal attention and care Declan was lavishing on him. Before he could formulate an answer, Sean's stomach growled and he couldn't contain his blush. Declan chuckled. "How does a sandwich and some soup sound?"

"I'm not picky," Sean murmured.

Declan brushed his fingers over Sean's cheek. "Don't move, okay? I'll be back in a few minutes."

Sean nodded and watched Declan leave the room. He touched his cheek where Declan had and wondered at the way his skin had tingled from the brief caress. He frowned and then winced as it pulled at the bruises on his face. Maybe the skin had reacted to being touched because of the beating. It made sense. He could tell he was healing at a faster rate than ever before and he didn't understand it. Since he could remember his injuries had always taken the same amount of time as a human to heal. He could already see fully out of the eye which had been entirely swollen shut just that morning. Something had changed and he didn't know what.

He didn't get the chance to think further into it before Declan returned with a tray of food which he set across Sean's lap. "I hope you don't mind if I eat here with you," Declan said as he took a second plate from the tray.

"No, I don't mind," Sean said. He picked up the two-tiered sandwich with two types of meat and cheese on it. The white bread with seeds in it wasn't like any he'd ever seen. He had never eaten anything like it and he eyed it uncertainly. How was he supposed to fit that in his mouth? He pulled it apart into a half sandwich and began to eat. Amazing flavors exploded across his tongue and he closed his eyes, moaning at such decadence. "Oh," he whimpered in pleasure.

His stomach grumbled loudly in the silence as he devoured the entire sandwich in what felt like seconds, loving the different textures of the bread, the crunch of the seeds, the tang of the mustard, and sweetness of the mayo. The turkey tasted smoky and divine while the ham seemed to have a bit of sugar on it. Sean would have licked the plate if Declan hadn't been in the room with him. He blushed when he realized Declan was staring at him, his own sandwich untouched. Sean dropped his gaze to the tray, nervously grabbing the spoon.

Steam rose off the bowl of soup and Sean ladled some out carefully, blowing on it to cool it off some before taking the scoop into his mouth. Again, the taste was so unlike anything Sean had ever eaten. Whenever Carl would allow Sean or the others to eat, they were lucky to get cold leftovers or things from a can. He'd never let them have something so exquisite or flavorful before. Sean managed to keep his moans to himself this time, but he couldn't quite contain his happy smile as he enjoyed the food. To his disappointment, the bowl emptied before he was ready for it to be. He wanted to ask for more, but felt it would be rude and didn't know if it were right to do so. Instead he set the spoon down on the tray.

Declan surprised him by placing half of his sandwich on Sean's plate. "I'm full already. Why don't you go ahead and finish that for me?"

Sean looked at Declan, hesitant but hopeful. "Are you sure?"

He gave Sean an encouraging smile. "I'm sure. Go ahead."

"Thanks!" Sean dug into the sandwich wholeheartedly. His stomach gave a pained protest when he finished, but Sean couldn't have been happier. He sank back into the pillows with a tired, but full, sigh. He'd eaten so much his belly even looked a bit distended. He couldn't remember ever feeling so satiated before. "That was the best thing I've ever eaten," he said, his voice slurring with sleepiness.

Declan smiled again and moved the tray from the bed. "That was nothing. Wait until you try my spaghetti. Ronnie says it's the best in the world."

Sean grunted as Declan helped him lie back down. He probably wouldn't have done it if he hadn't been on the verge of falling asleep again, but since he'd first caught sight of Declan's hair, he'd been fascinated by the golden locks. They were simply beautiful. Sean slid his fingers through the silken strands, grinning goofily as how soft they felt on his skin. "Pretty," he murmured.

A chuckle rumbled in Declan's throat. "You like my hair, huh?"

"Uh hmm," Sean sighed. His eyes were mere slits by then and he could barely form words. "'S soft."

Declan leaned down until the tip of his nose brushed over

Sean's throat. "Maybe one day soon you can feel it on other parts of your body."

Sean frowned and wrinkled his nose. "Could tickle."

"Perhaps," Declan murmured as he pulled back. "Are you ticklish, Sean?"

Sean nodded, face serious. "Very."

"Interesting to know." Declan pressed a gentle kiss to Sean's forehead. "Get some sleep, baby."

Grumbling, Sean wanted to argue. He'd slept so much already. But his body seemed to agree with Declan because he passed out rather quickly, the conversation melding into a part of his dreams, and it became something he forgot about by the time he awoke the next morning.

This time when Sean awakened he found himself alone and his body had healed even further. Sean slipped from the bed, careful not to agitate his ribs which still seemed tender, but nowhere near as painful as the day before. He made his way to the bathroom to relieve himself. Looking in the mirror afterward, he gaped at how the bruises had already become yellowed and appeared to be over a week old rather than a matter of days. How was that possible? Even the ones on his ribcage were fading.

"Sean?" Declan called through the door.

Sean opened the door and stared at Declan, confused. "What did you do to me?"

Declan frowned. "What are you talking about?"

Gesturing to his face and body, Sean replied, "I have never healed this quickly before. You must have done something."

A look flashed too quickly over Declan's face for Sean to identify. "You're a shifter. You heal faster than a human."

"No," Sean denied. "I am a shifter who has never shifted. I heal just as slow as a human."

Surprise dominated Declan's features. "You've never shifted?"

"No. This prevents me from shifting." Sean pointed at the collar. "My father hates... hated... shifters. He didn't want me to shift. He came home one day with this and has never once taken it off."

The surprise morphed into anger and Sean stepped back, suddenly scared at the way Declan's mood had changed. He didn't really know Declan and, despite how kind Declan had been since Sean's arrival here, it didn't mean the man wouldn't lash out at him. He didn't understand why Declan had grown mad, but if Declan intended to start throwing punches, Sean didn't want to be the nearest object.

Declan must have seen his instinctive reaction. "I would never hurt you," Declan said stiffly, hands balled into fists at his side. "Ever."

Sean flinched at the offense in Declan's tone and he could see the hurt in Declan's eyes. "I-"

"We will see about getting the collar removed," Declan interrupted him, moving away from Sean to stand at the window, his back to Sean. "I have never heard of such a thing before, but I know of someone who might be able to help."

Sean felt guilty as hell and he didn't know what to do. "I'm sorry," he said quietly, shuffling his feet in discomfort.

"It's fine. You don't know me and I truly hope to change that." Declan turned from the window to look at Sean. "If you'll give me the chance."

Flushing, Sean wrapped his arms around himself. He nibbled his bottom lip for a second and then nodded. "Okay."

Declan smiled and came forward, placing an arm around Sean's waist. "You really shouldn't be walking around just yet. Not until the doctor gives you the all clear. Then I can show you my home and introduce you to the streak."

"Is it okay for me to see Sam and the others again?" Sean asked as Declan helped him back into bed.

"Of course," Declan replied. "I'll send them in after breakfast. Would you like something to eat?"

Sean nodded eagerly, his stomach choosing that moment to growl loudly. Declan laughed huskily and pulled the blankets up to Sean's waist. "It's good to see I won't have to force you to eat. You're far too skinny and need to get some meat on your bones."

Embarrassment flooded Sean and he looked down at his lap, picking at the sheets. He knew he wasn't anything to look at. His ribs stuck out against his skin from lack of nourishment over the years and he felt like he was all elbows and knees in his five foot eleven frame. A gasp exploded from his lips when Declan gripped his chin and forced his face upward. "Don't," Declan growled gently. "You're beautiful and will only grow more exquisite as you heal."

Then Declan did something Sean never would have anticipated in a hundred years. He kissed him. Sean parted his lips in surprise, his breath leaving him in a tiny rush of air, as Declan cupped the side of Sean's face and then brushed his mouth over Sean's. Sean had seen kisses on TV during the times he'd been able to sneak a peek while upstairs at his father's and he'd always wondered what it felt like, but nothing had prepared him for the warmth or the softness of another person's lips on his own. The tendrils of feeling it sent through him were unlike anything he'd ever experienced and Sean didn't want it to end when Declan pulled away. He was tempted to follow and barely managed to restrain himself, staring at Declan, eyes wide in wonder and shock. Declan ran his thumb over Sean's bottom lip, rough calluses dragging over the smooth flesh causing even further electrical shocks to Sean's system.

"I'll be right back," Declan rasped.

Sean could do nothing more than nod mutely, watching as Declan left the room. His body felt hot and tight, and he pressed a hand over the stiff length between his thighs. He'd gotten hard before, but rarely, and never because of another person. He squeezed and bit back a moan. What was happening to him? None of the sensations running through him were things he understood. Sean released his penis and slumped against the pillows. He needed to get his body under his control before Declan returned.

6

DECLAN

When Declan had seen Sean's utter enjoyment at something as simple as a sandwich he'd been furious. If he could bring Sean's father back from the dead and kill the son of a bitch all over again he would have. There'd been no way to miss just how deprived Sean was from the outside world. He knew there were a lot of things he still needed to know about Sean, but it seemed Sean had never been taught even the smallest of things. Declan intended on making it his life's mission to show Sean everything and anything his mate desired.

He smiled on his way down to the kitchen, his lips tingling at the remembered feel of Sean's mouth under his. He'd purposely kept the kiss light, not wanting to press for more, certain Sean had never experienced a kiss before. He'd been right if Sean's expression had been anything to go by. The innocent wonder on Sean's face made Declan's heart ache at just how much Sean had missed out on in life and his balls tighten at knowing he'd be the first to touch Sean in such an intimate way. His tiger relished the fact Sean was untouched, the beast prowling beneath the surface of his skin, yowling to go back upstairs and claim their mate before anyone else could dare try. Not that anyone would go near Sean without his permission. None of the other males had even been upstairs since Sean's arrival in Declan's home. They knew Declan would gut them if they even tried. It would take all of Declan's self-control to even allow Sean out of his home before he'd placed his mark on Sean, but as long as Declan was with him, it would have to be enough.

Victor sat at the table chatting with Rose while Sam and Tara were attempting to get Vicky to eat. Vicky immediately brought her gaze to Declan the moment he stepped into the kitchen. He'd already been downstairs once, but the girls hadn't been awake yet. "Good Morning, Vicky," he greeted with a soft smile.

She never took her eyes off of him as he stepped to the stove and dished out eggs, bacon, and home fries for Sean. He slathered toast with butter and jam and set it on the plate with the other food. "Would the three of you like to visit with Sean after his breakfast?" Declan asked.

"Yes, please, if that's all right," Sam replied. She studied Declan and he knew she was a very intelligent young shifter. "Sean's your mate, isn't he?" she asked bluntly.

Tara hissed at Sam as the others fell silent. Declan continued to put everything on a tray for Sean and, once finished, he turned and moved to squat beside her, looking at her. "He is," Declan answered quietly. "But he isn't aware of it. I would ask that you not tell him as I don't want to scare him. He has a lot to deal with right now."

Sam gave him a shrewd look, but after a few moments hesitation, nodded. "Don't hurt him."

"Never," Declan promised, reaching out to touch her shoulder. "I'll come back downstairs to get you once he's finished eating."

Tara glanced at Declan. "Is he okay?"

"He's doing much better. He may even be up and around tomorrow."

The girls shared a look, but didn't say anything. Declan knew the reason Sean had healed so quickly was because he'd shared his life force with Sean. They were bound and Declan's strength flowed through Sean's veins now which meant Declan's abilities as an alpha also could be tapped into by Sean, including his body's natural ability to heal faster. Declan couldn't share this with them though. He needed to get that damned collar off of Sean and soon.

After pouring a glass of orange juice and adding it to the tray, he lifted his bundle and carried it upstairs to his bedroom. Sean sat staring at the window, watching the leaves of the tree rustling in the light breeze. Declan cleared his throat to alert Sean to his presence and entered the room to place the tray on Sean's lap. The sheer joy shining from Sean's face at the sight of the food before him almost shattered Declan's heart. For the first time since he'd been a child, Declan actually felt his eyes burn with the possibility of tears. He kept his movements slow and easy as he settled down onto the bed beside Sean.

"While you spend time with the girls, I am going to give my friend a call. I believe he may know how to remove the collar," Declan managed to get out.

Sean shrugged a thin shoulder, his attention solely on the food. "If he can't, it's not like I haven't lived with it my entire life."

Declan scowled. "We'll get it off, Sean. I promise you."

Sean looked at Declan, his brow furrowed. "I didn't mean to upset you."

Declan shook his head. "You didn't upset me, but you have to know it isn't normal to not be able to shift, Sean. Do you even know what kind of shifter you are?"

"No. My father wouldn't tell me and the one time I

asked..." Sean didn't finish and Declan could only imagine what Sean's father had done in retaliation of Sean asking.

Blood boiling, Declan struggled to remain calm. "What happened to your mother?"

Sean toyed with his fork. "My father used to talk about her leaving him and me, abandoning us. He would call her awful names and say she left us for another man, a shifter. Carl would say the shifter stole her away from him."

Declan knew it was possible for a human and a shifter to be mated and it was even possible for a human and a shifter to have a child if they weren't mates. He'd seen it happen before within his own streak. But there was no way a mother would have left her child behind even if she had met her intended mate after the fact. Something smelled off about the lies Sean's father had told Sean. He could hear the hurt in Sean's voice and see it in his face. "Listen to me, Sean," Declan said firmly, "No matter what your father told you, your mother never would have left you behind willingly. Understand me?"

Sean tipped his head forward, allowing his crudely cut hair to cover his still bruised features. "If she didn't le-leave then it would me-mean he di-did something to her," Sean whispered, his hold tightening on the fork.

Wincing, Declan realized Sean would rather believe his mother had abandoned them rather than the possibility she could be dead. "It could also mean he wasn't really your father, Sean," Declan offered.

Breath hitching, Sean whipped his head up to stare at Declan, eyes wide. Declan could see the idea had never occurred to Sean, but it had to Declan. With the fact the bastard had apparently kidnapped so many other shifter children over the years and kept them for unknown periods of time, it was entirely possible Sean was the man's first abduction. "What do you remember of your childhood, Sean? What's your first memory of your father?"

He saw Sean struggling to think back. "I remember being in the basement," Sean murmured. "I remember him being mad because I was crying and asking for my mom."

Fury coursed through Declan, but he tamped it down. Right now Sean needed him not his anger. "Do you ever recall him being with your mom?"

"I don't know. I don't remember her." Sean sounded agitated, his voice strained.

Instead of trying to push Sean further, Declan took hold of Sean's hand and held it in his, tracing the back of it with his index finger from his other hand. "Enough dark thoughts for now. Finish your breakfast and then the girls can come to visit."

Sean flexed his hand in Declan's. "I'm sorry if I upset you."

"Stop," Declan chastised softly, bringing Sean's hand to his lips for a brief kiss. "You didn't upset me. I'm the one who should be apologizing for upsetting you. I shouldn't have brought up the subject while you're still healing. I'm an idiot for doing it."

Sean tilted his head curiously. The action set off a niggling thought in the back of Declan's mind and he tried to capture it, but it slipped away before he could. It reminded him of someone yet he couldn't place the person. He released Sean's hand and pointed at the food. "Eat," he instructed.

"Yes, sir," Sean answered.

At first, Declan thought Sean was being serious, but he caught a twinkle of laughter in the sapphire eyes and he reached out to flick the burnished lock hanging closest to him. It made his heart swell to see Sean already teasing him. Declan laughed. "Impertinent cub."

A red hue rose beneath the yellowing bruises and Declan fought the urge of his tiger to lean in and kiss Sean again.

The small taste earlier had left him hungering for more. He wanted to devour the sweet, sweet man beside him. He knew Sean was nowhere near ready for Declan to claim him so he would bide his time until then. "I've gone ahead and had Rose order you some clothing. It should be here in the next couple of days. Whatever you don't like or doesn't fit right, we can return," Declan said as Sean resumed eating.

"You didn't have to do that," Sean protested.

"Are you planning on going around without clothes?" Declan asked. "Because the clothes you wore when I brought you here literally disintegrated when I removed them." Dismay covered Sean's face and Declan felt guilty, but he didn't apologize. "Don't worry about it, Sean. I have plenty of money and it is my job as your alpha to take care of you."

Surprise replaced the dismay. "My alpha?" Sean queried.

Declan grinned. "Of course. You're part of my streak now."

"I don't know anything about being in a streak," Sean replied.

"We can teach you," Declan said, waving away Sean's concern. "Finish eating. While Sam and the others are visiting with you I'll give my contact a call about the collar. See if they know of a way to remove it."

Sean touched the aforementioned object, grimacing. "I really don't think you'll be able to. My father said I'll never shift."

Declan scowled. "Your father was wrong. We will get that infernal collar off and you will shift, Sean. I promise you we will find a way."

Sean gave Declan a hopeful look. "You think so?"

"I know so," Declan growled. He knew without a doubt the collar had to be magicked. If Sean had worn it since childhood, it had to have grown with him to prevent choking him, which meant it had to be enchanted somehow. He didn't want to scare Sean any more than the younger man had been in his life as it seemed Sean had no clue about other preternatural beings aside from shifters and he didn't share the concept of there also being sorcerers in the world.

Once Sean had cleaned his plate and drank the glass of orange juice, Declan took the tray from Sean's lap. "I'll send Sam, Tara, and Vicky upstairs. You're not to leave the bed as you're still healing."

"Okay," Sean murmured.

Declan smiled at him and leaned down before Sean knew his intentions to steal another brief kiss. "I'll be back in an hour or so to check on you."

He left the room and headed downstairs where he deposited the tray in the kitchen and then told the girls it was okay to visit with Sean. Then he went into his office and shut the door. Taking a seat, he turned on his laptop. While it started, he grabbed the cell phone on his desk and dialed the number he knew quite well.

"Hunter."

"Kyle, it's Dec."

"When do you need me?"

"As soon as possible."

"Two days."

"See you then." The call disconnected and Declan set the phone back on the base. For Kyle not to ask questions meant he must have been somewhere he couldn't. Declan had been hoping to discuss the collar and find a way to remove it sooner, but he knew if anyone could figure out how it would be Kyle. He wondered if maybe the house his mate had been kept in held any secrets. He called Victor to his office and made a request for Victor to take a couple of others with him to search the house and the surrounding property and bring back whatever information or paperwork they could find. Victor didn't question Declan's orders or ask for any further details. He merely nodded and left to do as requested.

Figuring he'd give Sean and the others time to themselves, Declan spent the next hour answering emails from other clans and dealing with streak business. He had been letting a lot slide the last few days because of Sean's arrival at the compound and needed to catch up. It was mostly minor squabbles amongst disagreeing members and other packs reaching out to discuss trade agreements. Declan also found an email from one of his members who was currently traveling with his family, Arthur and Nicole Bianca and their teenage son Austin. They were the rarest of shifters in his clan, white tigers. There weren't many of them left in the world and Declan had been reluctant to let them travel so far, but they'd insisted, wanting to go see family in their native land of Russia. He'd only let them go when they'd promised to contact him twice a week while they were gone to let him know they were okay. He knew that probably made him seem like a dictator, but they'd already lost one child years ago, he couldn't allow them to be so far out of his reach without being kept abreast of their movements.

The email stated they were well, had located their family, and would be returning home soon. They hoped everyone was doing well and they looked forward to seeing their streak members soon. Arthur went on to talk about how their homeland was beautiful and they were grateful to Declan for allowing them the freedom to return to Russia to see it. He also attached photos of the three of them with family members and then singles of Arthur and Nicole or just Austin at some tourist location. Declan smiled, happy to see they were enjoying their trip. He sent off a quick reply, telling them to be safe and that no thanks were needed.

Standing, Declan went to the french doors overlooking the back of the house. His skin twitched and he could sense his tiger needing to be free for a little while. He cracked open the doors before stripping his clothing and setting them aside. With a seamless shift, he took on his animal form and padded softly outside into the sunlight. The warmth caressed his fur and he yawned and stretched, kneading the grass beneath his large paws. Sometimes setting his tiger loose after being in his human form for several days was a bit like being contorted into a small confined space for a long period of time. Bones cracked, muscles stretched and burned. It felt fantastic.

Declan tossed his head back and let out a loud roar which a few others nearby returned in eagerness. He flopped down in the grass and rolled around for a moment or two then launched to his feet and took off running into the forest. The trees rustled overhead in the wind, whispering of the coming autumn days. His claws dug into the earth, eating up the ground as he darted around trees and over fallen logs and branches. He chased after a jackrabbit until it disappeared into a burrow, missing it by a hairsbreadth.

After letting off some of the restlessness in his blood, Declan returned to the main house and once back inside his office, shifted and dressed again. Eagerness to see his mate sent him out of the study and up the stairs. He found Sean alone, asleep, and approached the bed, smiling gently. He reached down and brushed a strand of hair back from Sean's cheek only to frown when Sean whimpered and flinched. "Hey, baby, it's just me," Declan murmured, hoping to sooth Sean.

Sean's eyes flew open. Fear and panic almost swallowed the irises whole.

"Easy," Declan rumbled in a soft tone, sliding the tips of his fingers along Sean's neck in a light caress.

"Declan?" Sean said, his voice shaking.

Declan lowered himself to his knees beside the bed,

instinctively understanding that towering over Sean wasn't a good idea. "Yes, Sean, it's me."

"I-I'm sorry," Sean mumbled.

"For what?" Declan asked, confused, still touching Sean. His tiger loved the feel of Sean's smooth skin. He wanted to bury himself inside the smaller shifter and never surface.

Sean shook his head as tears dampened his lashes.

Declan sucked in a deep breath at how much the sight of Sean crying caused his chest to tighten. He brought the hand stroking Sean's skin up to cup Sean's cheek. His heart clenched when Sean leaned into his palm unconsciously. It was clear his animal knew their connection. "Are you afraid of me?" Declan asked, pained at the thought.

"No," Sean whispered.

"Then why are you sorry?"

"For being so much trouble."

Surprise held Declan mute for a moment and then Declan gave a low growl causing Sean to jerk and blink at him in confusion. "You aren't trouble, Sean. You're-" Declan cut himself off. He couldn't reveal to Sean just yet about them being mates. "You're the reason my nephew and all of the others are still alive. You're amazing and strong and so much more than words can begin to describe. But never believe you are trouble. I don't want to hear you say that about yourself again. Understand?"

Sean swallowed hard and nodded at Declan, but it wasn't fear Declan scented from his mate. Arousal wafted from Sean once more sending heat straight to Declan's cock. He bit back a groan as the zipper on his jeans bit into the straining flesh between his thighs. His cock jerked when Sean licked his lips nervously and Declan couldn't stop himself. He rose from the floor and covered Sean's mouth with his own. This time the kiss was anything but placid and loving. It was passionate and lustful. Declan plunged his tongue inside Sean, dying for a taste of the man meant to be his. His hands fisted into the sheets beside Sean as he fought his natural urge to grab the man and strip away the barriers between them, wanting nothing more than to claim the beautiful shifter for his own.

A gasping moan reverberated against Declan's eardrums and he eagerly swallowed it. Declan slid a hand beneath Sean to cup the back of his head, holding him steady for the ravaging kiss. His body hummed with the need to dominate Sean, but he would never do anything to harm Sean. His mate was still healing. He forced himself to break the kiss and buried his face in the pillow beside Sean. Declan could feel his skin trembling as he kept his weight off Sean's prone form and tried to gather himself.

"Declan?" Sean asked uncertainly near Declan's ear. But it was the touch of Sean's hand on his side which caused Declan to raise his head.

"I'm sorry," Declan rasped.

A healthy red flushed Sean's cheeks and his lips were swollen from the hard kiss. "It's okay."

"No, it's not. You're still injured and I-" Declan broke off his words.

"I liked it," Sean admitted softly.

Declan groaned at the innocent words. His dick jerked inside his pants. Sliding away from Sean, Declan perched on the edge of the bed, one leg bent at the knee while the other dangled over the side. "You have no idea what you do to me."

He heard Sean's breath catch and smiled. He took Sean's hand in his, brought it to his lips, and kissed the backs of Sean's fingers. "How would you like to come downstairs for dinner tonight?"

A smile lit Sean's face. "Yeah?"

"I think you're up for it. Just promise me you'll let me know if it's gets to be too much."

Sean eagerly nodded. "I will."

"Good. It'll be just us, Rose, the girls, Ronnie, and maybe one or two others."

"I'd like to see Ronnie again," Sean said.

"I'm sure he'll be happy to see you, too."

Declan spent the remainder of the afternoon with Sean telling him about the streak, how many members they had, and how there were other clans out in the world as well. He also explained about the Council of Shifters, an elite number of elders who watched over their kind and ensured they did nothing to endanger themselves or others like them. He relished the fascination he saw on Sean's face as he talked and would spend the rest of his life doing whatever he could to see such an expression on his mate's features. The only interruption came in the return of Victor and the others, but Declan forewent hearing the report until after the evening meal, not wishing to ruin the time he spent with Sean with bad news.

When it was time for dinner, he helped Sean put on a clean pair of sweatpants and a T-shirt another streak member had loaned them until the clothing Declan had ordered arrived. Sean trembled with eagerness as Declan helped guide him down the stairs to the dining room making Declan happy he'd suggested Sean join everyone despite his injuries.

7

SEAN

The rest of the house matched the opulence of the bedroom, in Sean's opinion anyway. He'd never seen such beautiful hardwood floors, plush carpeting, and shining furniture before. The gleaming oak of the staircase caught his eye the moment they stepped out of the bedroom and Sean stared in wonder. Everything in his father's place had been dilapidated, falling down, or dirty. The railings in the house had been missing spindles or were entirely gone. Most of the walls throughout the hallways leading into the dining room Declan led him to were white. Some had paintings or mirrors and others had pictures of what Sean was certain were streak members. He could only hope Declan would let him explore further once he'd healed properly. The need to see more itched beneath his skin.

But it was the sheer breathtaking display of food on a long dark cherry dining table which caused Sean to stop, his mouth dropping open in shock. He'd never seen so many different and wonderful dishes in his life. His stomach growled and clenched at the same time. Plates of greens, meats, baskets of bread, glasses of what appeared to be water, and what Sean knew to be some type of potato with cheese on top covered most of the surface.

Too many varying scents of shifters tantalized his nose on top of the food. He saw Sam, Tara, and Vicky already seated at the table, and he recognized the woman named Rose sitting close to the head of the table with Ronnie next to her. But it was the sight of an unknown man with dark blond hair, light blue eyes, and goatee which caused him to tense. He didn't even realize he'd tightened his hold on Declan's forearm until Declan brought his hand down on top of Sean's. "Easy, baby," Declan murmured. "This is Victor, my beta. He would never hurt you."

"Hello, Sean," Victor greeted, voice smooth and warm.

Sean slowly relaxed and gave a tremulous smile. "Hello."

"Sean!" Ronnie cried, jumping from his seat to rush up to him. He threw his thin arms around Sean's waist and hugged him.

Sean smiled and touched the top of Ronnie's head, returning the hug halfway, still holding onto Declan.

"Careful, Ronnie," Declan grunted out a warning. "He's still not completely healed."

"I'm fine," Sean admonished Declan softly when Ronnie backed away as if his tail were on fire and he appeared crestfallen. "I barely feel it anymore. Promise."

The grin returned to Ronnie's face. "I wanted to come see you, but Mama said you couldn't have visitors yet."

"Well I'm okay enough now so you can come visit me whenever you'd like," Sean replied, releasing Declan to lean forward and ruffle Ronnie's hair.

Ronnie scowled at the childish gesture, straightening his hair out in a huff. "I'm not a little kid."

Sean bit back a laugh and tried his best to give Ronnie a solemn expression. "I'm sorry. I won't do it again."

Ronnie gave a short nod in acceptance of Sean's apology. He grabbed Sean's hand and tugged. "Come sit next to me!"

Declan sighed. "Ronnie."

"Please?"

Sean glanced at Declan who gave him a small nod. He smiled and followed Ronnie the short distance to a chair near the head of the table. Ronnie pulled it out for him as well. "Thank you," Sean said.

Declan took the seat at the end of the table, to Sean's left. Sean smiled at Vicky and the other girls across from him. No one moved to take any food as Declan took the plate in front of Sean and began dishing food onto it. They waited until Declan had placed the food back in front of Sean and also filled his own plate before they served themselves. Sean wondered at the dynamic in confusion, but the food distracted him and he picked up his fork. There were green beans, the potatoes with cheese, rare strips of what appeared to be beef of some kind, and a roll. He didn't even know where to start.

He scooped a bite of the potatoes and stuck it in his mouth. The explosion of flavor surprised him. He'd only ever had potatoes from a can before or left over cold French fries that his father had thrown away. A quiet moan escaped his lips and he stuffed in another forkful. The cheese tasted creamy and amazing. It wasn't until he'd finished all of them that he saw a number of eyes trained on him. He flushed and dropped his fork on the plate.

A low growl came from his left and Sean startled, whipping his head toward Declan to find the man glaring at the others. Fascination kept Sean's gaze on Declan for several heartbeats as Declan's eyes and teeth had partially shifted. Fangs had dropped down from Declan's gums appearing large and fearsome. Yet they didn't scare Sean. If anything he felt the same heat building in his lower belly he had earlier when Declan had kissed him. Declan's nostrils flared suddenly and the green eyes which had become rounder and more cat-like in his partial shift pinned Sean in place. Sean twitched in his chair for some unknown reason and he could feel his face and throat growing warm again.

The others in the room faded away and Sean leaned forward in his chair, his lips parting on a swift intake of air. He almost fell out of his seat in the desire to be closer to Declan. A cough brought both of them out of the stupor they seemed to have become lost in because Sean blinked and shook his head, grasping the table to keep from tumbling to the floor as he realized just how on the edge he was. Embarrassment flashed through him and he tipped his head forward, allowing his hair to hide his face.

Declan's strong hand slid over the back of his neck, surprising him yet again, and Sean jumped. "Let's eat, everyone," Declan said, squeezing Sean's nape reassuringly before releasing him.

Sean didn't resume eating right away. Instead he waited and watched the others from beneath his hair. They seemed to be ignoring him now. So he resumed eating, this time slower and less eagerly, sensing it wasn't normal for someone to enjoy it as much as he did. The conversation flowed around him for a while, but Sean concentrated on keeping his movements on par with everyone else's. He didn't want to cause Declan to be ashamed of him. The idea gave him pause. He wasn't sure why he cared so much. Maybe because the man had done more for him than anyone else in his life. Declan had saved his life after all and taken him into his home.

"Sean?"

Looking up, he realized Sam must have asked him something because she looked at him with an expectant expression. "What?"

"I asked how you were feeling."

"Oh. I'm much better."

Sam smiled in relief. "That's great. Declan is taking good care of you, huh?"

For some reason the question seemed rather leading and Sean tilted his head at the odd gleam in her eye. "Yes, he is." He didn't understand subtlety or innuendos. "Why?"

"No reason. Tara and I are going to tour the streak's compound tomorrow. Rose said we can go pick out some clothes in town too. Is there anything you want us to get for you?"

Sean shook his head. "I'm okay."

Sam frowned. "Are you sure? You can't stay in the same clothes forever."

Declan chose then to interject. "I've already taken the liberty of ordering him some items online. They should be here in the next day or so."

"Oh! That's great. You want us to get you anything to do?"

"I never thought of that," Declan admitted. "I have a library full of books. Would you like to have something to read?"

Sean tensed and looked away, shame flooding him. He almost didn't see the quick shake of Sam's head at Declan. His stomach twisted and he set his fork down beside his plate, the remainder of his food no longer tempting. "I need to use the bathroom if that's okay?"

"Of course. You don't need to ask," Declan replied. "Do you need help getting there?"

"No, I'm fine."

"It's just down the hall on the right."

Sean stood and walked out of the room, careful not to jar his still healing ribs. He located the bathroom easily enough and entered, closing the door behind him. His father had never taught him to read and there hadn't really been a chance to learn while taking care of the other cubs. In fact, most of the things he did know were things he'd taught himself or he'd learned from the other cubs and they weren't much. He knew how to make basic meals, simple fair really, and he knew how to do laundry, how to sew, another skill he'd gained through trial and error. But real-world things like reading, math, and other things most children were taught in school he didn't have a clue about. Sam and Tara had done their best to try and help him, but there hadn't exactly been a whole lot of material for them to practice with. They'd taught him what they could.

Pushing away from the door, he looked in the mirror at himself. The bruises had faded even further and were just patches of yellow mottled with tiny blotches of pale purple. He touched his eye, the one which had been most damaged, and wondered at how fast he'd healed. He leaned in closer to peer at the skin. His father had always hated how long it took him to get better after a particularly bad beating so for him to be up and around in a matter of days meant something had changed, Sean just didn't know what.

Are you all right, baby?

The sound of Declan's voice in his head caused Sean to jerk backward from the counter and he banged his elbow on a towel rod which in turn caused a pang in his ribs. He hissed and wrapped an arm around his midsection. How the hell could he hear Declan inside his mind?

Sean?

Sean wasn't sure how to answer Declan. He closed his eyes and figured if he thought the reply Declan could "hear" it. *I'm fine.*

Do you need me?

No.

The idea of Declan being able to talk to him mentally

seemed invasive and Sean wondered if Declan could see his thoughts too.

I can only hear your thoughts, Sean, and only when you're upset or let me in.

How? A soft sigh drifted through Sean's mind and Sean frowned. Declan seemed hesitant to answer him. Why? *Declan?*

I'll explain it to you eventually, baby, but for now, please just understand it's not a bad thing. Are you certain you don't need my assistance returning to the table?

For the first time in a long time, Sean actually started to feel angry. He didn't like having things hidden from him and he was beginning to think Declan saw him as a child, especially considering how often Declan called him baby. He may not have had a childhood like other normal people, but he had been through a whole hell of a lot more than most and didn't deserve to be treated like he'd break. *I'm fine*, he snapped back.

Silence met his reply and Sean sensed Declan wasn't happy with his response, but he couldn't have cared less right then. The whole evening had become overwhelming very quickly. Aside from everyone looking at him like he was a bug underneath a microscope when he'd been eating, the idea Declan could see inside his mind scared the hell out of him. He wouldn't be able to hide the things he'd gone through or the way Declan made him feel and it seemed somehow more terrifying than when he used to wait for the times his father would go into a rage and use him as a punching bag.

He opened the bathroom door and instead of going toward the dining room, he made a right hand turn and wandered in the direction of the back of the house. A door sat open at the end of the hallway and he saw a small light on, beckoning him forward. He entered what looked like an office or something similar. A large L-shaped desk with a small TV on it faced the door. The walls were lined with shelves of books and there was a couch underneath a window with a couple of doors leading to the outside. A fireplace, currently unlit, had a pretty fluffy brown rug in front of it and Sean had the urge to go roll around on it to see if it were as soft as it seemed.

Something sent him to the desk though and Sean ran his fingers over the shining smooth surface, smiling at how cool it felt beneath his fingers. The room smelled strongly of Declan so he felt pretty certain the space belonged to Declan. He pushed a large leather chair away from the desk and sat down in it gingerly. The air squished out of it in a rush and Sean let out a small chuckle at how it almost engulfed his smaller form. He snuggled into it, closing his eyes and breathing in the scent of tiger shifter clinging to it. He curled his fingers over the armrests and used his feet to swing the chair back and forth. A happy giddiness swept through Sean. Being surrounded by Declan's scent gave him a sense of safety he had never experienced in his entire life.

A creak alerted him to someone's presence and Sean opened his eyes to see Declan standing in the doorway, full lips curved into a slight smile. "I wondered where you'd gotten to," Declan murmured.

Guilt flashed through Sean and the peace he'd felt seconds ago vanished. He stood abruptly and stepped away from the chair. "I'm sorry. I-"

Declan moved further into the room. "It's okay. Sit back down."

Sean shook his head and inched his way around to the front of the desk, hands clasped behind his back. He looked everywhere but at Declan. "You must like to watch a lot of TV," Sean mumbled.

"What?" Declan asked with a confused look.

He pointed at the monitor on Declan's desk. Understanding and something else chased over Declan's features. "You've never seen a computer before?" Declan asked.

Frowning, Sean tilted his head. The other children had mentioned things called computers and video games, but Sean hadn't expected to ever have the chance to use one or see one so he'd never tried to learn too much about them. "No. What do they do?"

Declan motioned for Sean to return to the other side of the desk. "I'll show you."

Sean cautiously followed Declan, who insisted he sit back down in the chair. He tried to refuse, but Declan gave him a look which Sean couldn't deny so he lowered himself into it, tensing when Declan came in close to hit a button on a strange object on top of the desk that had letters on plastic squares. "This is the keyboard, that's the mouse which you use to navigate through the menus and windows, and the screen is your monitor."

The "TV" lit up and a picture of Declan with Rose and Ronnie covered with other objects appeared. Sean stared in awe at the images. Declan placed his hand on a rounded plastic item he'd called the mouse and Sean saw a little arrow on the screen move when Declan moved the mouse. Sean couldn't help the noise he let out. "What is it for?"

"What?"

"The computer. What is it for? Why do you have one?"

Declan crouched down beside Sean. "People use them for many purposes. Business, playing games, storing files. It all depends on what they need it for. I mostly use mine for streak business and communicating with others."

"You can talk with other shifters through here?" Sean asked, peering at the monitor. "I don't see a telephone."

Declan chuckled and brought his free hand to rest on Sean's knee. "There is a way to connect a microphone to the computer so you can verbally speak to someone through it if necessary, but you can also e-mail someone, which is an electronic letter of sorts. Maybe I can show you how to do that someday soon. Would you like to see one of the video games?"

Sean frowned. "I don't think I'd be very good at it."

"That's okay. Everything takes time to learn." Declan squeezed Sean's knee lightly, sending a thrill through him. Sean watched as Declan clicked on several things and a window came up with rectangular objects he recognized as playing cards. Carl McNeely may not have done much, but he had been a gambler so Sean knew what cards were. "This game is called Solitaire. It's a pretty easy game. You see those four blank squares there at the top?"

Nodding, Sean listened as Declan explained the rules and began shifting cards around on the screen using the mouse. His heart beat fast against his ribcage, his mouth dry as he breathed through parted lips. When Declan finished and won the game, bright colors exploded across the screen and Sean squeaked, his eyes widening further.

"Do you want to try?" Declan asked.

Biting down on his bottom lip, Sean hesitated. He didn't want to look even more foolish in front of Declan. Declan took the decision out of his hands by carefully picking up Sean's hand and placing it on the mouse. He guided Sean and the mouse on how to start a new game as well as through the first few simple moves. The weight of Declan's hand on top of his caused electric tingles to race down Sean's arm and into his chest, but it was the strange ache left behind when Declan removed his touch which confused Sean. He didn't understand any of the emotions Declan triggered inside him and most of them he had never known and had no way of identifying what they meant.

"Sean?" Declan rumbled near his ear, disturbing him

enough to recognize he'd been sitting there staring at the screen instead of trying to play.

Pushing aside everything else for now, Sean started clicking and dragging the cards on the screen, imitating what he'd seen Declan do, but when one just returned to its spot, he frowned. He tried again and it still wouldn't stay.

"It's because they aren't alternating colors," Declan explained. "See these here," he pointed at the others, "they're all red and then black and then red again. You can't place two black cards on top of one another."

Sean nibbled his bottom lip in concentration and even though it took several games he managed to win one. A huge smile broke over his face as the fireworks exploded on the screen. "I did it!"

Declan grinned at him. "You did. Well done, baby."

"Why do you call me that?" Sean asked abruptly, wrinkling his nose. "I'm not a baby."

Declan blinked in surprise at his question. "It's an affectionate term. An endearment."

"En-endearment?" Sean repeated hesitatingly. He'd never heard the word before.

"It's a nickname someone gives to another person they care about. It isn't because I see you as a child, Sean. Far from it," Declan replied.

"Oh."

Standing from the crouching position he'd been in for so long, Declan held out his hand to Sean. "Come on. I think it's time for you to get back to bed. You've had quite a bit of excitement tonight and the doctor hasn't given you the all clear to be walking around just yet."

"I'm really all right," Sean protested.

"Until the doctor says you're okay for more than light activity, I'd rather you not strain yourself." When Sean would have complained again Declan interjected, "Please, for me."

Giving in with a sigh, Sean nodded and placed his hand in Declan's. "Okay."

"Thank you. I'll have the doctor swing by tomorrow to examine you."

Declan escorted Sean back to his room and remained a watchful presence as Sean settled into bed. Despite his exclamations of being fine, Sean couldn't quite stifle a yawn as he burrowed into his pillows. "Good night, baby," Declan said.

"Good night, Declan."

Sean watched as Declan left, closing the door behind him. He lay there and stared at the ceiling above him for a while, thinking over dinner and everything that had transpired over the evening. He couldn't get over his awe of the computer and the card game, but his embarrassment at how little he truly knew about everything edged out his joy of winning. He didn't know how to read, he had no skills, and had never gone to school to learn anything. Sean's skin fairly itched with shame at how stupid and simple he must seem to everyone. Those thoughts whirled around in his mind for quite a while before he managed to slip off to a restless sleep, dreams of a disappointed Declan haunting him.

8

DECLAN

Declan closed the door behind him, tightening his fingers on the doorknob momentarily. His tiger scratched at the surface of his skin. It wanted him to claim his mate and he wasn't sure how long he could hold onto his instincts. He knew Sean desired him. He scented Sean's arousal, especially earlier in the dining room, but Sean was nowhere near ready to accept him or his position as Alpha-mate. The sheer mountain of insecurities housed inside Sean seemed almost unsurpassable. Declan needed to make Sean aware of their connection first. He just hoped Sean could get past the self-doubt he'd felt in Sean's mind at the dinner table. Sam's words from earlier came to mind. *"Sean can't read."*

He'd never imagined just how much Sean had been robbed of in his life, even just the simplest things. He wanted to give Sean everything, to show him the world, to teach him what being alive meant. Getting the damned collar off would be the first start. He headed downstairs to find Victor, anxious to hear what they had found earlier in the day. Victor waited for him in the living room, a somber expression on his face. Declan gestured for Victor have a seat and Victor shook his head. "Tell me," Declan commanded after he'd sat in his own high back chair near the fireplace.

"It is almost beyond words, Alpha," Victor began, pacing back and forth. He stopped near the hearth, placing a hand on the mantel. "We searched the house first. I have never seen such filthy and horrid living conditions. The basement where the children were kept was only part of it. But what we found behind the house... Alpha, there were... graves."

Victor ran a hand over his face, rubbing at his eyes. Declan could see they were reddening as though Victor were on the edge of tears. "About a dozen or so."

Declan caught his breath and he shoved forward to the edge of his seat. "Are you certain?"

Victor nodded. "Y-yes, Alpha. They had markers. Stones. Each marked with a name."

Acidic bile rose to the back of Declan's throat, burning, threatening to bring up the dinner he'd consumed a mere hour ago. Somehow he knew without a shred of doubt the person who'd buried those bodies wasn't the bastard whose throat he'd torn out, but the very shifter who lay in Declan's own bed upstairs. He wanted nothing more than to go to Sean and gather him into his arms. Another crack formed in Declan's heart for Sean and he found his claws were out and sheathed in the arms of the chair in which he sat.

They would have to try and locate the clan of each child. The only way to do that would be to unbury them and try to identify them. Declan knew they would have to question Sean, to see if he could reveal anything about the children, whatever they could use to find their homes and give their parents closure. The idea of causing his mate even further pain sent rage pulsing through his blood. Every time he gained new knowledge of Sean's past and the man Sean called father the more Declan wished he'd drawn out the son of a bitch's death longer.

"What else?" Declan growled.

"We didn't find anything in the house except damaged or dirty furniture, clothing, and rodents. There were no signs of anyone having lived there except the children and the man who took them, and we didn't find any papers anywhere in the house aside from old newspapers. I'm sorry, Alpha."

Disappointment bit deep, but Declan held it in. He'd been hoping for something. He knew Kyle would have a way to find an answer on how to remove the collar, but he felt the impatience to see Sean's true form and knew if only Sean could shift then maybe Sean would recognize the connection between them. "It's okay, Victor. It was only a shot in the dark. Thank you for searching. We will need to see if we can locate the clans of the children buried there. It may open old wounds for some, but at least they will have closure."

"Do you want me to send some of the streak members out there to begin exhuming the bodies, Alpha?"

"Not yet, Victor. I don't wish to disturb the dead until we must. I want to see if we can find the families first."

"Forgive me, but…" Victor trailed off and glanced at the ceiling, saying without words what Declan had already thought.

"I have already considered what's on your mind, Victor, and I will speak with Sean once I am certain he is well enough. Until then see if you can gather information on the missing children from nearby clans, but be careful not to alert any of them. I don't want to cause any hysteria or have anyone digging up those graves without care or thought to the others buried there."

"Right away, Alpha."

"Once you have the information, bring it to me."

"Of course."

Declan dismissed Victor, but didn't move immediately. He couldn't imagine what kind of a monster would do such a thing to innocent children and then make another child dispose of the bodies. It horrified him the whole thing had been on the edge of his territory and he hadn't even known. Tomorrow he would assign new patrols stretching to the outskirts of his borders. There would never be another chance for this to happen. And he swore the moment he could, he'd burn that fucking house to the ground and every horrible memory Sean had with it.

The next morning, Declan stopped in to see Sean first, happy to see the bruises had faded even further. "I'll bring your breakfast and then place a call to our doctor. We should have you on your feet today."

"Could I maybe eat breakfast downstairs today instead?" Sean asked hesitantly.

"Are you sure you're up for it? I want you to make sure you eat everything on your plate." Declan didn't want a repeat of the night before when everyone had made Sean nervous about the way he'd eaten.

Sean nodded. "I'm fine. And… I'm sorry about last night. I shouldn't have left like that. It was wrong of me."

"No," Declan grunted. "They were wrong for making you feel bad. You have nothing to apologize for."

Sapphire eyes met his and Declan could see a shadow of the beast lurking behind them. It frustrated him to no end to not know what kind of shifter Sean was. He lifted a hand to touch the length of hair grazing Sean's shoulder. "We really should see about evening out your hair. Do you like it this long?"

Sean shrugged. "I've never thought about it. Sam or Tara

always used whatever we could find to keep it as short as we could. My father-" he cut himself off.

Declan knew whatever Sean had been about to say would have made him even angrier about the situation his mate had been in. "I kind of like it this length. You have such delicate features. With your long neck and high cheekbones, it suits you."

A light dusting of pink rushed to the pale skin of Sean's cheeks and he dropped his gaze to the comforter over his lap. Declan smiled softly. He leaned down. "Sean?"

Sean lifted his head again in question.

"Kiss me," Declan murmured.

Surprise caused Sean's eyes to widen a fraction and his lips to part. Declan could hear Sean's heart beat increase and Declan's tiger prowled within him. It pleased him when Sean moved in and pressed his lips over Declan's, but Sean kept the kiss short, a mere fluttering of butterfly wings. Declan cupped the back of Sean's head and dragged him in for a deeper kiss, thrusting his tongue inside Sean's mouth, seeking the taste of Sean.

He felt Sean grip his shoulders and wondered if Sean intended to push him away, but satisfaction roared through him when Sean only dug in his fingers and held on tight. Declan snaked his free arm around Sean's waist, pulling him closer until Sean straddled his lap and their hard cocks were aligned. It pleased him to find Sean as aroused as him. "Sean," Declan growled into Sean's mouth.

A small moan sank into Declan and he thrust his hips upward, grinding them together. Sean gasped and gave an involuntary jerk of his pelvis. Declan could feel Sean trembling and forced himself to break the kiss and ensure his mate wasn't in pain. Sean's cheeks were flushed, lips swollen, and his eyes were closed as he panted. Declan's nostrils flared as he tried to scent anything above Sean's arousal. Sean's eyelids flickered open and Declan could see lust in the deep blue. "Declan?" Sean rasped.

Declan leaned his forehead against Sean's and breathed in deeply. He berated himself for losing control yet again. He needed to keep from being alone around Sean until he'd prepared Sean. "Declan?" Sean questioned again, this time his voice quivering with uncertainty.

Raising his head, Declan threaded his fingers through Sean's hair. "It's okay, baby. I'm sorry. I lost control."

Sean frowned. "I don't understand."

"I was too rough."

Comprehension dawned on Sean's features. "No."

Declan traced over the stubble burns along Sean's chin. "You're still healing."

Frustration curtained Sean's face. "I'm fine! I liked what we… uh … what we were…"

Tenderness caused Declan to chuckle at Sean's stammering. He placed another soft kiss to Sean's lips. "I know you did, baby." He slid his hand down between them to cup Sean's erection through the thin sweat pants, giving it a small squeeze, and relishing the gasp Sean set free. "Do you truly understand where what we are doing will lead, Sean?"

Again, confusion lit Sean's gaze.

"Do you know what sex is?" Declan asked.

Sean seemed to shut down then and he looked everywhere except at Declan. "Like what my father did to Sam and Tara?"

"No!" Declan growled. "What that man did to them was rape."

Declan could sense Sean becoming overwhelmed again as he had the previous night and decided to let it go. He kissed Sean's temple. "It's okay, Sean. We can discuss this another time."

Sean shook his head. "No. I-I just… I want to know. I've

seen things. On T.V. My father would watch them. He would do things to Tara and to Sam. Horrible things. Is that what you want to do to me?"

"God, no!" Declan exclaimed, horrified Sean believed him capable of it. He set Sean down amongst the sheets and stood. He paced to one side of the room and back again. This hadn't been what he'd expected to discuss this morning. The information Victor shared with him the previous evening weighed heavily on him, but so did the need to clarify the difference between rape and making love to his mate. "Do you truly think I could do that to you, Sean?" he asked, stopping at the window to gaze out over the streak compound.

"You want to have sex with me," Sean said.

"Yes, but I would never hurt you. Ever. What your… that *man* did to the girls wasn't done out of care and affection for them. He did it to degrade them, to cause them pain. When sex is between two consenting adults it's a beautiful, wonderful, amazing thing. It feels right and it feels good."

"Why?" Sean asked.

Declan turned to look at Sean, frowning. "Why what?"

"Why do you wa-want to have sex with me?" Sean clarified.

There was no way Declan could get out of telling Sean the truth this time. He approached the bed and sank down on the edge where he grabbed Sean's hand and held it in his own. "There are many legends in the shifter community, Sean. Not having grown up with your kind, it may be hard for you to understand this, but shifters are born with a soul mate, another half, one who is our life mate. When we find them we know it by scent alone. It is rare to encounter them, and some of us go our entire lives without ever meeting our mate."

Sean nodded. "Sam told me about them. She said her parents were life mates. She said she couldn't wait to find her own, but hoped whoever he or she was would be able to accept her after what my father had done to her."

Declan shuddered and brought Sean's wrist to his mouth. He gave it an open mouth kiss. "Her life mate will not care. They will accept her no matter what because what happened to her wasn't her fault. Sam is an amazingly strong shifter, passionate and beautiful. She will make someone a fine mate someday."

A small growl bubbled up in Sean's throat, surprising both of them. Declan chuckled. "No need to be jealous, Sean. She is not my mate and I swore I would never take someone as such unless they were my life mate."

"I'm sorry," Sean said helplessly.

"Don't be. I love that you're already feeling the pull so strongly."

"The pull?"

Declan took a deep breath. "Sean… what I'm trying to say is, you are my life mate. I knew it the moment Ronnie returned here with your scent on him."

Shock widened Sean's eyes. "What?"

"Can't you sense it? Haven't you noticed the connection we have? How my scent calls to you? How aroused you get whenever we are in the same room together? Or the way we can talk to each other without words? Have you ever been able to do that before?"

"But I-"

"You know something is different. It's why you're healing so quickly. Part of the bonding between us has already begun and as the ties strengthen more and more of my abilities will become part of you."

Sean stared at Declan, speechless.

"I didn't intend on revealing this so soon, but I couldn't let you believe something meant to be special between us could ever be so dark." Declan caressed the back of Sean's hand with his thumb. "I need you to know in your head and your heart I would never hurt you and I would give my life to protect you, Sean. You are my life mate. My tiger knows it and I know it."

When Sean still didn't respond, Declan's heart fell into his stomach. He smiled sadly. "I will not do anything until you can accept and understand everything, Sean. I would never force you to accept me. Even if you never do." He set Sean's hand, palm down, on Sean's thigh. "I will get your breakfast and call the doctor to come in and examine you. We'll see if we can't get you the all clear today. I'd like to show you the streak's lands and introduce you to some of the others. Just rest here for now."

Declan stood and walked to the door. His chest had never been tighter. He knew he'd laid a lot on Sean just then and it was naïve to think Sean would just accept everything so easily, especially since his mate hadn't been raised with shifters, but he couldn't quite help feeling rejected.

"Declan."

He stopped and spun around, hope rising.

"I thought it was okay for me to eat downstairs this morning."

The balloon popped and Declan gritted his teeth while forcing a smile. "Of course. Let me help you."

"I can do it," Sean said, pushing the blankets back and sliding from the bed.

Declan attempted to take Sean's arm, but Sean shook his head. "I'm okay. Really."

They went downstairs together. The girls were already seated at the breakfast table with Ronnie while Rose cooked breakfast. Tara and Sam stood and came around to hug Sean, who returned the greeting enthusiastically. Declan couldn't stay there and watch the way Sean eagerly accepted their affection so soon after what Declan's tiger deemed rejection. "I'll go call the doctor," he murmured and left the room.

It almost seemed as if the big, bad alpha of the Royal Taiga Streak was running away with his tail between his legs and it chafed something fierce inside of Declan, but he had no idea how to repair the damage he'd done that morning. The only plan he had was giving it time. He reached his office and closed the door partway. After he placed the call to the doctor, he didn't return to the dining room. Instead he chose to remain in the study and take care of some of the streak business, losing himself in the day to day goings on.

9

SEAN

The happy chattering of Sam and Tara at breakfast couldn't force the whirling thoughts of what Declan had revealed to Sean out of his head. How could Declan possibly want an unlearned, inexperienced nobody like him? But Declan's confession of them being life mates made it even worse because it meant Declan didn't have a choice.

All of the food Sean consumed tasted like ash on his tongue and he didn't even notice Sam and Tara exchanging concerned glances more than once. It wasn't until after Rose and Ronnie disappeared from the dining room that Sam demanded to know what was wrong. "What is going on with you, Sean?"

Sean realized the table had been cleared and the only plate left sat in front of him. "No-Nothing."

Sam scowled at him and she stood, waddling around to perch in the chair to next him. She smacked him on the shoulder and he grunted. "Damn it, Sam. What the hell?"

"Don't lie to me, Sean. We've been through too much together to start lying now. What's up?"

He gazed at Sam and saw how good she truly looked. She had a healthy glow about her now. Her skin no longer appeared pale and any bruises were gone. Her hair had been trimmed, her eyes had a happy sparkle to them, and she even wore clothing that fit her pregnant slender form properly. "Tell me about mates again, Sam."

She sucked in a breath and he saw a light come on in her eyes. "He told you."

"You knew?"

She nodded. "I saw how he was with you. Only a life mate would care so much about a stranger."

Sean frowned. "So there really is no choice about how he feels about me?"

Sam's brow furrowed. "What do you mean?"

Tipping his head down to hide his face, Sean fidgeted with his fork. "Someone like Declan couldn't possibly want someone like me."

"What the hell is that supposed to mean?" Sam demanded. "Someone like you? You mean someone brave and kind and beautiful? Someone who sacrificed eating more often than not in order to ensure the other cubs would have food? You are a wonderful person, Sean, and Alpha Declan would be crazy not to want you. Did he tell you he didn't want you? Is that it? Because if he did I'm going to kick his ass."

She made to stand, but Sean stopped her, grabbing her hand. He furiously shook his head. "No. He… he told me he wants to cl-claim me. But how can he possibly want to? I can't even read, Sam. I'd only embarrass him."

Plopping back onto the chair, she smacked him on the shoulder again. "Damn it, Sean. You can learn to read and anything else you set your mind to! I'll teach you. Declan is the kindest alpha I've ever met."

"Exactly!" Sean cried. "He would never tell me the truth

because of how kind he is. I can't believe he truly wants someone whose father was a monster!"

Tears stung Sean's eyes and his nose burned. He hadn't allowed himself the luxury of truly crying in a long, long time, but he very much wanted to give into the urge at the moment. Sam grabbed his shoulders and turned him toward her. She peered into his face, not giving in until he met her gaze. "Do you truly believe he was your father, Sean? Because I don't. I think you were another victim, a child he took from their family."

Sean trembled. He couldn't deny how he'd wondered the same thing over the years. "I don't know," he whispered.

"I do," Sam replied with conviction. "Because a man without a soul like Carl McNeely could never spawn a kind, loving person such as you, Sean. Declan has no idea how lucky he is that you are his mate."

"I agree," a deep voice came from the doorway and Sean tensed, his eyes widening and his breath stuttering inside his lungs.

He raised his gaze to meet the deep emerald green of Declan's. A soft tenderness radiated out toward him, something Sean had only ever seen on the face of one of the actors on TV when he'd caught a glimpse, and Sean shivered at the warmth the look ignited in his belly. Declan came further into the room and crouched down beside his chair to look at him, one hand coming to rest on his knee. "The mating bond only tells us who our true mates are, Sean, it doesn't make us love them. Your heart and the way you have cared so selflessly for the other shifter cubs have shown me the kind of person you are inside. That's who I see. Nothing else matters."

"But-" Sean didn't finish because Declan placed a finger over his lips.

"No buts, my mate. None of it matters. Understand?"

Sean nodded, heart thudding almost painfully against his ribcage.

"Good," Declan said. "The doctor will be here shortly to examine you. If he says it's okay for you to be up, I would like to show you your new home."

"Okay," Sean murmured.

Declan smiled, clearly pleased, and stood. He stroked a hand over the crown of Sean's head. "I think it would be best if he saw you in your room though. He's going to need privacy. Are you finished eating?"

"Yes," Sean answered.

Humming, Declan glanced at Sean's plate. "There's still quite a bit of food there."

"I am full," Sean assured him.

"Okay. If you're sure, but you're to let me know if you get hungry." Declan waited for Sean to stand and then took his hand, leading him out of the room. Sean glanced at Sam and Tara who gave him wide grins. He still didn't know what was expected of him, but went along with Declan for the time being.

The doctor arrived about ten minutes after Declan had ensured Sean's safe return to the bedroom. Sean hadn't been conscious when the doctor had been there before so he tensed when the strange dark-haired man appeared in the doorway with Declan close behind. "Sean, this is Dr. Cameron Green. He's going to make sure you're well enough to be up for light activity."

"Hello, Sean," Cameron greeted, slowly coming toward the bed.

Cameron had well-kept dark brown hair with light hazel eyes. There were laugh lines at the edges of his eyes and Sean could just make out a dimple in one of his cheeks. A strong cleft indented the rounded chin beneath full lips. Sean noticed a silver earring flash in Cameron's right ear when the man turned his head. "You're looking so much better than the last time I saw you," Cameron commented as he set a small black bag down on the stand beside the bed.

Sean didn't reply. He just watched everything Cameron did. Cameron took out several items and laid them on top of the comforter. "I'm going to take your blood pressure, temperature, and a few other vitals first, Sean, then I'm going to check your ribs and arm, see if we can't take that cast off. I'm sure you're dying for a shower by now."

Biting the inside of his bottom lip, Sean nodded. Cameron picked up an odd object with something dangling off of it. "This is a blood pressure cuff. I'm going to wrap it around your upper arm, okay? Then I'm going to pump air into it with this," he pointed at the black plastic thing hanging on the end of it, "and it's going to tell me how your heart is functioning while I listen to it with this." Cameron lifted the end of another item around his neck.

"I need you to remove your shirt, Sean. Can you do that for me?"

Sean started to get nervous and glanced at Declan who stood nearby, arms crossed over his chest, watching them. "I... I guess."

He hesitatingly reached for the bottom of the shirt. A low rumble came from Declan and Sean let go of the shirt instantly, terrified he'd done something wrong.

"Declan," Cameron grunted. "I need to examine him. If you can't control yourself, you'll need to step outside."

"No!" Sean whimpered, petrified of being left alone with Cameron.

Declan was by his side in a heartbeat. "It's all right, baby. I won't leave you," Declan murmured, sliding an arm around Sean's shoulders.

Sean turned his face into Declan's chest and breathed in the familiar scent. He didn't want to appear weak in front of

Declan, but the idea of being around a large, unknown male scared the hell out of him. "I'm sorry," he whispered.

"Don't. It's okay."

Cameron remained quiet, seeming to understand Sean needed a minute to gather his courage. Sean finally managed to pull himself away from Declan enough to grip the edge of the shirt once more and skimmed it over his head. He felt Declan tense beside him, but there were no more growls. Cameron slid two ends of the object around his neck into his ears and then wrapped a part of what he'd called a blood pressure cuff around Sean's upper arm. "It may feel tight, but just try to relax."

The round disc was cold as it came to rest on his inner elbow and Sean jumped. He watched in fascination, his wariness fading away as Cameron pumped the plastic object in his hand and the cuff got stiffer. Cameron didn't even seem to pay attention to Sean at all as he listened to whatever sounds he wanted to hear. A grunt came out when Cameron finished and unwrapped the cuff. "Good, good. Now I am going to listen to your heartbeat."

He placed the disc over Sean's chest, pressing in for about ten seconds. "Good. Now, can you lean forward a little bit?"

Sean did as he asked, very aware of Declan's arm slipping down to his waist to support him. Cameron placed the disc on his back close to his shoulder blade. "Now breathe in, good, now out." He moved it over to the other side of Sean's back. "Again."

Cameron pulled the ends out of his ears, wrapped the object around his neck again, and picked up a notebook. He made some notations in it. "Do you feel any tenderness on your ribs still?"

"A little," Sean admitted, leaning into Declan's side.

"When you are sitting or just when you move?"

"When I move around."

Declan huffed, but didn't say anything.

"It's good to get some exercise. Lying in bed all day doesn't stretch the muscles or work out the kinks." Cameron set the notebook and pen down. "I'm going to press on the area a little. I need you to tell me if it hurts at all, okay?"

Sean nodded, tensing as Cameron moved in closer and put his fingers on the area where his father's boot print had already faded. He had to bite his lip and fight the urge to squirm as Cameron prodded the area. "That hurt?"

"No," Sean responded through clenched teeth.

Cameron frowned, pushing on the spot again. "You sure? You tense up when I do that."

"I'm sure," Sean replied, struggling to keep from jerking away from Cameron.

Cameron trailed his fingers down a little further and this time Sean couldn't quite stifle the giggle. A smile tilted the corner of Cameron's lips. "Ah, ticklish I see."

"Very."

"Sorry. We're almost done. Any pain?"

"No."

"Here?"

"No." Another snort came free much to Sean's utter embarrassment. He felt Declan's frame shudder beside him and he glanced at him to see Declan's eyes dancing with mirth. Scowling, he poked Declan in the side who jolted at the nudge.

"Sorry, love," Declan murmured, nuzzling Sean's temple.

"Well, it appears your ribs have healed quite nicely," Cameron said, sitting back. "I'd like to do some blood work, make sure there's nothing else going on. Is that okay?"

Sean frowned. "Blood work?"

Cameron slid a needle and a vial from the black bag and Sean mewled in terror. He tried to climb over Declan to escape. "No! No! Stay away!"

Declan wrapped his arms around Sean. "Easy, baby. Cam, put that fucking thing away!"

Sean struggled against Declan's hold, crying at being restrained. "Let me go! Please! I promise I'll be good!"

"Shh, Shh. It's okay. Jesus. I've got you, baby. I swear no one is ever going to hurt you again." Declan rocked Sean while whispering soothing nothings into his ear.

At some point Cameron slipped from the room, leaving them alone, and Sean eventually tired himself out. He lay against Declan's chest, staring at the far wall, wondering when Cameron would be back and when the agony would begin. What had he done? Why did they want to hurt him? He'd begun to believe he was safe here. Had it all been a lie?

"Talk to me, Sean."

The deep rumble at his back surprised him and Sean jumped.

"What did he do to you?"

Sean didn't understand. Wasn't that what they were going to do to him?

"What was in the needle, Sean?"

He shook his head weakly along Declan's shoulder. He didn't know. All he knew was the sheer torture it left behind.

"He injected you with something?"

"Yes," Sean rasped.

"God, baby, I'm so sorry. I wish…" Declan pressed a kiss to Sean's bare shoulder and another to Sean's throat. "If only I had known you were right there, on the edge of my lands…"

"What did I do?" Sean asked.

"What do you mean?"

"Why did he want to hurt me?"

"Because your father was a sick man."

Sean gave a shake of his head. "The doctor."

Declan sucked in a deep breath. "Did you think I would

let him do that to you? Did you think I wanted him to hurt you?"

"He had a needle," Sean replied simply.

A shudder ripped through the large body behind him and Sean frowned.

"Listen to me, Sean. Hear what I am telling you. No one, *no one*, will ever hurt you again. Me especially. Do you understand me?"

Sean tilted his head enough to be able to see Declan's profile. Furrowed lines creased the area between Declan's brow. There were more around the outside edges of Declan's mouth. The goatee and stubble didn't hide them. Sean reached up and traced them with the tip of a finger. Declan nuzzled into the palm of Sean's hand, tactile and wanting.

"I'll tell Cameron to forget the blood work," Declan said softly. "I don't ever want to hear you cry again, okay? The only sound you should ever make is laughter."

Pursing his lips, Sean eyed Declan. The fear and panic in Sean's veins had dissipated and he no longer wanted to get away from Declan. In fact, he had become very aware of being shirtless and Declan's muscular, furred arms were wrapped tight around him. He drew his knees up to his chest to cover the reaction his body had to Declan's closeness. "I don't think anyone can laugh all the time."

Declan poked Sean in the side eliciting a small laugh from Sean. "No?"

"Declan, don't," Sean said.

"And if I do?" Declan asked, repeating his previous movement again.

Sean tried to grab at Declan's hands, but he couldn't stop him and before long Declan had Sean pinned beneath him, relentlessly tickling the hell out of him. Peals of laughter bounced off the walls as Sean begged him to stop and attempted more than once to snag Declan's hands, but it wasn't until fat tears of joy were rolling down Sean's temples into his hairline and Sean's lungs felt on fire that Declan stopped. Declan gave him a smug smile. "See?" Declan taunted.

Scowling without heat, Sean pushed at Declan's immovable pecs. "That's so not right."

"Laughter looks good on you."

The frown died away and Sean stared up at Declan. His fingers flexed against the planes of Declan's hard chest and he pulled his bottom lip between his teeth. He wanted to ask Declan to kiss him, but didn't know if he had the right.

"You don't have to ask," Declan murmured before bending his head to brush his mouth over Sean's.

Sean had forgotten Declan could hear his thoughts if he let him and his cheeks heated at knowing Declan had been able to catch something so intimate. Declan lifted away and smiled at him, trailing the backs his fingers over Sean's throat. "I think we should see what Cam's decision is and if he thinks you're well enough. I want to show off my mate to the streak."

Swallowing in nervousness, Sean nodded. "Okay."

DECLAN

eclan rose off the bed, reluctant to let Sean go. The sheer terror in Sean's cries echoed in Declan's ears and his tiger wanted to be set free, to rip apart whoever caused his mate such pain. He buried the urge, ensuring Sean couldn't feel it through the bond between them. There were no known agents in this world which could cause a shifter to feel anything close to the agony Sean seemed so frightened of and the idea of such a thing existing concerned Declan greatly. Who would create such a disgusting toxin? And why? The questions whirled through his mind quick as lightning bugs as Declan opened the door to beckon Cameron to return. It seemed he not only had the collar which he needed answers to.

Cameron came forward from where he leaned against the wall. "Everything all right, Alpha?"

A leopard shifter, Cameron had come to Declan's streak three years ago when the pack he'd been part of was attacked by a pack of rogues lead by a scarred Alpha wolf and most of the members were killed. Cameron had barely escaped with his life. Declan had absorbed three others into his streak while the other six remaining members had traveled to other packs to be with family. There were only two other leopard shifters in the Royal Taiga Streak besides Cameron. "Everything's fine. Don't even show him a needle."

Cameron gave a brief nod. "I don't need to do the blood work. He is doing much better than when he was brought here. I believe we can remove the cast as well."

Declan stepped back and allowed Cameron into the room, watching carefully as Cameron approached the bed and Sean as if he would an injured animal. "I'm sorry if I scared you, Sean," Cameron said. "If it's okay, I'd like to remove the cast on your arm. See what your mobility is."

Sean consented, but never looked away as Cameron began cutting away at the cast. Declan returned to Sean's side and clasped Sean's free hand in his. He would do everything in his power to ensure he kept his promise to Sean.

"Can you move your arm for me, Sean?" Cameron asked once the cast had been removed. "Bend it like that. Any pain? Soreness?"

Sean shook his head. "No."

Cameron made some notes on a notepad. "I would like to get an x-ray, if at all possible. Just to make sure. Would you be able to come to my clinic?"

"We'll be there," Declan assured him. "When?"

"As soon as possible. I don't want to risk damaging the bone further since we removed the cast already."

"What's an x-ray?" Sean asked.

Cameron blinked then smiled. "I take a picture of your bone so we can make sure it's healed."

Sean frowned. "How?"

"The machine sends a shot of radiation through your arm and bounces back an image of the bone, giving me a clear view of whether or not the break has healed or if there are any fractures still remaining."

"Wow. Really?"

Chuckling, Cameron replied, "Yep. It's rather fascinating stuff. There's also machines that can do the same thing with your heart, lungs, and other organs."

Sean's eyes widened further causing Declan's heart to clench in his chest. "Is he okay to be up, Cam?"

"He's healthy enough to do some light exercise. I wouldn't recommend he do any marathons or anything just yet. But walking is fine. Is there a reason he hasn't shifted to heal the damage?" Cameron asked.

"I can't shift," Sean replied. He said it so matter-of-factly, as if it didn't make any difference in the world, but Declan sensed his sadness. "The collar prevents me from doing so."

"I see." Cameron leaned in closer to peer at the collar. "Well we'll just continue using old fashioned medicine to keep you on the road to recovery. Alpha Declan, if you could get him to the clinic for the x-ray that will help a lot."

"As soon as he is dressed."

"I'll head over there now to get things ready then," Cameron said and stood. He gathered his things and left the room.

Declan went to the dresser where he'd stored more of the borrowed clothing. "Fredrick and Tomas's parents sent over some clothing for you until what we ordered arrives. Brigette's cousin Alexi is about the same size you are. They may be slightly big on you, but shouldn't be too much so."

He took out a pair of jeans, a T-shirt, and a pair of under-wear and brought them back to the bed. "Do you need help getting dressed?"

Sean gave Declan a look. "I'm not a child."

Declan sighed. "I know that, ba-Sean." He figured it best not to call Sean baby while Sean was feeling as though he were being coddled. "I'm just concerned you're not entirely healed yet."

"You heard what Dr. Cameron said. I'm fine. Besides, I've dealt with worse than this and had to keep taking care of the others."

"Things are different now. You don't have to take care of anyone but yourself."

"I can get dressed by myself. I promise."

Declan eyed Sean, scenting the air for dishonesty but found none. He relented. "All right. I'm going to let Rose know where we're going. Meet me by the front door in ten minutes?"

"Okay."

He set the clothing down beside Sean and left. His tiger prowled beneath his skin, yowling for him to return to his mate, but he knew he had to show he trusted Sean or risk breaking the tentative trust they were building between them.

Declan sought out Rose and told her where he was taking Sean. By the time he returned to the entryway, Sean already stood by the front door, waiting for him with hands held in front of him. Declan smiled. "Eager, are we?"

Sean nodded. "I'd like to be outside."

Declan winced. He knew Sean hadn't gotten much chance to spend time outdoors with being held in the basement, other than when he'd apparently had to bury those children or whatever else his father had forced him to do. "Would you like to take a walk before we head over to the clinic?"

"Can we?" Sean asked excitedly.

"For a little bit."

Sean reached for the door handle, too enthusiastic to wait. Declan laughed and followed behind Sean. He couldn't help his tiger's instinct to protect Sean and grasped Sean's elbow as they walked, pointing things out, explaining the ways of the streak. "Everyone does their share. We don't hide from the outside world, but we do tend to stick to our own as do many of the other shifter packs. The humans would use us for experiments or hurt us out of fear if they knew of our existence.

"There's a daycare that the parents are able to leave their children at while they go about their daily tasks or jobs. The nearest town is about thirty miles south of here. Usually we take whatever we grow, craft, or wish to sell there. Many of the business owners have contracts with the streak."

"Do the humans come here?" Sean asked, peering around curiously.

"No. We do not allow them on our land. My great grandfather bought two thousand acres of land for the streak before this area had developed as much as it has. There are other houses and cabins littering the area, but we're relatively safe to wander the forest in our animal forms as much as we need." Declan waved at Micah Rivers, a bobcat shifter, who called out a greeting from his front porch.

"How many shifters are there in your streak?"

"There are a little over two hundred. Now more with you, Sam, and the others."

Sean stopped and looked at him. "You consider us part of your streak?"

Declan turned Sean toward him. He raised a hand to cup Sean's cheek. "Of course, Sean. You're my mate. The moment I scented you was the moment you became a part of me and a part of this streak. The girls are your pack. They refuse to leave you which means they belong here, too. For as long as they wish it."

The blue of Sean's eyes became so bright it almost hurt and then Declan found his arms full of Sean, his slender arms around Declan's waist. "Thank you," Sean whispered.

Tenderness swamped Declan and he carded his fingers through Sean's jagged locks. "You do not have to thank me, Sean. I would do anything for you."

Sean nuzzled his cheek into Declan's chest in an almost feline way. Declan had a sneaking suspicion Sean was some sort of cat shifter. The smaller male seemed way too tactile to be any other type. "Come on, we need to get you seen to and I think those stitches need to be removed too so we can finally get you into a shower and then see about having your hair trimmed." Declan touched the threaded flesh on Sean's collar bone and forehead. "Cam didn't have a chance to take these out earlier."

A small sigh came free, but Sean stepped away. "Okay."

They continued to the clinic, Declan still describing and explaining the ways of his streak to Sean as they went. There were two female wolf shifters with their children in the waiting area when they arrived. "Alpha Declan," they greeted in unison.

"Is everything okay, Lisa? Heather?" Declan asked.

"Everything's fine. Christian has a minor stomach bug. Think he picked it up at the daycare," Lisa explained.

Heather smiled. "Same with my youngest Richard. He's been under the weather. Was hoping Dr. West could prescribe something to settle his stomach."

"Dr. West?" Sean murmured.

The two women zeroed in on Sean then who immediately stepped behind Declan a fraction at the sudden attention. "Lisa Lunera and Heather Memphis, this is Sean, my mate," Declan announced proudly, drawing Sean to his side.

The two women gasped and stood, congratulating Declan. "That's so wonderful, Alpha!" Lisa exclaimed, holding her hand out to Sean.

Sean tentatively took it, appearing uncertain, and Declan nudged Sean forward with a gentle palm. "Lisa is the owner of the daycare I mentioned before and Heather helps oversee the accounts and inventory of the streak. She's Victor's cousin's wife."

Lisa smiled, warm and inviting, and clasped his hand in between two of hers. "Look at you. Such beautiful skin! Like porcelain. I'm so jealous."

A becoming blush stained Sean's cheeks pink and Declan hid a grin. "We're here to see Dr. Green. Sean is still healing from his ordeal."

"Oh, I heard the rumors!" Heather exclaimed, clucking her tongue. "Such an awful thing! You were one of those children, Sean?"

The flush faded away along with Sean's smile and Declan could sense Sean's unease. He placed his hand on Sean's shoulder. "I think Dr. Green is ready for us," he said, glancing at the nurse who sat at the front desk.

"Oh, of course! Welcome to the streak, Sean!" Heather said.

"Thank you," Sean whispered.

"I hope your little ones feel better," Declan said as he led Sean toward the back of the clinic.

Cameron appeared in one of the doorways. "In here, Alpha."

Declan coaxed Sean into the room and helped Sean onto the table Cameron indicated. First, Cameron made short work of removing the stitches. Though the wounds had healed significantly, slashes of pink still marred the paleness of Sean's flesh. He never left Sean's side, holding onto Sean's hand tightly while Cameron did his thing.

Then it was time for the x-rays. Cameron had Sean lay down and brought a portable machine over to the side of the table. He kept up a steady stream of explanation while positioning Sean's arm for the best image possible. "We will need to step out of the room, I'm afraid," Cameron said, apology evident in his tone.

Sean gave Declan a worried glance and Declan bent down to kiss his forehead. "I'll be just outside that glass." He pointed to the big window. "I'm not leaving you, baby. There's nothing to fear here."

Taking a deep breath, Sean nodded and gave a rushed, "'K."

Giving Sean a tender smile, Declan nuzzled Sean's temple. "A few minutes and I'll be right back by your side, Sean."

There was no doubt Sean felt nervous, but the trust he showed in Declan soothed the wound torn open from earlier when Sean believed Declan capable of hurting him. Declan watched through the window as Cameron ran a couple x-rays on Sean's arm. The instant Cameron indicated he could return to Sean, he shot through the door and helped Sean sit up. He knew an outsider would believe he showed his Achilles' heel with his mate, but the knowledge of just how close he'd come to losing Sean before he'd even found him weighed on Declan's shoulders heavily and he would challenge any who dared to call him weak.

"Was that it?" Sean asked.

"Yep. See? Didn't hurt, right?" Declan asked.

"No."

"Let's go into Cam's office while he waits for the images to print."

Sean never stopped looking around, absorbing everything around him like a sponge, as they made the short trip to Cameron's office. Declan thought back to what Sam had told him about Sean not being able to read and wondered what else Sean had never been taught. Unbidden images of carnal pleasures rose to Declan's mind and heat pooled between his thighs, his balls growing heavy with seed and the desire to fill Sean despite knowing he could never impregnate him. The idea of being the first to touch Sean so intimately made his cock throb and his fangs ache to taste the smooth, pale flesh Declan had seen so many times over the last several days while helping Sean dress and changing his bandages.

Taking a deep breath, Declan fought to get his body under control. Cameron would no doubt scent his lust the moment he stepped into the room. Sean seemed none the wiser, his shifter traits buried beneath the human ones. Declan curled his fingers over the arms of the chair he sat down in and held on tight, nerves fracturing as his tiger battered the surface of his control, throwing itself at his skin in an effort to break free and claim their mate. His fangs broke free from their gums and Declan closed his eyes, which were no doubt flickering between human and tiger.

"Shit." The swear word came from behind him and Declan couldn't hold back the yowl he released. "Alpha, please," Cameron gasped, dropping to one knee and tilting his head to the side. "He's not ready. You know that."

"What's going on?" Sean asked, voice trembling.

Declan swung his head to stare at Sean, his entire body quivering with the need to pin Sean down and fuck him, mate him, make him theirs before anyone else could take him away from them. He dragged in a deep breath, struggling to remain in control, but Cameron's next words shattered the tenuous grip he had.

"Sean, you need to slowly come toward me."

SEAN

Sean had been studying the tidy little room they sat in when something changed. There were so many fascinating things around him, things he'd never seen, even on the TV when he'd gotten the opportunity to watch it. The strange machine Dr. Green had called an x-ray scared him at first, but when it didn't do anything except make a couple of noises his fear died off and curiosity took its place. Now he perched on the edge of a chair, wanting nothing more than to stand up and have the chance to poke at some of the assorted jars he saw sitting on a counter nearby. There were also several posters on the walls that, even though he couldn't read them, had images he couldn't stop staring at.

At first, a sweet scent hit Sean's nostrils and it quickly became tantalizing, something Sean wanted more of. He breathed in deep draughts, trying to identify the fragrance. He'd never smelled anything like it and it went straight to his belly and even lower, causing a strange reaction between his thighs. Sean's eyes widened a fraction and he clenched his legs together in hopes of hiding his hardening flesh.

But it was the purring from Declan's direction which

surprised him even more and Sean turned to stare at Declan. The sound intensified the heat he felt building inside of him. His back entrance throbbed as Declan's purring increased and Sean gasped, his chest heaving as he tried to breathe through the dizzying effects of whatever was happening. Distress pulsed through him when the doctor returned and Sean couldn't stop the odd sense of disappointment, but Declan's response to Dr. Green's appearance and Dr. Green's request for Sean to stand and come to him sent even more fire to Sean's groin.

"Alpha, he's not ready," Dr. Green protested.

Declan snarled at Dr. Green and Dr. Green stepped backward, out of the door. "All right. I understand."

Sean didn't. His head felt stuffed full of cotton and his body seemed as if it would be consumed by the flames licking along his veins. He whimpered and glanced between Declan and Dr. Green. A growl rumbled in Declan's throat whenever he looked away from Declan, forcing Sean's gaze back to Declan. "What's going on?" he asked.

"Just know Declan would never hurt you, Sean. The mating fever has hit him, hard, and he needs to claim you or he may very well tear the compound apart," Dr. Green explained in a gentle voice.

Sean frowned, not understanding what he meant. "Claim me?"

Declan slid from the chair to his hands and knees, purring again, and began to move toward Sean. His eyes were almost entirely cat now and Sean shivered at the way Declan licked his lips.

"I have to go. Just trust him, Sean. He won't hurt you."

Declan reached Sean and Sean touched Declan's cheek. "I do trust him," Sean whispered just as the office door closed.

The kisses he'd already shared with Declan previously hadn't prepared him for the one he received right then.

Declan surged upward to capture, no, to dominate Sean's mouth, in a kiss so powerful, so hungry it destroyed any thought Sean may have had to resist. He grasped Declan's muscular shoulders, holding on tight as Declan yanked Sean from the seat into his arms. Sean could do nothing except open his lips to the tongue seeking entrance, the hot flesh flooding his mouth in a desperate need to explore every unknown centimeter.

Sean's mind whirled at every new sensation, every new touch. He couldn't stop the cry Declan swallowed as Declan wedged himself between Sean's thighs, bringing their equally rigid lengths into contact with one another. Sean opened his eyes wide at the sheer pleasure as Declan rocked their pelvises against each other. No one had ever touched him like this before. Suddenly, he found himself airborne and then he was on his back on the desk, items clattering to the floor with the sweep of one of Declan's hands.

"Need you, mate," Declan garbled, his words barely legible as he dragged his mouth down Sean's throat. His lips, tongue, and teeth licked, sucked and nipped their way along Sean's skin as Sean ran his hands down Declan's back until he reached the hem of Declan's T-shirt where he pushed his hands beneath the fabric. The heat from Declan's flesh seared into Sean's palms the moment they came into contact. Sean moaned, tossing his head side to side as he tried to comprehend and deal with the multitude of feelings beating at his senses.

The sound of material ripping disturbed Sean until he realized Declan had literally torn the shirt from Sean's body. Sean started, but forgot in the next instant when Declan's mouth latched onto his nipple. "Declan!"

Flames licked along Sean's body with each hard suckle of Declan's lips at his nipple. Sean buried his fingers in Declan's hair and hung on for dear life, panting with need. Declan didn't linger there for long though. Wet, slick kisses explored his sternum down to his belly and a moist tongue dipping into his naval wrenching a whimper from Sean. Somehow Declan managed to drag Sean's pants and underwear down and off his legs without tangling them on the sneakers he wore. Sean's cock slapped against his abdomen, smearing a clear, sticky fluid which Declan lapped up, a rumble rattling inside Declan's chest.

Embarrassment caused Sean to cover his face with one hand while the other moved from Declan's scalp to his shoulder. He made a mewling noise when hot, damp heat blew across his shaft just before Declan engulfed the length in his mouth. Sean cried out, arching his back from the desk. Nothing in his life had ever felt so good. The noises coming from his throat sounded loud in the small room, but Sean couldn't hold them back. His entire body trembled as Declan suckled at his prick, large hands pinning Sean's hips in place on the desk, keeping him from moving away. Not that he would want to!

A tightness spread through his balls and up through his groin. Sean could feel something spiraling within him, getting ready to spring loose, and he didn't know if he should push Declan away or pull him closer and beg for him to never stop. His toes curled inside his sneakers and he dug his fingers into Declan's muscles. "Declan... I... I... please..."

His broken pleading only seemed to encourage Declan and the pressure of heat on his cock grew harder. Sean couldn't contain himself. He shattered, screaming Declan's name while clutching at Declan, his entire being quivering from the inside out. A buzzing sound filled Sean's ears and his vision went black just before his body went boneless upon the desk. He shuddered again and again, unable to determine what the hell had just happened to him.

He barely realized Declan moving over him or the sounds

of Declan digging through the drawers of the metal desk. It was only when he found his legs drawn up and felt a probing at the entrance to his backside did the satiation begin to dissipate and tension invaded his body. Purring rumbled nearby and Sean looked at Declan's face. Declan leaned down to capture his lips in a warm kiss as a slick digit invaded his channel. Sean gave a choked moan and jerked, surprised. Declan slid the finger out and then in again. It didn't hurt. It seemed strange at first, but the oddness quickly vanished to become pleasure once more.

Declan added a second slickened finger to the first one, stretching Sean's hole wider. Sean went rigid again, uncertainty invading him much like Declan, but when Declan hooked those fingers and brushed over something inside of him Sean's eyes widened and he gave a slight whimper. "Oh!"

A satisfied growl rattled in Declan's throat. He tagged whatever spot it was inside of Sean again and again until Sean was nothing more than a mass of trembling flesh. He heard the sound of a zipper and hot wet heat brushed over his inner thigh causing Sean to start slightly. He tried to look down, but Declan claimed his mouth for another kiss and Sean became lost in Declan's lips. Suddenly empty, Sean moaned in annoyance and canted his hips, seeking Declan's withdrawn fingers. A blunt object pressed against him this time, different from the slender digits. It wasn't until the new rigid column began to invade his body that Sean realized something unusual entered him. He stiffened again.

Declan mouthed the area where Sean's throat connected to his shoulder, his broad chest vibrating with a low purr. The sound combined with the slickness of Declan's tongue swirling over the sensitive skin relaxed Sean a fraction at a time and eventually his channel accepted what he came to understand was Declan. Sean gripped the back of Declan's shirt with quivering hands the moment the fabric of Declan's jeans scraped against his bottom, indicating Declan had seated himself as far inside Sean as possible. Sweat dampened Sean's body by then and he could barely breathe through the multitude of sensations inundating him. Something seemed to wrap around his chest and burrow its way inside his heart, tying him irrevocably to the big shifter who'd not only rescued him, but had done everything in his power to care for Sean from the moment Sean had awakened.

"Declan," Sean murmured, drawing his legs upward around Declan's waist, hooking his still-sneakered feet around the ankles to hold on tight. He didn't understand everything. In fact, he didn't understand much of anything right then, but one thing he did know was that he wanted Declan. When Declan moved, Sean sucked in a shuddering breath at how good it made him feel despite the stretched fullness.

Sean clenched around the large hardness which brought forth a deep growl from Declan and a sharp thrust of Declan's hips. Thrusts which didn't stop and Declan held tight to Sean to keep him from slipping away from him on each plunge into Sean's now receptive backside. The soft cotton of Declan's T-shirt dragged over the pulsing flesh of Sean's cock, increasing the already heightened pleasure crashing over Sean. Despite having already reached a pinnacle moments before, Sean knew he would lose himself again and clutched at Declan as hard as he could, afraid if he didn't he'd fly apart and never be whole once more. Sounds of sobbing echoed from the walls around them and Sean wondered vaguely who made the noises only to realize they were coming from him. Inane begging spilled from his lips as Declan continued to drive into him.

Pressure unlike anything Sean had ever experienced began to build within him. Tingles ran through his belly and thighs to his balls and he couldn't help the panting gasps bursting from his lips. It scared him how intense everything became until something suddenly snapped and a pleasure crashed over him so immense it stole his breathe. Pulsing jets of hot liquid splashed across his abdomen, almost scalding him with their heat.

A loud roar penetrated the fog dampening Sean's mind and then a bright flash of pain followed by another wave of sheer bliss. Something shifted then. Sean could see a large tiger approaching him, padding toward him at a steady pace, staring as if it intended to pounce. Yet when it reached him and the moment changed, Sean found himself curled up against the warm, soft fur, and strong vibrations shot straight through his chest.

Sandpaper lazily drifted over his cheek and Sean giggled at the swipe of the tiger's tongue. He scratched the tiger behind the ear, grinning when it leaned into his touch and purred even louder. The bright orange and black stripes were beautiful and Sean marveled at their color against his own skin. The tiger began to melt away only to be replaced by Declan, who immediately swept Sean against his chest, capturing his mouth in a deep kiss. Sean moaned and wrapped his arms around Declan's neck, holding on tight.

Everything changed again and Sean found his viewpoint had become lower as though he were on hands and knees. Then he realized he'd shifted! He'd become the animal he'd been born to be, but before he could try to even gain a glimpse of himself, the same orange and black tiger tackled him into the soft grass. Sean let out a yowl of displeasure at being taken down in such a manner. Yowl? Only cats yowled, didn't they? He didn't have the chance to think much further into it because everything started to fade away and he found himself back in the doctor's office on the desk with Declan.

When he finally gathered his faculties enough to think, he

found Declan lapping at his shoulder while shudders wracked Declan's large frame. Sean could feel Declan still inside of him and when he tried to move Declan gave a low rumble, holding him in place. "Declan?" Sean murmured.

The sound of Sean's voice or maybe Sean whispering his name seemed to bring Declan back to himself and Declan raised his head, blinking his eyes as though he'd just awakened. Sean saw horror enter Declan's features. "Sean? Did I… Oh god. I'm so sorry, Sean."

Sean winced as Declan slid free from him, the flesh tender after the new experience. He didn't understand why Declan regretted what they'd done. He sat up and tried to cover himself the best he could with his hands. Did Declan not really want him? Sean couldn't blame Declan considering he had nothing to offer the powerful alpha.

"No!" Declan gathered Sean into his arms, resting his chin on top of Sean's head. "No, Sean. Never believe I could ever not want you. But this isn't how I wanted it to happen. I didn't want to claim you until you were ready, until you knew what it meant, and certainly not in a place such as this."

"I don't understand," Sean replied, his voice muffled against Declan's chest.

"I know you don't and that's why I'm angry at myself, at my tiger, for giving in to the mating fever. There are things you don't yet understand about being mates and I wanted you to have the choice because so many have already been taken away from you."

There weren't many times in Sean's life where he could count his heart hurting from being happy, but hearing Declan's words sent a sharp stab deep into his chest, straight to said organ. Tears welled up and trickled down his cheeks. He may not understand what had truly happened, but he did remember what Sam had told him about mates; how they were two halves of the same soul and once they found one another they never let go. The knowledge of Declan being his mate finally sank in. He'd been given a gorgeous, strong, fierce tiger prince to spend the rest of his life with.

Declan tightened his arms around Sean. A chuckle rumbled beneath Sean's ear. "Haven't I been telling you that same thing, baby?"

Sean tilted his head enough to look at Declan. "I don't des-"

A fierce glare stopped the words on Sean's lips. Declan cupped Sean's cheeks, using the pads of his thumbs to wipe away the tracks of Sean's tears. "You deserve it more than anyone I've ever met, Sean. After everything you've endured no one is more deserving than you to be happy and safe. I don't want you to ever believe otherwise. Don't forget, we're tied now. Here," he tapped gently on Sean's temple, "and here," he placed his palm over Sean's heart. "I know what you're feeling and thinking, mate, and I will do everything in my power to ensure you realize how precious you are."

Sean flushed. He opened his mouth to protest Declan's words, but snapped it closed with an audible click of his jaw when Declan gave him a look. Self-consciousness set in when he realized he was still naked in Declan's arms and the red hue in his cheeks deepened. Declan carded his fingers through Sean's hair with a husky laugh. "Better get used to it, mate, because now that you've accepted me, you aren't sleeping alone ever again and I never wear clothes to bed. Ever."

Eyes widening, Sean met Declan's gaze. His breathing deepened and he felt his body respond. The green of Declan's eyes darkened, but before Declan could do more than bend his head, a tentative knock sounded. Declan sighed and leaned his forehead against Sean's. "The real world calls. We still need to hear the results of your x-rays. Besides, I would prefer the next time I indulge in your delectable body it be in a real bed out of earshot of others."

Sean covered his face with both hands, a small sound of discomfort rattling in his throat, and Declan kissed his cheek, amusement radiating from him. "You tore my clothes," Sean pointed out when he could speak.

Declan bent down and picked up the tattered T-shirt, eyeing it. "Hmm… I guess I did. At least your pants seemed to have survived." He handed the bottoms to Sean and then tugged his shirt over his head. "Here."

"I'll swim in that!" Sean exclaimed.

"No one sees my mate," Declan said, his tone deadly.

Sean took the shirt and pulled it on. It fell to his knees causing Sean to grimace. He looked as though he wore a dress or something.

"We'll return to the house so you can get a different one. Besides, the clothing we ordered for you should be in sometime today or tomorrow." Declan ran his palm down Sean's arm in a soothing caress before calling out, "You can come in now, Cam."

The door opened a fraction and Dr. Green stuck his head in first, peering at them to make sure they were decent. Sean saw the doctor's nose twitch and sniffed the air himself. A sharp tang of something decidedly Declan clung to the room for sure. Declan grinned when Dr. Green gave them both a look. "You couldn't have waited until you got back to your house?" Dr. Green groused as he came fully into the room, leaving the door open, no doubt to let the scents dissipate.

"Sorry, Cam. Someday you'll know how it is though." Declan sat in the chair he'd been in previously and, surprising Sean, tugged him down into his lap. At first, Sean tried to climb off, uncomfortable at being held in front of Dr. Green, but Declan refused to set him free and he eventually relented. "So, how's the arm looking?"

Dr. Green had been in the process of picking up the items Declan had shoved off the desk when he'd set Sean on it before and he straightened, turned on the light of some square box on the wall, and grabbed up some black plastic sheets. Sean watched in fascination as Dr. Green proceeded to shove those plastic sheets into clips on the square box which revealed there were actual images on them. He made a sound of astonishment and stared as the doctor started to talk. "Everything looks good, Alpha. The bone has healed quite nicely. There's not even a fracture left behind. I would say he's good to go with just about any type of activity. I also took an x-ray of the broken rib as well. It has also set without any issues."

"That's great news, Cam. There are no lingering problems then?"

"No, but if it's all right with Sean, I'd like to speak to you in private for a moment, if I may?"

Sean shrugged and nodded.

Dr. Green smiled gently. "If you'd like, you can watch T.V. in the waiting room. Nurse Holt can show you."

"Okay," Sean replied.

Dr. Green hit one of the buttons on a phone on his desk. "Nurse Holt, would you please come escort my patient to the waiting room? I need to speak with Alpha Declan for a few moments."

No more than twenty seconds had passed before an older woman with graying dark brown hair appeared in the doorway. "Nurse Holt, this is Sean. Sean, this is Becky Holt. She's-"

"Wolf," Sean interrupted, eyes widening. There had been only one other wolf shifter besides Tara over the years. One of the cubs, a young girl, had been a wolf. She'd only been in the basement with them for four years. The day after her eleventh birthday he'd been forced to bury her. His father had killed her before he'd had a chance to do to her what he'd done to Sam and Tara. The woman standing in front of him smelled almost exactly like her. "Gina," Sean whispered.

Becky's pretty silver eyes widened in shock. "What did you say?"

Sean shivered and shook his head. "I'm sorry. I-I-"

"What's wrong?" Declan asked him, concern in his voice.

"Why did you say my daughter's name? How did you know it?" Becky demanded, coming closer. "Do you know where she is?"

"Becky, you forget your place," Declan snarled, standing while still holding Sean close.

Becky immediately cowered, craning her neck toward Declan in a show of submission. "Forgive me, Alpha."

"I'm sorry," Sean whispered, burying his face against Declan's bicep. Bile rose in his throat as the memory of Gina's broken body rose in his mind. He felt Declan jerk and rage crashed over Sean causing him to flinch.

Declan cupped Sean's nape in a calming manner. "Shh, baby. I'm not angry with you. I'm furious that bastard put you through so much."

"Please," Becky begged. "Tell me where my daughter is."

Sean couldn't speak past the lump choking him and Declan seemed to understand. He coaxed Sean into one of the chairs and then slowly approached Becky, placing a hand on her shoulder. "I'm so sorry, Becky."

Those words seemed to be enough to make her understand Gina was dead because she let out a wailing cry and collapsed against Declan, who gathered her close and allowed her to sob in his arms. Sean's heart broke for her and the parents of the other children who were buried out behind the house. He had done his own mourning for each and every cub over the years. The last one a mere three months before Ronnie had been taken and the whole rescue had happened.

Once she'd calmed enough, Dr. Green called her husband and sent her home for the day. He situated Sean in the waiting room himself with the remote for the T.V. and showed him how to use it. Sean didn't really feel like watching anything anymore. A dark cloud had settled itself over his heart and he let the remote drop to his lap as he thought over all of the children taken during the course of his life. His father had never shown any of them mercy. It was a blessing the seven of them had made it out alive. Fredrick and Tomas were back with their parents. Sam, Tara, and Vicky were alive even though none of them knew where they belonged. Sean knew with more certainty than ever he'd made the right decision to let Ronnie escape despite the beating he'd received which had almost ended his life. If Sean hadn't taken the chance, who knew how many others Carl McNeely would have murdered.

1 2

DECLAN

"I thought you should know what else I found on the x-rays, Declan," Cameron said after he'd closed the door.

Cameron only addressed him as Declan when they were alone, despite the many times Declan had told him it wasn't necessary to call him Alpha unless in front of another streak or pack. Declan tensed. "What is it?"

"Sean's body has been through quite a number of traumas over the course of his life. Aside from the slight limp he has in his gait from the improperly set bone in his leg, there have been other broken bones in his ribs and the same shoulder area. Without having a full scan from head to toe, I can't truly know the extent of the damage to the rest of his body, but I'm going to make an educated guess and say they'd reveal having gone through the same level of stress."

"What are you telling me, Cam?"

Cameron took a deep breath and looked Declan in the eye, face serious. "He may never be able to shift, even if you do get the collar off, Declan. I don't know if his body will be able to handle the change."

A cold chill spread over Declan. "But you don't know that

for sure."

"No. Again, I can't tell without doing a full body scan, tests, an MRI even. It could cause him unbearable agony to change or it could heal the damage. In fact, I'm not even sure removing the collar is a good idea right now until we know for sure."

Declan swore, his hands wrapping around the metal handles of the chair he sat in so tightly they bent outward. He wanted to spare Sean any further pain, but it seemed at every turn he failed to do so. How could he tell this to Sean? Even now he could feel Sean's distress over the situation from mere moments ago and the children Sean had cared for over the years. Declan wanted to break something, to tear it apart with his bare hands, to rend the flesh from someone and rage at the heavens to explain why someone with such a gentle soul would have to endure so fucking much.

"Do you have the equipment here?"

Cameron shook his head. "No. You'd have to take him into the city. I don't have the MRI machine here for tests like that."

"Schedule it. As soon as possible." Declan stood.

"Declan?"

He looked at Cameron.

"Sean may appear fragile, but he's stronger than you may believe him to be. He spent years being abused and survived when others didn't. That says a lot about his inner and outer strength."

"I know it, Cam. He's stronger than me because I know I would never have lived through so much and come out the other end as sweet and kind as he is," Declan replied, his expression somber.

Cameron smiled, though there was no humor in it. "Victor told me about the graves, Declan. To prepare us for exhuming the bodies. We need to identify them and start notifying the parents. It's awful Gina is dead, but at least now Becky knows what happened to her daughter. It's the not knowing that's the worst, I think. The constant wondering where they are, are they alive or dead, is someone hurting them? Those questions will haunt those parents until they know the truth."

"I understand, Cam. I already planned on talking to Sean to try and see if he at least could remember their names, anything about the children, to help locate their clans. But this… this just made it all the harder. I saw her, Cam. I saw Sean as he buried her. I saw the things the son of a bitch did to her before death gave her release from the nightmare. To know this happened on the edge of my lands and I didn't even know it!" Declan snarled, fangs dropping and claws breaking free from his fingers. "I have already begun reworking the patrols, to push them out toward the borders. There is no chance of this ever being a possibility here ever again."

The sympathy on Cameron's face caused Declan to scowl even harder. He blamed himself for being lax in his duties as alpha. This never would have happened if he had done more, pushed his people for more, felt a need for better security at the edges of his lands. There hadn't been any strife amongst any of the clans in over fifty years. His father had pulled the patrols in closer to the compound a little over thirty years ago. He'd done it to protect the streak and their members better rather than being so widespread after a random rogue shifter attack one night in the compound left two female lionesses wounded and a male wolf dead. Declan had never seen any reason to change them when he took over ten years ago after his father's death, but now, after seeing this, he would have the borders patrolled at least once or twice a week to ensure this couldn't happen again.

"It's not your fault, Declan," Cameron murmured. "You

couldn't have known. No one could have. Most streak members never even go out that far."

"It doesn't make it okay!" Declan protested, clenching his hands into fists, uncaring as the claws cut into his palms. Blood spilled over his fingers. "My life mate suffered so much and even now continues to do so because I wasn't the alpha I should have been."

Cameron came around to Declan's side. "Stop, Dec. You can't continue to take the blame on your shoulders like this. It's not healthy and it won't help Sean. He's going to need you to be there for him. He's never shifted from what you told me so he has never accessed his animal half. Right now, he's safe from any harm. His mental link to his other side hasn't been established so there's no chance of spirit rot."

Declan's breath caught in his throat and his chest almost caved in. He hadn't even thought of something so vile. It was something he'd never wish on anyone. Spirit rot left the shifter an empty shell, hollow and lifeless. Declan had only ever seen it twice in his life and he could never forget the way the two who'd gone through it had wasted away to nothing before their souls had been set free. "We need to get him those tests immediately, Cam," Declan whispered.

Cameron set his hand on Declan's shoulder. "We will, Dec. I'll set it up as soon as possible. Until then, try not to worry. I just wanted you to be aware of Sean's situation. I also think Sean should talk to Amanda."

Meeting Cameron's gaze, Declan nodded. "I'll arrange it."

Amanda Binson was their resident human therapist and one of the very few humans to know of their existence having had a sister who mated a lion shifter in the streak. She worked in the nearby city, but had learned to apply quite a bit of her skill to the members of the streak. "I'll do the same for the three girls, too. The youngest, Victoria, won't even speak. I think all of them could use someone to talk to."

Declan gave a distracted grunt. His skin itched and he needed to be with his mate. "I'm going to take Sean home."

He stood, but Cameron stopped him. "Dec?" Turning his head, he looked at Cameron still seated in the chair beside him. "Don't forget Sean is stronger than you think."

"Yeah," Declan murmured and then left the office.

Sean had his knees drawn to his chest, his arms looped loosely around them, when Declan entered the waiting room. A smile tilted the corners of Sean's lips and Declan held out his arms, his heart swelling when Sean instantly flew into them. He embraced Sean close, rubbing his chin over the top of Sean's scalp in an attempt to ensure his scent was all over him. "I'm sorry I took so long," Declan said.

"It's okay. Can we go home? I'm a little tired."

Sean's easy use of the word home sent warmth through Declan. "Whatever you want, gorgeous." Declan reluctantly released Sean, but kept an arm around Sean's waist. "Cameron is going to schedule some further tests for you in the city. Something he feels is necessary before we can remove the collar. Okay?"

A slender shoulder lifted in a careless shrug. It hurt Declan's spirit how easily Sean accepted the lack of connection to his animal half. He supposed with Sean never having shifted there couldn't be any sense of loss, but he couldn't understand how Sean just didn't seem to care. He kept quiet until they were back at the house and Sean had removed the borrowed sneakers and was about to get into bed. "Sean?"

Sean looked at him, pausing with his hand on the comforter. "What's wrong?" he asked when he saw whatever it was on Declan's face.

"Do you not want the collar removed?"

Lips parting, Sean dropped the blanket. He sat down on the edge of the bed, setting his hands in his lap. "Why wouldn't I?"

Declan took a seat next to Sean. "You just don't seem affected by the idea of finally being able to shift. Don't you want to?"

Sean wouldn't look at him. Instead he stared at his lap. "I don't know," Sean whispered.

"Are you scared?"

Another shrug met his question. Declan felt a flash of fear from Sean, but it slithered away quickly. It seemed Sean was learning how to hide things from him already. Reaching out, he cupped Sean's chin and tilted Sean's head enough to meet his gaze. Sadness dampened the beautiful sapphires. "Why, Sean?"

"It's wrong," Sean whimpered, closing his eyes.

"What is?"

"Shifting."

Declan made a sound of shock. "Shifting is a beautiful thing, baby. It's a part of who you are."

"No," Sean denied, shaking his head.

"Open your eyes, Sean." At first, Sean refused, but Declan demanded again, "Open your eyes."

Sean's eyelids fluttered upward, revealing turbulent blue orbs.

"You are a shifter, baby. It's an integral part of your being. There is nothing wrong with it. That… human didn't understand what you are and made you fear it. I will teach you to love yourself, to love being a shifter. There's nothing more freeing than changing into your animal half and becoming one with the forest."

Sean's lips trembled and Declan ran his thumb over the lower one. "I want to run with you in our animal forms, mate. I need to feel the earth beneath my paws and know you are beside me with every stride. I know there's a beautiful creature just waiting to be set free inside you."

"Does it hurt?" Sean asked.

"Maybe a little at first, but eventually it becomes a change your body welcomes."

Declan could see the curiosity growing in Sean. "What kind do you think I am?"

Smiling, Declan ran his fingers through Sean's hair. They hadn't gotten it trimmed as he'd been meaning to. "Some kind of cat. Maybe even a tiger like me, Rose, and Ronnie."

"Really?' Sean asked, eagerness echoing in his voice.

He hummed. "We won't know until we can remove the collar. Tomorrow my friend Kyle should be here and he can hopefully tell us how to take it off."

"Maybe I can shift tomorrow?"

Declan stifled a wince. "Maybe. We'll see what happens. Why don't you get some rest and we'll talk some more later?"

Sean wrinkled his nose at Declan. "I'm not tired now."

The act reminded him of Ronnie and Declan chuckled. "You will be once you lay down. Come on, get under the covers and relax."

"Will you… lay with me?" Sean asked shyly.

"Of course." Declan toed off his shoes before standing and helping Sean onto the bed. He tapped Sean's hip gently. "Over, gorgeous."

The moment Declan settled his large frame beside him, Sean snuggled up close to Declan, sliding a slender arm across Declan's chest. Declan didn't know if it was the mating bond or the innocence Sean still had despite everything that made Sean accept him and their connection so quickly. He knew there were still quite a number of things to work out, but they would do it together.

"Declan?"

He grunted.

"Is it… do you think my mom's still alive?"

The words hit Declan square in the sternum. "I don't know, baby, but something tells me she just might be."

Sean didn't say anything for a long moment then, "He wasn't my father, was he?"

Declan breathed out a deep breath before replying. "I don't think so."

Sean went silent and for a while Declan thought he'd fallen asleep, but a wet heat spread over his chest and salt stung Declan's nostrils. "Hey, now," Declan murmured, stroking his hand down Sean's back.

"Why? Why would he lie?" Sean choked. "Why did he tell me my mother was dead? Why did he hurt all those kids?"

"He was a sick man, Sean. Sick people do things we'll never understand." Declan continued to caress Sean, touching Sean wherever he could to try and soothe him. He just let Sean cry himself out until Sean lay atop his chest, trembling from time to time. If Declan could have, he would take away every ounce of pain Sean had suffered through, but all he could do was be there for Sean whenever he needed him. He rubbed his chin over the top of Sean's head. "Sleep now, baby."

Eventually Sean calmed down enough to drift off to sleep. Knowing the things Sean had endured over the years caused pain to endlessly dig into his heart. How Sean could possibly have survived so much seemed beyond fathomable yet Declan couldn't be prouder of him. Despite everything, he'd tried his best to protect the other cubs.

Declan didn't know who Sean's parents were, but he'd bet both their lives the son of bitch he'd already killed wasn't one of them. Tomorrow he'd start having Victor search through the news stories from around Sean's birth up to five years after to see if there were any reports of a missing child around the same time. Maybe they could locate Sean's parents. He figured they belonged to one of the surrounding packs. McNeely hadn't exactly been consistent. Some kidnappings seemed to be several months apart while others were years apart. If the number of graves Victor had found plus the six they'd rescued along with Ronnie were any indication, he snatched an average of one per year.

Declan clenched his jaw and nuzzled Sean's temple. This entire time this shit had been going on at the end of his lands and he hadn't known. Guilt, fury, and sadness all enveloped him in a hard cloud of regret. If only he'd pushed the patrols out further instead of just letting the status quo go on after his father's passing. He could have saved Sean so much sooner than he had, saved him from the countless beatings and broken bones. The idea of Sean suffering even further if they removed the collar broke his heart even more. He didn't want to lose Sean, not when he'd just found him, but the risk to himself was also significant now with their souls tied as one. If Sean died, so would he.

Sean didn't stir, even for dinner, and Declan just let him sleep through, knowing he needed the rest. He kept watch over Sean the entire night, unable to sleep with the number of thoughts roiling around in his head, and the fingers of sunlight filtering through the curtains alerted him to the dawn of a new day. A day when Kyle would be arriving to tell them if it would be possible to remove the offending piece of leather around Sean's throat. Declan pressed a kiss to Sean's temple and slid from the bed. He grabbed a quick shower and dressed in a pair of worn blue jeans which hugged his legs in all the right places, a white t-shirt, and an emerald green sweater with the sleeves rolled up to his elbows.

Sean still slept when Declan exited the bedroom and he headed downstairs to get a cup of coffee and prepare a tray for the two of them. Rose sat at the kitchen table with Ronnie, Sam and Tara. "Good morning, Uncle Dec," Ronnie said.

Declan smiled tiredly. "Good morning, Ronnie."

Rose gave him a concerned look and followed him to the counter. "You sleep at all?"

Shaking his head, Declan grabbed a mug and poured a cup of steaming coffee. "Too much to worry about."

"What did Cam tell you?" Rose asked.

Declan gave a grim look her way. Her eyes rounded. "Is it bad?"

He lowered his voice to the slightest sound, not wanting the others to hear him. "If the collar is removed and he shifts it could kill him."

Rose gasped, drawing the attention of the others for a split second. "What are you going to do?"

"I'm still going to talk to Kyle."

She scowled. "Why'd you call him?"

Rose had a love/hate relationship with Kyle. Ever since they were cubs they'd been at each other's throats. She didn't approve of the job he held and made sure he knew it. "You know he's the only one who can help, Rose," Declan replied, grabbing a couple of plates to load up with eggs, bacon, and toast. "He's the only one who is going to know how to remove it, if it can be removed that is."

"Is Sean going to be able to shift?" Tara asked from the nearby table.

Declan didn't really want to answer, but after everything they'd all been through he didn't feel right ignoring her. So he told her what he could. "Maybe. It's hard to know if the collar can be removed or not."

A troubled look came over Tara's features. Declan asked, "What's wrong?"

She bit her lip, but eventually answered. "Sean's father tried putting collars on a couple of the others. At least from what Sean has told us. They didn't survive. Within a matter of weeks, they died."

Shock and horror came over Declan. "Other cubs were subjected to the same collar?"

Rose gave a quiet sob beside him as Tara nodded. "There were a couple of the others who shifted to try and escape. That's really all I know though. It happened before we were there and Sean didn't want to talk about it."

Declan couldn't believe just how much Sean had suffered over the years at the hands of Carl McNeely. How Sean survived… Declan could barely stomach the idea of Sean witnessing those awful things. "Thank you, Tara."

She nodded. Declan filled a glass with orange juice and added it to the tray with some napkins and silverware. He picked up the tray and headed upstairs. The bed was empty as he entered the room, but the sound of the sink running confirmed Sean's whereabouts. When Sean came out, Declan told him, "Get comfortable. I brought breakfast."

Sean protested while climbing into bed, "I could have gone downstairs."

"I know you could have, Sean. I just wanted to have breakfast alone with you." Declan set the tray over Sean's lap and settled beside him. "Eat."

He seemed to accept Declan's explanation and tucked into the food. Declan picked at his food, his appetite non-existent. He prayed Kyle had good news.

Once Sean finished, Declan nudged his plate toward Sean to encourage him to eat more. Sean eyed the food, but asked, "Aren't you hungry?"

"Not really. Go ahead."

With a happy sigh, Sean tucked into the food and Declan smiled indulgently. He ran the fingers of his left hand over the side of Sean's neck, touch catching on the collar for a second. How anyone could possibly do something so heinous to anyone as innocent as Sean caused rage to boil through Declan's veins. He hid his emotions behind a fake half smile and after the second plate had been cleaned, he slid off the bed and lifted the tray. "Why don't you get dressed and we'll head downstairs, okay?"

Sean nodded and stood, but hesitated at the foot of the bed. Declan frowned. "Something wrong?"

At first, Declan didn't think Sean would answer, but then he turned toward Declan and asked, "What did you do to me?"

Taken aback, Declan set the tray on the nightstand and approached Sean. "What do you mean?"

Sean tugged on his lower lip with his teeth. "I don't know what you did, but somehow the limp I've had for longer than I can remember is gone. I've never been able to walk normal." He looked Declan in the eyes. "I know whatever you did to save me when I should have died changed me."

Declan grasped Sean by the shoulders. "I did what I had to in order to save you, Sean. You are my mate and I would give my life for yours. That's all that matters."

Shaking his head, Sean replied, "I can feel it. When you're around me. Something is different." He touched his chest. "In here."

Exasperated, but also impressed at how intuitive and intelligent Sean was, Declan said, "We're mates, Sean. Our souls are bound because I claimed you. You feel it within you."

It wasn't a lie, but it also wasn't the whole truth either. He didn't want Sean to know about what he'd actually done to save him. Uncertainty still danced in the depths of Sean's eyes, but he seemed to accept what Declan said. "Okay."

Declan pulled Sean close and hugged him tight for a split second before releasing him. "I'll see you downstairs."

Sean nodded and Declan grabbed the tray and left the room.

13

SEAN

Sean watched Declan leave the room. In his heart, he knew Declan hadn't been totally telling the truth, but he couldn't get the strong alpha to admit to what he'd really done to him. Turning, he pulled a t-shirt and jeans from the dresser drawer Declan had shown him a couple of days prior. It didn't take long to dress and then he headed down to the dining room, stopping at the bottom of the stairs when he heard a giggle. His breath caught in his throat when he realized the sound had come from Vicky. His butt hit the stairs as his knees gave out and his throat tightened.

Out of every cub who'd ended up in the dingy basement, Vicky had been the most impacted psychologically. She hadn't spoken a word since the first time Carl beat her for shifting in fear. Sean had tried for a long time to get her to speak. To hear her actually laugh was like a fist to his stomach and a sledgehammer to his heart. He would never be able to do enough to thank Declan for saving the cubs he'd come to love and care for over time. Even if he'd died in that dingy, dark basement, he wouldn't ever regret letting Ronnie go. Just for Vicky to be able to feel safe enough to giggle in such a happy way meant more to him than anything else in the world.

"Hey, you okay?" Ronnie asked, coming out of the kitchen and spotting him on the stairs.

Sean nodded, unable to speak. Ronnie came closer and frowned. "Why are you crying?"

Reaching up, Sean touched his cheek and his fingers came away wet. He managed a wobbly smile. "I'm more than okay, Ronnie. I couldn't be happier."

"You cry when you're happy?" Ronnie asked, tilting his head a bit.

Sean laughed quietly. "Yeah, I suppose I do."

"You're weird."

Laughing harder, Sean shrugged. "I guess I am."

"Do you wanna see my room?" Ronnie asked. "I can show you my Pokemon card collection. I've got one of the rarest cards out there." He puffed out his chest in pride.

Sean had no clue what a Pokemon was, but he nodded. "Sure, Ronnie. I'd like that."

Ronnie eagerly grabbed his hand and tugged Sean back upstairs. "My favorite Pokemon is Charizard, but Dennis, that's my friend, his is Pikachu. I told him everyone likes Pikachu so he should pick another favorite, but he refused." Ronnie rolled his eyes at Sean. "There are so many different ones."

Sean just allowed Ronnie to rattle on as he led Sean to his room. He looked around curiously when they entered. There were a number of colorful posters on the wall, some looked like movie posters or something. He moved closer to a nearby shelf which held several plastic figures.

"Those are my Avengers action figures!" Ronnie exclaimed excitedly, coming close to Sean's side. "See, that one is Captain America and that's Thor. My favorite is The

Hulk." He pointed at a large green figure. "Have you ever seen the Avenger movies?"

Sean shook his head. He had never really seen any movies actually. "No," he murmured.

"Oh, we should watch them! Have a movie night with me, you, Mom, and Uncle Dec!"

"Sure." Sean wondered what his life would have been like if he'd grown up normal. Would he have seen those movies? Would he have been enamored with them as Ronnie appeared to be? And what about being attracted to someone? Is it possible he wouldn't feel so stupid for not knowing how to kiss someone, to touch them? The memory of what Declan had done to him sent warmth running through his body. Surely he would have known exactly how to react, what it meant, and definitely how it felt.

Ronnie took a black book from his desk. "These are my Pokemon cards. See," he jabbed his finger at a card of a strange looking orange creature. "That's my Shadowless First Edition Charizard! Dennis searched it on eBay once and it sold for eight-hundred dollars!"

Another term Sean had never heard of. "eBay?"

"Oh, yeah, it's an online site where people sell things. Uncle Dec let me pick out an item for my birthday last year from there!"

"That sounds nice," Sean murmured. Envy bit deep and shame followed closely on its heels. He shouldn't be envious of Ronnie's childhood. He should be happy the little boy had such a great life. Embarrassment caused him to turn away from Ronnie's collection in a quick motion. "I think we should go back downstairs. Declan is probably looking for me."

Ronnie didn't seem to notice his swift change in mood. He followed Sean back to the dining room. Declan came out of the kitchen at the same time. "There you are, gorgeous."

Sean gave a weak smile. "Sorry. Ronnie wanted to show me his Pokeme collection."

Declan choked. "Excuse me?"

At the same time, Ronnie exclaimed, "It's my Pokemon collection!"

Sean had no idea why Declan seemed shocked by Ronnie sharing the cards with him and frowned. "Was that not okay?"

Declan cleared his throat. "No, no, it's fine. I misunderstood. Kyle should be arriving in a little bit. Why don't we go to my office? Victor will show him in once he gets here."

"Okay." Sean brushed off the confusion and trailed behind Declan to the same room as the other night.

"Would you like to play Solitaire again?" Declan asked.

Sean shook his head. He knew he had been ignoring the possibility of finally being able to shift, but now that the chance could be here his stomach felt tight. Would they be able to remove the collar? Apprehension tinged with excitement kept him fidgeting and he wandered around the office, staring at the books he couldn't read.

"Are you nervous?"

Shrugging, Sean fingered the spine of one of the books. "I guess."

"Everything is going to work out, Sean. I promise."

He furrowed his brow and twitched a little. Heat trickled through him. He'd promised the same thing to more than one of the cubs who hadn't survived. "You can't say that."

"Why not?"

"Because you don't know if that's true or not. You can never promise everything is going to be fine." Sean glared at the floor.

He sensed Declan moving closer to him. "Things always work out the way they're meant to, Sean."

Anger trickled through Sean and he lifted his gaze to

Declan. "Meant to? Were those cubs meant to die? Were they meant to be beaten and killed? Is that what you're saying?"

Declan winced. "That's not what I meant."

"Then don't promise everything is going to be okay, because it's not!" Sean shouted, chest heaving, fists clenched at his side.

Declan stepped into Sean's space and wrapped his arms around Sean. "You're right, baby, I'm sorry. I'm sorry you had to go through something so horrible and that I couldn't save you sooner. I'm sorry you had to bury those children. That's something no one should ever have to do."

Sean started crying at Declan's words and he buried his face against Declan's chest. He sobbed his heart out, grieving for the loss of the cubs he couldn't protect, for the childhood he'd never had, and the innocence of the cubs who'd been rescued with him. He hadn't broken down so many times in a matter of days since he'd been a child. The first time he'd cried in front of his father, the man had beaten him and broken his left wrist. After that he'd struggled to cut himself off from his emotions and eventually succeeded.

Once he'd quieted down to mere hiccups, Sean became aware of Declan rubbing his back and the sound of his heartbeat underneath his ear. "I'm so-sorry," Sean said shakily.

Declan shushed him. "Nothing to be sorry about. You needed to let everything out. I'm the one who should apologize for using platitudes when we don't know what is going to happen. I won't lie to you. There are risks involved with removing the collar."

Sean savored the chance to be comforted, to be held, knowing someone actually cared about his pain. He heaved a sigh which caused his body to shudder. "I guessed."

Declan rubbed his chin over the crown of Sean's head. "I just want to protect you, Sean. To never let anyone or anything hurt you again."

Digging his fingers into the back of Declan's shirt, he hadn't even realized he'd wrapped his arms around Declan at some point, Sean nuzzled at the hard pec beneath his cheek. "There's no way you can stop me from ever being hurt."

"I can try," Declan replied fiercely. "I will fight whoever I have to in order to make it happen."

Sean gave a shaky laugh. "What if I hurt myself? You going to protect me from me?"

"If I have to," Declan declared.

Sean's laugh became a humorous chuckle and he leaned back to wrinkle his nose at Declan. "I'm a bit of a klutz so you're going to be a busy man."

Before Declan could respond, a knock came at the office door. "Alpha?"

Declan released Sean, but grabbed his hand and tugged him over to the sofa. "Come in."

Victor, a man Sean found very stoic and serious, entered the office with a tall, muscular dark-haired male just behind him. "Mr. Hunter is here."

Rolling his eyes, the guy said, "When are you going to stop calling me Mr. Hunter? I'm not my father."

"I'll leave you to your business, Alpha," Victor said, ignoring the other shifter, and left the room.

"Kyle," Declan bid, waving a hand at the leather armchair across from the couch. "This is my mate, Sean."

Kyle nodded his head in a respectful manner and sat in the chair across from them, placing one ankle on his other knee. Sean couldn't help but notice how good-looking Kyle was. The man had ragged cut black hair which fell across his forehead and bright green eyes, which seemed almost electric. Sean also observed a scar close to the man's right eye, giving him a rakish appearance. Kyle's gaze seemed fixated on the collar around Sean's throat. "Good to meet you, Sean."

"Hi," Sean murmured, pressing closer to Declan.

"I called you here, Kyle, because-"

"The collar," Kyle interrupted.

Declan nodded. "Yes. There's no clasp, no way to cut it off, not even with scissors or wire cutters."

Kyle sat forward, studying the leather. "I have only ever seen this kind of magic once. Only a powerful witch can remove it."

Sean's heart sank and he twisted his hands together. Declan laid his hand on top of Sean's. A scowl adorned Declan's face. "I should have known. Do you know of any who can take it off?"

Kyle didn't answer immediately. He never looked away from the collar or Sean, studying both. "Who put the collar on you?"

Sean swallowed hard and started to sweat. Declan answered for him. "A man who we believe abducted him as a child and pretended to be his father. He hated shifters from what Sean has told me and didn't want Sean shifting."

Rage flared over Kyle's face and he snarled. "Disgusting humans," he spat.

Declan shook his head. "Not all humans are the same."

"Most are," Kyle growled.

"I have known many and even have several here in the compound who are very much supporters of shifters."

"I need to get in touch with a contact to locate a witch powerful enough to remove it, Dec. It won't be easy and honestly, if the collar has been on him as long as I suspect, there may be even more risk than usual."

Declan nodded. "Understood. When can we expect to hear?"

"Give me a couple of days. My contact tends to... disappear when they wish to be alone."

"Thanks, Kyle. You're free to stay here for the time being if you wish."

Kyle tipped his head in thanks. "I'll take you up on that offer. I can use some rest."

"Complicated assignment?"

"Something like that."

Declan stood and held out his hand to Kyle. "I appreciate any help you can give. The room upstairs, second door on the left, is unoccupied at the moment. It's yours as long as you'd like."

Kyle shook Declan's hand. "I'll send out some inquiries now."

Sean remained seated on the sofa, staring at a point on the wall across from him. The idea of being unable to choose whether to remove the long-worn strip of leather around his throat actually rattled Sean. He'd seen so many awful things done by his father and even been victim of those things himself over the years. But those didn't upset him as much as the glimpse of actually being able to shift into whatever animal form he could take for the first time in his life only to have it taken away. Sharp pains echoed out from his chest and Sean struggled to breathe.

"Sean? Baby?" Declan's voice sounded miles away, muffled down a long tunnel.

Strong hands gripped his shoulders and shook him slightly causing Sean to look up at Declan's face. Gasping, Sean threw himself against Declan and began sobbing, great gulping cries that wrecked his throat and caused his entire body to shudder with each sound he made. "God, baby, you're breaking my heart," Declan rasped, tightening his hold on Sean. "I've got you, sweetheart."

He didn't have any clue how long he cried, but Sean felt exhausted to the core when he finally calmed down enough to return to awareness. Embarrassment swamped him and he pulled away from Declan only to stare in horror at the huge wet spot on Declan's shirt. "I'm sorry!" he exclaimed, voice destroyed. "I keep crying all over you!"

Declan shushed him and tugged him close again. "It's just a shirt and I suspect you haven't let yourself cry in a long time. You're still processing the traumas of your past and crying jags are to be expected."

Sean couldn't find the strength to move away a second time and just lay wrapped in Declan's embrace.

"Do you want to talk about what upset you just now?"

Swiping a hand over his cheek, Sean shrugged, biting his lip.

"Come on, Sean. Talk to me," Declan prodded. He pressed a kiss to the crown of Sean's head.

"I-I thought I mi-might finally be able to sh-shift and-" Sean cut off, his throat tightening once more.

"You thought you'd be able to find out what you are. Who you are," Declan finished for him. "You will, Sean. I promise. We will get that fucking collar off and you'll shift and we'll be able to run together as we were meant to."

"Bu-but Kyle said-" Declan stopped Sean.

"It's not impossible to remove it, baby. We just have to find the right witch." Sean tried to protest again, but Declan squeezed him lightly. "Stop, Sean. We *will* remove the damn thing."

"Okay," Sean whispered, still not convinced.

Declan gripped Sean's chin between two fingers and tilted his head up until their eyes met. "Trust me, sexy, because there is one thing you have yet to learn about me and it's how stubborn I am until I get what I want. And there is nothing I want more than to see you in your animal form and to run with you through the trees on our land."

A tiny flicker of hope ignited in Sean's heart and he gave Declan a tiny nod to which Declan smiled. "See? That's my beautiful mate."

Sean could feel his face heat up and he knew he had to be blushing at Declan's words. "I'm not," he murmured.

"Not what?" Declan asked. "Beautiful?"

Sean nodded.

Declan scowled without heat at him. "Don't ever think that, Sean. You are the most beautiful, sexy, amazingly strong person I have ever met."

The sincerity in Declan's voice spoke to Sean's heart and he caught his breath. He'd felt a hard tug in the depths of his heart. Warmth settled into his chest, a strangeness he'd never experienced before.

"Everything all right, baby?" Declan's voice rumbled beneath Sean's ear.

Sniffling, Sean replied, "Yeah."

Declan tightened his hold for a split second and then said, "Let's go take a walk. Get some fresh air and I'm sure you could use the chance to stretch your legs."

"Okay."

They both stood from the sofa and Sean allowed Declan to lead him out of the office, down the hallway, and through the front door. A light breeze drifted along Sean's skin and ruffled his hair as they walked. Sean noticed several other people watching them as they walked, curiosity on their faces. "They're curious about you. They now know you're my mate."

"Oh," Sean whispered. He didn't know if he should feel uncomfortable about the scrutiny or just enjoy the time outside in the sunlight.

Declan wrapped his arm around Sean's shoulders and pulled him close to his side. "They're going to love you, Sean. You don't have to be worried."

Doubt shrouded Sean, but he figured he'd trust Declan to know what is best so he brushed away his uncertainty and leaned into Declan. Sean could see the place was laid out like a little town. "You said there were a little over two hundred who live here?"

"Yes. Just over."

"That's a lot, isn't it?"

"It's actually a low number for most clans," Declan replied. "We've built our numbers quite significantly over the last thirty years, but many packs outnumber us two-to-one."

"Do you think my pa-parents are in a nearby pack?" Sean asked.

"It's possible. There are several spread out over a three-hundred-mile radius from here."

Sean bit his lip at the possibility of having a family. What would they look like? Would they even recognize him or want him after all these years?

Declan stopped walking and tugged Sean close. "Your family is going to love you, Sean. I'm sure they have missed you all these years."

"You think so?" Sean whispered.

"I know so."

"Alpha Declan!"

Sean started and peered around Declan's shoulder. Cameron rushed toward them. Declan turned to greet the doctor. "Cam, everything okay?"

"Yes. I was able to secure a spot at the hospital to run the tests we spoke of."

"Great news, Cam. When?"

"This afternoon at three."

Declan frowned. "Sooner than I expected."

"It's either at three today or there isn't space for another month." Cameron glanced at Sean. "I also wanted to ask if there's been any information regarding what we talked about."

"Not yet, Cam." Declan growled at Cameron, surprising

Sean. "Too much has gone on for me to ask those questions yet."

Cameron stepped back and tilted his neck toward Declan. "Of course, Alpha. I didn't mean anything by it. Just anxious to get the answers for so many others."

Declan sighed. "I understand, Cam. I just need you to bear with me. I cannot help my protective instincts."

"Completely understood. I'll be at the hospital waiting for you at 3 p.m. It will take about thirty minutes to get into the city."

"We'll see you then," Declan replied.

Sean looked at Declan as Cameron walked away. "What was it he wanted to know the answer to?"

Declan grimaced. "I'd rather we head back to the house before we talk about that."

Wariness hit Sean hard. "Okay."

The peacefulness of the sun and fresh air evaporated and they were both quiet on the return trip to Declan's study. They stopped just inside the door as Declan beckoned Victor to follow them. Victor seemed to sense something serious happening and trailed behind them in silence. Sean couldn't help but get nervous about whatever seemed to be going on. Victor sat at the desk while Sean sat on the sofa.

Declan seemed hesitant to start and Sean watched the large shifter prowl the office for several moments before Declan came and sat beside him. He took Sean's hand in his and caught Sean's gaze. "I need you to know I wouldn't ask this of you if it weren't important."

"O-okay," Sean murmured, uneasy.

"I need to know about the graves, baby."

14

DECLAN

Declan watched Sean's face closely as the words left his mouth. Despair flooded Sean's features. Causing his mate anymore pain sat like a rock in Declan's chest, but he needed to know. "I know it hurts to talk about them, Sean, but their families need to know what happened to them. If it's too much, at least tell me their names and we'll go through the records we can find to locate any missing children with those names."

Sean swallowed hard several times and he finally managed to croak, "I'll tell you."

"There were twelve?"

"Fourteen," Sean whispered. "It started with Yuri, a seven-year-old panther cub. My fa-Carl killed him because Yuri bit him. He kept hitting Yuri over and over again until Yuri didn't move or make a-another s-s-sound."

Grief twisted Sean's features. "Then it was Destiny, a rabbit shifter. She was only two. H-he sn-snap-"

"Stop, baby!" Declan rasped. "Just names and if you know what kind of shifter they were. You don't need to relive their deaths."

Sean took a deep breath and nodded. "Hector, seven years old, a bear shifter. Charlie, six years old, a hawk shifter."

Declan reined in his need to roar in rage and break the closest piece of furniture as he listened to Sean recount each child. He glanced at Victor to see the man writing the names and shifter breeds down. It would take time for them to find as many of the families and clans as possible.

When Sean finally finished, Declan could hardly breathe. To know so many had suffered and Sean had witnessed it all, dealt with burying them, it shattered his heart. He wished with all of his soul he'd been able to save Sean from the years of pain and death. Declan crushed Sean to him in a hard embrace. He buried his face in Sean's hair. "I'm so sorry, baby. No one should ever have to live through something like this."

A shudder wound its way through Sean and Sean rested his forehead on Declan's shoulder. "They deserved more."

"You deserved more," Declan breathed. "You'll never have to see anything like that again. I swear it on my life."

Declan turned toward Victor. "Have Cameron provide instructions on exhuming them to prevent disturbing the bodies more than necessary, Victor, and make sure someone is with Becky when they bring back Gina."

Victor gave a brief nod and left the room, the sheet of names in one hand. Nothing could ever make Declan understand how anyone could possibly do what the psycho Carl McNeely had done. He hoped the bastard burned in hell for eternity.

Sean had remained quiet and Declan returned his attention to his mate. Shoulders hunched, Sean stared down at the floor, pure anguish hanging over his slender frame. Declan knew Sean had been through so much, but there were so many things still left to deal with and he had no idea how he could protect Sean from what was to come.

"Sean?"

He raised his gaze to Declan's.

"We need to get ready to head into the city, baby. Today is the only day we can do the tests Cameron suggested before you can shift."

Sean gave a nod. "Okay."

Declan took Sean's hand in his as he led him out of the room. Once they were in the car and on the road, Declan glanced at Sean. "I just need to ask you to not mention shifters in public, Sean. The general human population doesn't know about shifters and it would be very bad for all of us if they found out."

Sean nodded, staring out the window and watching the trees rushing by. "I understand."

Grimacing, Declan tightened his hold on the steering wheel of his Chevy Tahoe. Being a fairly large man and taller than most due to his genetics as an alpha tiger shifter, Declan couldn't fit into something smaller. He typically ended up uncomfortable or with a crick in his neck. He reached out and grabbed Sean's hand, squeezing his fingers lightly. "It'll be okay, Sean."

A slight shrug is all Declan saw from Sean's direction. He knew Sean's detachment from most situations wasn't normal, but they needed to deal with one thing at a time. The next event which broke Declan's heart even further was the sheer wonder on Sean's face as the city came into view. Even the gas station had Sean with his face stuck to the window, watching the people, the cars, and the new sights. "What's that?" Sean exclaimed as they passed a bakery window with cakes and treats displayed.

Swallowing hard, Declan managed, "It's a bakery. Do you want to stop in before we head back home after the tests?"

Sean looked over his shoulder at Declan, pure excitement on his face. "Can we? Oh, please?"

Declan cleared his throat and gave a grin he knew didn't reach his eyes and was shaky at best. "Of course. We'll get anything you want."

The idea of the sweets seemed to distract Sean and, even though he displayed curiosity of the things around them as they continued their drive through the city, it kept his mind preoccupied from the tests as far as Declan could tell. When they got into the hospital, Sean's gaze never lingered anywhere for long. Declan would explain things to Sean and what they were before Sean could ask. The nurse at the desk directed them where to go, sending them to a set of elevators. Sean jumped when the doors opened and Declan guided him into the elevator. He hit the button for the third floor.

A slight tang of fear hit Declan's nose causing him to pull Sean closer to his side. "It's all right," he murmured.

Fine tremors shook Sean's body and Declan urged the elevator to hurry. It dinged at their floor and he led Sean out immediately. They followed the signs to the imaging department where another attendant indicated for them to take a seat.

They weren't on their own for long when Cameron greeted them at the small waiting area. "Declan. Was the drive in okay?"

"Fine. We're going to stop at Harley's bakery on the way back to the house."

Cameron smiled. "Sounds amazing. He makes some of the best pastries! If I ate there every day, I'd weigh three hundred pounds in a quick minute."

Declan laughed. "I don't know about that, Cam, but I agree, his pastries are almost sinful."

"Why don't you two come this way?" Cameron beckoned and led them through a door and stopped beside a huge window. Declan could see the MRI machine through the glass and hoped Sean could handle it. Being enclosed in a little tube like that wasn't easy. Declan's tiger prowled restlessly beneath his skin at knowing Sean would be separated from them.

"Sean, I need you to change into the hospital gown the nurse left for you on the chair. Just put your clothing into the small lockers nearby, okay? No one will touch them."

Sean nodded and entered the room, closing the door behind him. Declan leaned against the wall and waited, arms folded across his chest. Cameron gave him a sympathetic smile. "He will be all right, Dec."

Declan nodded, but didn't relax. Sean joined them moments later, barefoot and wearing the usual white and blue paper thin gown. He held the back shut with one hand and flushed, eyes trained on the floor. Declan moved around to shield Sean's backside and he tied the cloth closed better, ensuring no one could see Sean's bottom. "It's okay, baby," Declan murmured close to Sean's ear.

He could feel Sean's uneasiness as Cameron led them into the room with the giant window. "This is an MRI machine, Sean. It's basically a way for me to see your internal organs and bones so we know what to expect if you go to shift."

"If?" Sean asked softly.

Hiding a wince, Declan placed a hand on Sean's shoulder. "When."

Sean gave a small nod and Declan squeezed Sean's shoulder in comfort. Cameron smiled, but Declan could see Cameron's uncertainty about whether Sean would be able to or not. "I need to see what kind of damage has been done to your body, Sean. To ensure it's safe for you to shift."

"Okay," Sean whispered.

"Climb up and lay down on your back, head toward the machine," Cameron instructed. He hovered near as Sean wriggled his way onto the platform. "While the tests are running, you can't move, Sean. I need you to remain still in order to get the images we need."

He handed a small rubber ball attached to a cable to Sean. "If you start to panic or need to pause the tests, squeeze this. It'll alert me and I'll immediately halt the scan. I'll be able to talk to you through the speakers in the machine."

"C-Can Declan stay with me?" Sean stuttered, nervousness obvious in his features and tone.

Declan swallowed hard and gave Sean an encouraging look. "I'll be right outside that window, Sean." He pointed toward the nearby room where another man sat behind a computer. "Just like when Cam took the x-rays. Remember? If you need me, you just tell me, okay?"

Sean took a deep breath and tried to give Declan a smile which didn't form completely. Declan leaned down and kissed Sean, trailing his fingers over Sean's cheek in a light caress. "I love you, Sean."

Surprise widened Sean's eyes and Declan kissed Sean again. "I'll be right outside, baby."

Declan fought his tiger's instincts to remain at Sean's side. He balled his hands into fists and held onto the scruff of his tiger's neck. They had to do this. It was important to know the extent of the damage to Sean and if his shifting could hurt him further or even kill him. Declan practically held his breathe as the machine started. Nothing in his life had ever prepared him for a mate who was as traumatized as Sean, but he wouldn't trade having Sean in his life for anything.

The entire test took about thirty minutes. Declan never once looked away from the monitor centering on Sean's face. If Sean even looked panicked, Declan would stop the test, but his mate did him proud and never once appeared flustered. The moment Cameron gave him the all clear, Declan was in the room and by Sean's side in seconds. He gathered Sean close to his chest, breathing in the distinctive scent of Sean's skin. "You okay, gorgeous?"

Sean nodded against him. "Yeah," he replied. "It wasn't all that scary."

Declan chuckled and nuzzled Sean's temple with his nose. "You're so brave, Sean."

A snort of disbelief came from Sean. "I just had to lay down in a tube. That's not brave."

Declan stroked a hand down Sean's arm. "You have more courage than you can possibly know. You didn't know what would happen, but you still remained calm the entire time."

Sean shrugged. "I trust you."

The faith Sean had in him caused Declan's breath to catch and he hugged Sean a little tighter. "Cam will meet with us once you're dressed again."

Declan helped Sean off the table and back to the room where he waited outside while Sean re-dressed. They sat for twenty minutes in the small waiting area, not talking, just holding each other's hand tight. Cameron appeared in the entrance and beckoned for the two of them to follow. He led them into an office with a large window behind the desk. "Have a seat," he said, motioning to the two chairs in front of the desk before he moved around to sit on the other side.

Sean watched with curiosity as Cameron started doing something on the computer. He pointed at a monitor on the wall beside them where they could see skeletal images. Declan winced when he saw the multitude of jagged lines over several of the bones. "The good news is there are no areas which cause me great concern regarding the previous fractures and broken bones. There are quite a number of them which never set correctly, but none of them have fused beyond repair. I believe a shift would heal everything completely."

"Really?" Sean whispered, hope shining from his bright

blue eyes. Declan swallowed hard and balled his free hand into a fist.

"What's the bad news, Cam?"

Cameron sighed. "Right to the point, Alpha."

"Can Sean shift?"

"Yes," Sean sucked in a deep breath, "but the first time he does it's going to hurt. Greatly. Every bone which didn't set properly before will break again during the initial change."

Rage at knowing his mate would have to feel those injuries again roiled within Declan. He clenched and unclenched his jaw several times until he could control himself. "Is there any chance of pain killers being administered?"

Cameron shook his head. "I'm sorry, Alpha, but no. It's going to be hard enough for Sean to connect with his other half. Drugs would merely stunt the chance he could successfully shift fully. It may even lead to him being stuck in half-form."

"Wi-will it hurt every time?" Sean asked.

"No, Alpha-mate. Only the first time. After your first transformation, you will be wholly healed and able to change between forms as naturally as we do now."

Sean nodded his head. "I understand."

"No," Declan grunted.

Cameron frowned. "Alpha, your mate will-"

"I said no," Declan growled and stood. "I will not let him go through any further pain."

Sean also stood from his seat. "But I want to shift," he protested.

Declan paced the short length of the office, shaking his head and running one hand through his hair. He muttered beneath his breath. He couldn't let Sean go through all of that again. The feel of Sean's slender fingers wrapping around his forearm stopped him in his tracks. Declan looked down at his mate, anguish no doubt obvious on his face. He brought his hand up to cup Sean's smooth cheek. "I can't," he murmured, pained.

Sean nuzzled into Declan's palm. "Please, Declan. Seeing you, seeing the others and how happy they are in their other form, I need to know what that's like. I have to know."

Nothing in Declan's life had prepared him for the day he'd find his mate only to have to watch him suffer through a pain he couldn't fight or stop. But seeing the hope, the longing, in Sean's face made him realize he couldn't deny Sean something so integral to his being. Taking a deep breath, Declan gave a brief nod. "All right."

Happiness lit Sean's features. "Yes?"

"Yes," Declan managed.

Cameron had all but been forgotten in those moments, but reminded them of his presence when he spoke. "There is still the matter of the collar."

Sean's face fell and Declan glared at Cameron. "We're dealing with that. Kyle is already in touch with his contacts."

"Kyle?" Cameron murmured. "He's at the compound?"

"For a few days."

"I see."

"When Sean goes through his first shift, I want you there, Cam. Just in case."

Cameron nodded, seemingly distracted. "I'll be there, Alpha."

"Thank you, Dr. Cameron," Sean said quietly.

"Please, call me Cam or Cameron," he replied. "And you're very welcome, Alpha-mate. I'm just glad there was good news to be had."

"Is there anything else we should know, Cam?" Declan asked.

"I am going to prescribe some vitamin D and calcium tablets for Sean to take, starting today. The extra nutrients may help speed up the process of the healing once the shift is complete." Cameron grabbed a tablet from the desk, scribbled down on two sheets, and tore them off. He passed them to Declan. "I also think it would be a good idea for Sean to get regular exercise until then. Start with walking for at least thirty minutes a day and increase ten minutes each week. Until we know when the collar can come off, it will be beneficial in the long run to raise his strength as much as possible."

Declan took the prescriptions from Cameron. "We'll get these filled before we leave the city. Is there anything else?"

Cameron shook his head. "Not right now. Keep me posted regarding the collar and when that may be anticipated to be removed."

"Will do, Cam. Thank you for your help today. I'm relieved to know Sean's life is not in danger if he should shift."

"As am I," Cameron agreed.

They bid Cameron goodbye and left. Declan helped Sean into the Tahoe and jogged around to his side of the car. Minutes later they were on the main road. "There's a pharmacy near the bakery. We'll drop the prescriptions to be filled while we check out Harley's, okay?"

Sean smiled at Declan, a smile so much brighter than any of the others Declan had ever seen on his mate's face. It seemed as if a great weight had been lifted from Sean and happiness just radiated from within him. Declan cleared his throat which had suddenly grown tight. The emotions coming from Sean made Declan feel as if his heart would burst from his chest.

Declan took Sean's hand and brought it to his lips. He

pressed a kiss to the back of Sean's palm. "You have no idea how beautiful you look right now."

Pink bloomed over Sean's cheeks and his full lips parted in surprise at Declan's words. "I-I..."

A small chuckle trickled from Declan as he lowered their entwined hands to his upper thigh. He parallel parked the SUV in front of the pharmacy, hopped out, and went around to help Sean down from the Tahoe. It amused Declan when he saw Sean was so flustered he didn't even notice their surroundings again until they were inside the pharmacy. The light of curiosity overcame Sean's face and Declan allowed Sean to lead him in whatever direction. They wandered up and down the few aisles in the store for several minutes. Sean stopping every couple feet to stare at something on the shelves.

On the one hand, Declan found it endearing, but on the other it stirred the still smoldering anger at the fucker who'd stolen so much from his mate. If he had anything to do with it, he'd damn sure help Sean to experience everything. "What are these for?" Sean asked, bringing Declan out of his own head.

Declan raised a brow when he saw they had stopped in front of the feminine hygiene shelf. "They're for women."

Sean frowned. "They're like diapers?"

A bark of laughter escaped Declan. He supposed they could be related to diapers in a way. "I think I'll let Rose explain what these are for when we get back, okay, baby? It's something only a woman knows the true secrets of."

Brows furrowed, Sean nibbled his bottom lip, confusion clear as day. "Okay. I'll ask Rose."

Declan couldn't wait to hear how she explained tampons and pads to Sean. "Why don't you go pick out a candy bar while I get these in for them to fill?"

Sean tilted his head a bit. "What's a candy bar?"

"It's chocolate."

Delight brightened Sean's face. "I had chocolate once. One of the cubs had some when Carl brought him to us and they shared it with me. It's so good. Can I really have one?"

"You can have as many as you want," Declan choked.

A sound of pleasure rattled in Sean's throat and Declan guided Sean to the rack of candy. It took every bit of control Declan possessed not to buy the entire stock just for his mate. "I'll be right over at the counter," Declan murmured and let Sean's hand go.

Sean made a noise of acknowledgment, but he didn't take his eyes off the array of boxes and packages. Declan ensured Sean never left his sight as he passed over the paper to the pharmacist and let him know they were going to be waiting for them. By the time the pharmacist finished processing the forms in the computer, Sean had two items in his hands. He seemed to be unsure of which one to settle on. Declan could see one was a Hershey's chocolate bar and the other was a package of two Reese's peanut butter cups.

He walked over, took both packages from Sean and returned to the counter. "We will take these as well."

"Declan," Sean whispered anxiously.

Ignoring his mate's protest, Declan paid for both candies and the prescriptions. "We'll be right next door at Harley's."

"Oh, Harley's is amazing," the pharmacist crowed. "You have to try his new salted caramel stuffed scone. It's to die for."

"We'll do that. Thank you," Declan said, smiling. He handed the bag with the chocolate in it to Sean. "Let's go next door and take a look."

Sean hesitated, but then accepted the bag from Declan. When they were outside on the sidewalk, Sean said, "I didn't need both."

Shrugging, Declan placed a hand on Sean's lower back and guided him to the bakery's front door. "I wanted to. You can have one on the way home and another for later."

The smell of bread, sugar, and various fruits assaulted them the moment they entered the shop. Several customers were already in the store. Two were seated at one of the four small tables chatting between bites of pastry while three more were in line to pay. The walls were a delightful shade of sunshine yellow with the counters and tables a bright white with chrome trims, both of which offset the lighter shade of yellow floor. It was almost too bright for someone with eyes as sensitive as Declan's. Pictures scattered across the walls illustrating Harley's first day of business along with many other major events in his life since separating from his pack.

None of the humans in the shop knew Harley's true nature of being a llama shifter. Declan only knew from scent. He also knew Harley chose to live without a pack because of how many horrors he'd suffered at the hands of his last one. Declan left an open offer for Harley to join his streak should he ever need those kinds of ties again.

Declan waved at Harley behind the counter. "Declan!" Harley boomed.

Sean started at the loud voice and Declan soothed him with the brush of his fingers along Sean's spine to his shoulder. "Sean, I'd like you to meet Harley, the creator of these amazing desserts."

Harley grinned and stuck out a beefy paw over the top of the display counter. "Nice to meetcha, Sean."

Declan encouraged Sean to return the gesture. It took a couple breaths before Sean placed his much smaller hand in Harley's. "You're a skinny one, aren't you?" Harley chuckled, squeezing Sean's fingers gently and letting go. "Now, what can I get for the two of you?"

Declan looked at Sean. "Is there something you see that you'd like?"

Sean shook his head and kept his gaze on the floor. Declan frowned. He slid a finger under Sean's chin and tilted his face upward until Sean's gaze met his. "Is something wrong, baby?"

15

SEAN

Everything Sean had experienced over the last couple of hours was entirely new to him. The test to scan his body had been overwhelming to say the least, but he'd managed to hide his discomfort well enough. Years of practice at hiding his fear from his father, no… from Carl had made him an expert at it. When Declan had insisted on buying the two packages of candy for him, he'd felt uncomfortable. He didn't want Declan spending so much money on him.

Now they stood in the bakery and he knew Declan expected him to choose some of the amazing looking cakes in the case before them. Yet Sean couldn't shake off the feeling he should protest even more. "I don't need anything," Sean murmured, closing his eyes and trying to pull away from Declan.

Declan didn't let him go completely, but he did remove his fingers from Sean's chin. "I want you to have everything, Sean. You're my ma-man and I want to spoil you."

Sean heard Declan stumble over what he expected had

been the word mate. It reminded him they weren't supposed to discuss things about shifters in the open. He bit his lip. "It just makes me feel wrong," he murmured.

"Why?" Declan asked as he took Sean by his elbow and moved them into a secluded alcove away from the others in the store.

"Because I don't have any way of paying you back," Sean managed.

Declan jerked as if struck. "You don't need to pay me back, Sean. I just want you to be happy."

"I am happy," Sean said, not realizing until right then that he was, in fact, happy. Happier than he'd ever been in his entire life.

A light Sean didn't understand flooded Declan's eyes. "Did I say something wrong?" Sean asked.

"No," Declan rasped. "Not at all."

"You look upset."

A wet chuckle emerged from Declan and he yanked Sean into a firm hug, burying his face in the space between Sean's neck and shoulder. The brush of Declan's warm lips over his skin sent a shiver down Sean's spine and he couldn't contain the small gasp of breath from his mouth. "Sensitive there, my sexy mate?" Declan whispered across Sean's ear.

Sean gripped the back of Declan's shirt when he felt the slickness of Declan's tongue trace the same path. "Declan," he panted.

When Declan pulled back, a hunger stared back at Sean from the depths of Declan's hazel eyes. "We will continue this back at home," Declan promised, his voice deeper and rougher than usual.

The idea of more of those strange, pleasurable sensations left Sean in a daze as Declan led him back to the counter. He barely registered Declan instructing the man named Harley to fill a box with one of every kind in the case. Declan chatted easily with Harley while he constructed a box and began placing items in it, Sean's hand clasped firmly in Declan's. He couldn't say how long they were in the bakery or when they returned to the drugstore to pick up whatever medication Cameron had given them. He couldn't quite be sure if those feelings were good or bad.

It wasn't until they were back in the Tahoe that Sean managed to clear some of the fog in his brain. Declan had taken Sean's hand in his as soon as he pulled into traffic, heading toward home. The heat and strength of Declan's thigh on the back of his palm sent strange tingles of electricity along his arm. Hairs on the back of his arm stood on end practically. "Declan?"

"Yes, baby?"

"Are you going to do what you did in Dr. Cameron's office again?" Sean asked, nervous but excited.

"Do you want to do that again?" Declan asked in return.

Sean frowned. "I don't know. I-I always thought it was supposed to hurt. It always hurt for Sam and Tara."

Declan growled, a low angry sound in his throat. Sean tensed, wondering if he'd said something wrong. The noise faded and Declan glanced at Sean for a moment. "What we did in Cam's office was *nothing* like what Sam and Tara experienced. Your body as my mate was prepared for it, ready to take me inside of you, despite how abrupt I started it. Sam and Tara did not want what was done to them. No one should go through what they did."

Sean fingered the hem of the shirt he wore. "I liked it," he whispered, staring at the speck of dust on the vent in front of his seat.

"I'm glad," Declan said. "I felt like an insensitive jackass afterward. I hope you'll give me the chance to show you just how much better it can be. My tiger didn't want to wait and sometimes he takes control in highly emotional situation."

"It gets better?" Sean asked, surprised. If it got any better, he'd probably melt into a giant puddle of goo.

Declan laughed and brought Sean's hand to his chest in a slight hug. "Baby, you haven't seen anything yet."

Sean blushed. He had no idea how to respond and just remained silent.

"Why don't you try one of the chocolates?" Declan prompted. "We'll be back home in about twenty minutes."

Excited at the reminder, Sean extracted his hand from Declan's, snatched the bag from the floor and opened it. He took out the one with the orange wrapping. The smell of peanut butter and chocolate made his stomach growl and his mouth water. He tore the plastic open and saw two little round disks inside. Picking one up, he saw a paper on the bottom. "Is the paper edible?" Sean asked, eyeing the underside of the chocolate disk.

"No. You take that off before you eat it."

Some crumbs of chocolate flaked off as he pulled down the edge of the black paper. He took a bite and his eyes widened before rolling into the back of his head. A loud moan rattled in his throat as the flavors burst over his tongue. He devoured the remainder of the chocolate disk in his hand then snatched the other one out of the packaging.

"Slow down or you'll choke," Declan admonished.

Sean managed to swallow the bite in his mouth. "They're so good!"

"I knew you'd like it." Declan chuckled.

Sean savored the remainder of the peanut butter cup, taking smaller nibbles instead. It was so much better than he'd ever imagined. Of course, he'd seen many different things on the T.V. whenever he'd been allowed upstairs, and he'd also seen images in the magazines Carl got in the mail. But he had never come close to understanding how amazing something could taste and smell.

By the time Declan pulled off the road and onto the one leading into the forest surrounding the compound, Sean had finished the first chocolate candy. After Declan helped him out of the Tahoe once they parked and Declan retrieved the box of cakes, Sean carried the bag with the remaining candy inside to find Sam and Tara. He heard a small giggle coming from the dining room and went in to find Vicky sitting with Rose and Ronnie. She still wasn't talking, but she sounded happy and Sean knew no matter what happened Vicky would be all right. "Sean!" Ronnie exclaimed and jumped from his seat to rush to hug him.

"Hi," Sean greeted, returning the hug.

Declan set a hand on Sean's shoulder. "Why don't you spend some time with Ronnie and the others while dinner is prepared? I have some stuff to take care of in my office."

Sean nodded. Ronnie grabbed Sean by the hand and tugged him over to the table. He sat and Vicky immediately moved from her chair to his lap. "Hey, sweetie."

Vicky snuggled up to him, laying her head on his chest and stuffing her thumb in her mouth. Sean sighed at the familiar weight. He set the plastic bag on the table and wrapped his arms around her. Rose smiled at him. "It's been hard keeping her out of your room. She is very attached to you."

Sean rubbed the bottom of his chin on the top of her head. "The feeling is mutual."

"Do you know anything about her family? Where she came from?"

"No," Sean replied with a shake of his head. "Before she stopped talking, she couldn't remember anything regarding her home. She told me her mother was in heaven and her father would miss her. Someone must be looking for her."

Rose sighed, her face saddened. "We'll find her father. If he's looking, there must be a report out for her. It'll just take a little longer to find him."

Sean didn't want to let her go, but she deserved to be with her family. He knew Sam and Tara did, too. "I know they want to stay here, but Sam and Tara's family should at least know they're alive."

"Victor has been trying to locate anything related to their packs. We've even asked them if they knew what area they were taken from. They don't want to leave you so they haven't been the most cooperative about their families."

"They may not remember. They were ta-taken a long time ago," Sean murmured, his voice cracking a bit. He could still see the two of them when they were first thrown into the basement with him. Scared, bruised, and crying, begging him to tell them why they were there. "Sam... she went through the most. My... Carl took her when she was seven. He preferred her over the others most times."

He heard Rose's breath catch at what he said without saying it. "She lost the first two babies because he would kick her in the stomach whenever she fought him. We-we almost lost her both times."

Rose stood and came around to where he sat with Vicky in his lap. Tears streamed down her cheeks as she bent to hug the two of them. Sean felt guilty for making her cry. "I'm sorry," he whispered.

"For what?" Rose rasped. She straightened and swiped at her face to clear away the tracks.

"For making you cry."

"Oh, sweetheart, don't ever apologize for something like that. You went through so much. All of you did. It breaks my heart to know the horrors you all suffered." Rose stroked a hand over Vicky's blond hair. "Did," she cleared her throat, "did he do anything like that to Vicky?"

"No."

Relief raced across Rose's features. "Do you know when she stopped talking?"

"Ca-Carl hated it when they shifted. Sometimes they couldn't help it. Fear triggered their shifts and Vicky... she couldn't stop herself. H-He hit her until she fell unconscious. After that, she never spoke again."

A noise in the doorway brought Sean's head round and he saw Sam standing there, Tara behind her shoulder. They were both crying quietly. Sean felt terrible. He hadn't meant to make them relive the things they'd suffered. "Sam. Tara. I-"

Sam shook her head and came over to stand by the three of them, Tara on her heels. "No, Sean. It's not your fault. You did your best to help us, to save us. If you hadn't been there, I-I would have died more than once. You saved our lives, Sean. We won't leave you."

"You belong with your families, Sam."

"You are our family, Sean," Tara said.

"We love you, Sean," Sam added. "You're everything to us."

Sean felt Vicky shudder against him and he looked down to find her also crying, silent tears soaking his shirt. Sam and Tara piled around the two of them, crowding as close as they could. Both girls wrapped them in a tight hug. Sean leaned into the warmth from them and closed his eyes. He found he had to swallow several times to get past the lump suddenly wedged in his throat. Tara's words about them being family couldn't be truer. "We love you, Sean," Sam murmured again.

"I love you guys, too," Sean choked, his voice trashed.

· · ·

Sean spent the remainder of the afternoon before dinner with the three of them, Rose, and Ronnie. Sam revealed that her unborn child was a boy and declared she would name him after Sean. He couldn't wait to meet the little one. Even despite how the baby began, it didn't mean the child deserved any less love or a chance at a great life. He also took out the chocolate bar and split it into pieces to share with everyone. Vicky's reaction almost mirrored his own causing Sean's chest to tighten at how much she'd already missed out on in life.

A few of the streak's members had arrived a short while ago, insistent on helping prepare dinner with the new additions to the alpha's household. Rose didn't seem to be too upset. They introduced themselves to Sean with either a small bow or clasp of his hand. "It's so great to meet you, Alpha-mate," the brown-haired female named Tanzie greeted.

"It's nice to meet you, too," Sean returned, still nervous around the others.

"Stop fawning over him, Tanz, and get in here and start chopping vegetables!" Sean glanced over at the tall blond who'd introduced himself as Matthew. The guy was huge! At least seven feet from Sean's perspective with super broad shoulders and sparkling lavender eyes, Matthew surely outsized even Declan. Matthew looked at Sean and winked, a smile curling full lips.

Tanzie rolled her eyes and shook her ponytail out behind her in a huff. "Shut up, Mattie. This is the first time we've had the chance to meet him. Declan has been keeping him to himself."

Rose chuckled, standing from the long table. "You wouldn't do the same thing if you found your life mate, Tanz?"

Sucking her teeth, Tanzie replied, "It wouldn't be such a celebrated event as the alpha finding his mate."

"Stop before you scare him away, Tanz," Jaylin, another streak member, admonished. His darker skin, a beautiful mocha color, reminded Sean of a panther cub who'd lasted a month before Carl… Sean didn't want to remember DeAndre or the sight of his brown eyes open yet unseeing as Sean buried him. The cub had only been seven years old.

Tanzie huffed. "I ain't scaring him off. Am I, Sean?" She looked his way.

Sean shook his head. "No, ma'am."

"See?" She looked at Jaylin and stuck out her tongue.

The dining room and kitchen were a bustle of activity between the four of them moving around to chop, mix, and whatever else they needed to do for preparation. Sean didn't get a chance to watch everything because Sam and Tara distracted him by telling him about their day and all of the exciting people they'd met. They also teased him a bit about his being called Alpha-mate.

By the time Declan appeared in the dining room, Sean's cheeks hurt from smiling so much. Declan came straight to Sean's side, leaning down to kiss his temple. "I can feel your happiness, mate," he murmured close to Sean's ear.

Sean looked at Declan and without hesitation grabbed Declan's hand. "Sam's baby is a boy. She's going to name him Sean."

Declan squeezed Sean's hand in his. "It's a beautiful name for a beautiful person."

Heat flooded Sean's face and Sean felt pretty certain he was blushing. There was a collective, "Awww," from the four adult females and a gagging noise from the other two men in the kitchen. The flames encompassing Sean's features got even hotter.

"Stop embarrassing him," Declan groused.

"Yes, Alpha," Tanzie drawled, winking at Sean.

Sean couldn't help it. A laugh bubbled up from within him and the sound pealed across the room, filling every nook and cranny. He never expected to be in a place like this, with people who cared about him, or to be free to giggle or cry or just be who he was. A week ago, he'd thought for sure he'd die in that basement without experiencing anything in life, with no one to mourn him or miss him, and buried in the yard like all the others.

"I love the sound of your laugh," Declan said, stroking a hand over Sean's dark hair. "We'll make sure you have every reason to keep doing it."

The laughter died off, but Sean's lips remained lifted in a smile. Declan sat beside Sean, not releasing his hold on Sean's hand. Everyone chatted and joked as they finished making supper. Sean offered to help, but the others waved him back into his chair. It wasn't much longer before everyone, including the man from earlier named Kyle, was seated around the dining table, heaping plates of fried chicken, green beans, and other sides steaming in front of them.

"Everything looks great," Declan said. "Thanks for helping with dinner, Tanz, Jay, and Mattie."

"No problem, Alpha," Mattie replied, grinning. "Gives us a chance to get to know the new Alpha-mate. So it's not just altruistic reasons."

Declan chuckled and reached out to brush the backs of his fingers over Sean's cheek. "Well, either way, it's appreciated."

Everyone, except Kyle, who remained quiet, chatted while passing dishes and serving themselves. It was only as Sean excitedly told Sam and Tara about the bakery and the pharmacy that he remembered Declan's prompt to ask Rose about what he'd seen in the store. "Rose?"

Rose glanced away from cutting up chicken for Vicky. "Sean?"

"Can I ask you something?"

"Anything, sweetie."

"What's a tampon?"

Silence reigned after Sean's question and he frowned. "Did I ask something wrong?"

Declan's booming laughter echoed through the house as Rose fish-faced at Sean.

16

DECLAN

Declan chuckled as he remembered Rose's astonishment and her fumbling around to answer Sean's question at dinner. He hadn't expected Sean to ask about tampons at the dining table, but it made for an entertaining scene, for sure. The look on Sean's face though had been priceless. He'd turned redder than Declan had ever seen him.

His thoughts turned to why Victor hadn't made an appearance at dinner. Tomorrow would be a day he'd give anything to skip over. The sound of the bathroom door opening brought Declan's attention up from the floor he'd been staring at. Sean looked stunning to him with slightly damp hair from his shower and dressed in one of Declan's t-shirts, which engulfed his still very slender form. He watched as Sean padded barefoot to the bed and pulled back the covers. "I know Sam and Tara said they didn't want to go back to their packs, but I still think we should try to find them," Sean said, frowning as he climbed onto the bed.

"I agree," Declan said. He thought back to those stolen

moments in the bakery and lust shot through him. Standing, he stripped his clothing off, tossing his jeans and t-shirt over the nearby chair.

"Do you think they're still looking for them?" Sean asked while straightening the comforter over his lap.

"Parents never give up looking for their child."

Crawling onto the bed, Declan dragged the comforter down and off Sean's legs, almost growling at the sight of the smooth, pale flesh. He wanted to taste and lick every inch of Sean's silky and perfect skin. Sean's eyes widened a fraction and Declan smirked as he slid both palms along the length of Sean's legs to his thighs. "I believe I made a promise earlier, mate."

A small gasp puffed from Sean when Declan suddenly nuzzled at the warm flesh of Sean's inner thigh. "Wha-what are you doing?" Sean murmured.

"Showing you how much better it can be," Declan rumbled just before he swiped his tongue over the same path as his chin and cheek. Sean jumped and this time a gasp exploded from him.

"Dec-Declan," Sean keened, his hands coming forward to grasp Declan's shoulders.

Declan purred, his tiger close to the surface, and he urged Sean to spread his legs. The shirt Sean wore rode high enough to bare the hard, slender cock Declan intended on tasting very soon. A small pearl of liquid dotted the tip and spilled over, trickling down the darkened pink shaft. Perfectly proportionate round orbs rested beneath Sean's prick with only a light dusting of hair. "Beautiful," Declan murmured a second before his mouth made contact with them.

"Oh!" Sean cried out, his hands moving to fist in the strands of Declan's hair.

He pulled one and then the other into his mouth, rolling them over his tongue. The pants and small whimpers Sean let forth caused Declan's cock to throb in anticipation, but he ignored the appendage, focusing solely on bringing Sean as much pleasure as possible. Releasing Sean's sac from his mouth, Declan used the flat of his tongue to lick along the underside of Sean's shaft and swirled around the head. A growl rattled in his chest when Sean's flavor burst across his taste buds.

But it wasn't the taste or the soft pants which caused his cock to soak the blanket beneath him with pre-cum. It was the slight cry Sean let out and the way his hips thrust toward Declan when Declan swallowed his dick to the root. Declan grabbed hold of Sean's hips, pinning him in place, as he feasted upon his mate's length. "Dec-oh!" Sean tightened his hold in Declan's short locks when Declan hummed while Sean was in his throat.

Seconds passed and then Sean tripped over the edge with loud lusty cries. Declan would teach his mate patience and how to hold out later. Right now, he just wanted Sean to feel sated and peaceful. Once he'd taken every drop Sean had to give, Declan released Sean's softening shaft and kissed a path over Sean's trembling abdomen, belly, and heaving chest until he had Sean's shirt completely removed and then he settled his long length over Sean. Brushing a strand of hair back from Sean's sweaty cheek, Declan smiled softly at him.

A look of complete satiation stared back at him, Sean's cheeks and throat flushed from his orgasm. Declan leaned in to nuzzle at Sean's throat, his lips instinctively finding the mating mark. He would spend the rest of their lives putting that look on Sean's face as often as he possibly could.

Reaching into the nightstand where he'd placed a tube of Astroglide the day before. "Ready for more?" Declan asked, his voice husky from his own restrained desire.

Sean gave a breathless laugh of bewilderment. "There's more?"

Chuckling, Declan unsnapped the cap and spilled some of the lubricant over his fingers. "So much more, sexy. So much more."

A strangled moan issued from Sean when Declan moved to his knees and began to probe at his entrance with one finger. Declan had to grab his cock by the base to stave off the imminent climax at the feel of Sean's body opening to the invading digit. "God, baby, you are so fucking tight."

Sean flushed even deeper, his sapphire blue eyes sparkling from lust. Declan slowly thrust his finger in and out of Sean, waiting for the muscles to loosen a fraction to add a second one. A fine sheen of sweat broke out over Sean's entire body. "Does it feel good?" Declan rasped.

Biting his lip, Sean nodded. "And a little strange, too."

A wicked smirk settled on Declan's lips and he pulled out only to push back in with a second finger. Sean shuddered and Declan hooked his fingers just right, passing over the one spot he knew could cause mind-numbing pleasure. Sean let forth a scream, his body bowing from the bed, and Declan watched in awe as Sean came a second time, his cock spitting white seed all over his soft belly.

Declan's tiger yowled with pride inside his head and Declan leaned down to clean Sean's belly of the salty fluid. "You have no idea what you do to me," Declan whispered against Sean's skin.

With a quickness Declan would probably regret later, he stretched Sean further by adding a third finger, watching with lust at the way Sean's body opened to him. The moment he knew Sean could accept him without pain he covered his hard cock with lube and settled himself between Sean's thighs. He nudged the head of his dick at Sean's entrance and inched forward centimeter by centimeter.

His gaze swung from Sean's face to where they were joined throughout the several moments, gauging if Sean were in any pain. The only thing Declan saw in Sean's eyes appeared to be desire. His entire body was covered in sweat and a fine tremble wracked his strong form by the time his balls met Sean's cheeks. Declan remained stationary, knowing if there were even an ounce of friction on his cock he'd blow. When Sean shifted beneath him, Declan hissed and grabbed hold of Sean's waist. "Don't move."

Sean froze. "Did I-did I do something wrong?"

Declan shook his head, gritted his teeth and reached out to cup Sean's cheek. "No, baby. I'm just too close. I need a moment or it'll be over before it starts."

Sean's confusion didn't clear, but he abided by Declan's word and held still. When the tingle in Declan's balls subsided, he gave a tentative thrust, relishing the whimper Sean gave. He captured Sean's mouth with his, kissing him soft and slow at first. The intensity of the kiss changed in tune with Declan's movements inside of Sean, his tongue reaching in to encourage Sean to duel with his. Soon the scent of their passion and the sound of skin slapping against skin filled the room.

He wouldn't last much longer and he gave Sean one last lingering kiss before trailing his lips down to the mating scar. "Declan," Sean moaned, his thin arms wrapped around Declan's back, fingers gripping the rippling muscles.

Declan opened his mouth over the area and, the second his climax hit him, his teeth shifted to his tiger's. "Mate," he garbled before he sank his fangs deep into Sean's shoulder.

Sean cried out and Declan felt the warmth of his come between them, following Sean over the precipice and flooding Sean's tight channel. Shudders ripped through Declan and he wrenched his teeth free from Sean's shoulder to roar his satisfaction to the heavens.

He collapsed atop Sean after, face in the pillow beside Sean's head. The moment he could control his body again he rolled the two of them to their sides, not wanting to crush Sean beneath his heavy weight. Sean gave him a drunken smile and Declan huffed a light laugh, tracing the ridge of Sean's brow with the tip of one finger. "Was that better?"

Sean nodded. "So much better."

Chuckling, Declan gathered Sean close to his chest. "Sleep, baby. Tomorrow is another day."

He felt Sean yawn and snuggle closer to him. "G'night."

"Night, sexy."

The next morning Declan left Sean with Rose and the others after making sure he'd taken the prescriptions Cameron had prescribed. He headed to his office for a report from Victor, dreading what he'd reveal. A grim expression met him when Victor entered a few minutes later. Declan motioned for Victor to have a seat in front of his desk. "Tell me."

Victor ran a hand over his face, the usual stoicism gone, grief and sorrow in its place. Declan knew it wouldn't be pleasant, especially if it affected Victor to this extent. "We've managed to exhume half of the bodies, Alpha. Dr. Green has been up all night directing the clan members how to safely and carefully extract them. It's not pretty, Alpha."

"I knew it wouldn't be, Victor. Were you able to identify any of the remains?"

"The Alpha-mate marked them all with identifying factors such as their names and age at the time of death. If it weren't for that, it would take much longer. I have only located three of the families so far."

"Where?"

Swallowing hard, Victor grimaced. "A cub from the Koda

Sleuth, a hatchling from the Cast Clan, and a cub from the Clan of the Claw."

Declan swore and shoved to his feet. He paced. Their relationship with the Clan of the Claw was tenuous at best. Panthers felt they were above the rest of shifters, better in every way. When they found out about their cub there would be hell to pay because it had happened on the edge of the Royal Taiga's land. "Fuck!" Declan raged, slamming his fist against the wall. "How? How did this happen, Victor?"

"It's not your fault, Alpha. The patrols were drawn in closer to the compound by your father after the attack on our clan many years ago. It couldn't be risked having the enforcers so far out."

"That was so long ago, Victor! We've grown in number since then. I should have-"

"Alpha," Victor interrupted, "you couldn't have known. No one could have. You can't continue to blame yourself."

"This could very well start a war with the Clan of the Claw. You know that as well as I do."

"I don't think it will come to that."

Declan snorted derisively. "Do you really believe that? The slightest thing can set them off."

"After the previous alpha passed, his youngest son, Luthor took over. There are rumors he isn't as arrogant as his father."

Declan frowned. "Why did Luthor become alpha when there is a first born? Casey isn't it?"

"Casey is a Seer, Alpha."

It wasn't uncommon for the first born of an alpha to not be an alpha. Declan figured it had something to do with nature ensuring the current alpha did not kill the first born in order to remain in position until they died. "Keep working on identifying them, Victor. I will reach out to the other clans to begin proceedings for transfer of the remains."

"As you command, Alpha." Victor stood and moved to the door. He stopped, his hand on the knob, and turned. "It's not your fault, Dec. You know there was nothing you could have done."

Declan waved Victor out of the office and went to his desk where he dropped down onto the chair. Placing his elbows on the desk, he covered his face and sighed. Maybe Victor was right, but how could he find any way to apologize for the other clans affected by his negligence?

He made the decision to call the three leaders to the clan compound to break the news to them. There would be others as time went on. With each body exhumed the number of meetings would grow. Allowing his hands to drop, Declan reached for the phone and began dialing.

Thirty minutes later he'd made a call to the three other clans and requested they arrive at the compound in two days' time. Perhaps by then they would have removed Sean's collar and there would be something good to celebrate during the dark times ahead.

A tentative knock on his door caused Declan to sit up straighter. "Enter."

The door opened and Sean slipped in, closing the door behind him. Declan didn't hesitate. He held out his arms to Sean who immediately climbed onto his lap. "You're sad," Sean murmured.

Declan leaned his forehead against Sean's. "A little bit."

"What's wrong?"

"My heart hurts, baby."

"Why? Is it bad? Should I get Dr. Green?"

The innocence behind Sean's questions almost brought Declan to tears, reinforcing just how much those children had suffered just miles from his home. "It's not that kind of hurt."

Sean frowned. "You said your heart hurts. What other kind of hurt is there?"

Declan hated himself even more right then. He cleared his throat, closing his eyes. "When you spoke of the cubs, the ones who died, the ones you were forced to bury, what did you feel?"

Sean stiffened and Declan tightened his hold on Sean, self-loathing raging through him. "Sad. Pain. Emptiness."

"The pain wasn't something any doctor can heal, right?" Sean nodded. "That's how my heart aches right now, baby."

It shocked Declan when Sean wrapped his arms around Declan and held on as hard as he could. Yet he shouldn't be surprised. His mate was a caregiver, selfless and generous. "Whatever it is will be okay," Sean whispered.

Declan had no idea how his mate could still be so optimistic, so positive, after everything he'd gone through. Maybe they could get through this without further bloodshed. Smiling gently, Declan breathed in the scent of his mate's skin. "You're right, Sean. Things will be okay. Especially now that I have you."

A flush covered Sean's features, but he smiled, a smile Declan could see all the way up to his eyes. His mate was the strongest person he'd ever met and he'd spend every day of their life together making sure he was worthy of someone like Sean. "Do you want to talk about it?" Sean asked.

He'd rather ravish Sean right there in his office, but he knew Sean needed to know what to expect in the coming days. So instead of hiding the truth from him, Declan told Sean about the three cubs and their connection to the three clans arriving in two days. Sean remained quiet, only listening, but Declan could sense the sadness Sean felt through their bond. He also started explaining the hierarchy and the way others functioned as a pack or sleuth. The Royal Taiga

Streak had many allies, but some were tenuous and there were others which were downright hostile to outsiders.

"You're worried they'll blame you," Sean said, astonishing Declan once more.

"I know they will."

Sean frowned, tilting his head quizzically. "Why would they blame you? You didn't take their children and you weren't the one who hurt them either."

"Anger and hatred don't see with reason, sexy. Many times they blind someone to the truth, but even so, it still happened on the edges of our land. How could we not have noticed? Not seen it was happening sooner?"

"But you couldn't have known!" Sean protested. "We had no neighbors for miles and my father always kept them inside. I was the only one ever allowed outside. No one could have known we were in there."

"We'd have smelled you all. I would have known you-" Declan was cut short by Sean covering his mouth with his hand.

"I'm not the smartest person having never been to school," Sean shook his head when Declan went to object and Declan remained quiet, "but I do know what we went through wasn't your fault. The only one to blame is Ca-Carl McNeely. He stole all of us, hurt us, and was an evil man."

Sean dropped his hand from Declan's mouth. "I still have a lot to learn about the world, about living and about people. But there is one thing I know with all my heart is that you are a kind and generous man. You are nothing like the man I called my father."

Threading his fingers through Sean's still uncut hair, Declan said, "Thank you for those words, baby. I will do my best to make you proud to be my mate."

"I already am."

Declan groaned and crushed Sean to him. "If I didn't have streak business, I'd repeat last night right here on my desk."

Sean blushed and said, "Couldn't someone walk in?"

A growl rattled in Declan's throat. "They know better than to enter without knocking."

As his words finished, a knock came at the door. Declan scowled and then sighed. "Duty calls, sexy.

17

SEAN

Sean tried to slip from Declan's lap when he barked "Enter!", but Declan refused to let him go.

The man from the day before, Kyle, stepped into the room, closing the door behind him. "Alpha Declan."

"You have news?" Declan asked.

"Yes. I was able to get in touch with my contact who did know of a witch powerful enough to remove the collar."

Sean tensed and Declan ran his palm along Sean's thigh in a caress. "How long will it take for them to get here?"

Kyle strode forward and sat in one of the chairs in front of the desk. "The witch is... not so easy to convince. I found their reticence suspicious."

Declan frowned. "Do you think they could be the one to have made the collar? To have put it on Sean?"

Tipping his head, Kyle said, "I think it appears to be so."

"Bring them to me," Declan demanded, standing and setting Sean on his feet. "I want the foul son of a bitch who could do such a thing to an innocent child!"

The last ended on a roar and Sean jumped, instinctively shrinking away. Declan calmed instantly and grabbed Sean, pulling him back to his side. "I'm sorry, baby. I didn't mean to scare you."

Sean pressed his face to Declan's side. "I remember them," he mumbled.

Kyle seemed interested and leaned forward in his seat. "Do you remember what they looked like?"

Biting his lip, Sean nodded. "My father… Carl never used their name, but he returned once to reinforce the collar. I don't know why. Something happened when I turned thirteen. Carl brought me upstairs and there was a man there. He forced me to drink something that tasted like sand then said a bunch of words in a language I didn't understand."

Declan's chest rumbled beneath Sean's ear and he somehow knew Declan was mad at the man instead of him. Looking up at Declan, Sean said, "The collar got hot, almost painfully hot, and then it was over. After that, I never saw him again."

"What did he look like?" Kyle asked.

Sean looked at Kyle. "He had light brown hair and purple eyes. I remember the purple because when he finished whatever he'd done they glowed. There was a scar on his right cheek."

Kyle swore and sat back. "Son of a bitch."

Sean flinched. Declan rubbed the bottom of his chin on the top of Sean's head. "Bring him to me, Kyle. I want the fucker right here in front of me where I can gut the bastard."

Kyle gave a nod and stood, stone-cold expression on his face. "I'll have him here tomorrow."

Kyle had only just left the office when another knock came. "Come in," Declan snarled.

A huge, blond-haired male Sean hadn't met yet stepped into the office. He almost seemed to shrink the space with his height and width. Sean stared at him wide-eyed when the man spoke in a voice so deep his eardrums vibrated with the bass of it. "Alpha... sorry to interrupt."

Declan shook his head. "Michael, you weren't interrupting. Please come in. I'd like you to meet my mate Sean. Sean, Michael is one of the streak's enforcers and a longtime friend of mine."

Gray eyes settled on Sean. Michael tipped his head in greeting. "It's good to meet you, Alpha-mate."

The title many of the streak members used toward him still unsettled him. He didn't really understand what it meant, but he certainly never dreamed to be the mate of an alpha, or anything really as he'd expected to die in his father's basement. Over the years he'd spent taking care of the cubs he'd learned a lot about packs, prides, and others from them. The chain from alpha to all those underneath him wasn't unfamiliar to Sean. If he'd truly understood what the others had explained to him, knowing he stood on the same level as Declan made him nervous. He wasn't good enough to be equal with Declan.

Declan tensed beside him and Sean wondered if he'd missed anything. Michael had started talking, but Sean remained locked in his own thoughts instead of paying attention. "Michael," Declan interrupted.

Michael stopped giving his report to Declan. "Alpha?"

"I need a moment with my mate. Will you please step out of the room for a few minutes?"

Michael nodded. "Yes, Alpha."

As soon as Michael had shut the door, Declan gripped Sean by the shoulders, turning him to face him. "I want you to hear me, Sean. You are perfect. You are stronger than anyone I have ever met and I don't ever want to hear you think you're not good enough again."

Sean's eyes widened. "I'm not-"

Declan glared at Sean. "Don't say it. You are more than

you think you are and anything else can be taught, learned, and experienced. You want to learn? I can arrange it with the streak's teacher. You want to travel? I'll go with you and we'll go anywhere in the world you want. No matter what it is, you are free to pursue whatever you want. I'll make sure of that. There is nothing and no one stopping you anymore. Understood?"

Biting his lip, Sean nodded. "Okay," he murmured.

Declan kissed Sean's forehead. "Why don't you go visit with Sam and Tara? I'll finish up with Michael and then we can go talk to Clarissa about starting you on lessons."

Sean nodded and murmured, "Okay."

He left the office and wandered down the hallway, lost in thought. Anything he wanted? But what did he want? He'd never had the choice before and never thought he would. How could he know what he wanted to do?

Lost in his thoughts, Sean barely registered exiting the house and going to the porch swing where he sat down. Saying he felt overwhelmed would be an understatement and he had no idea how long he remained there, staring off into the distance. Only the sound of his name really brought him to awareness. "Sean?"

He blinked several times to bring himself around. Sam stood nearby, frowning. "You okay?"

Sean shrugged and looked down at his hands on his lap. "I don't know what I want, Sam."

Sam came closer and sat in the swing beside him. "What do you mean?"

"Declan said I can do whatever I want. Learn whatever I want. But how do I know what that is?"

Sam wrapped her arm around him and leaned her head on his shoulder. "That's the fun part, Sean. Learning new things. Do you remember that time? Where he let us both upstairs at the same time because he'd made a mess in the kitchen and didn't want to get up from the couch? He wanted us both to clean it up."

"Yeah, I remember," Sean murmured, shuddering. After they'd finished, Carl had demanded Sean go back to the basement and he'd grabbed Sam, yanking her into his lap and starting to maul her. For the first time since Carl had kidnapped Sam, Sean bore witness to Sam's pain and degradation, even for the few seconds he'd found himself frozen in place before Carl had shouted at him again to get the fuck down to the basement. Sean had hated his father more than ever right then, but he'd been powerless to help Sam or stop Carl.

"There was a movie on the T.V. and I remember watching a woman riding a horse and I thought that's something I want to do. She looked so carefree and happy. Something I could barely recall feeling in my life."

Sean nuzzled at Sam's hair. He'd never known anything before the cold, damp basement or the terror his father had instilled in him.

"But I knew if I ever got free, if we ever got free, I wanted to be happy. Of course, riding a horse would be amazing also." Sam chuckled a bit. "My point is, Sean, you are free to discover what makes *you* happy and there are so many ways to find those things, too. You've never had a chance to live, to experience the normal things normal people do every single day. Cooking, horseback riding, reading, drawing, skydiving, and so many other amazing things await you. Don't be afraid to try anything and everything."

A shuddery sigh escaped Sean. "Thanks, Sam."

"You deserve everything, Sean, because if it weren't for you, Tara, Vicky and I would be dead. Not to mention Fredrick and Tomas and Ronnie. None of them would have been reunited with their family."

"Sam?"

"Hmm?"

"You need to find your family." Sam started to protest again, but Sean shook his head. "It's not right to let them continue to believe you're gone. They deserve to know you're alive."

"What if… what if they don't want me, Sean? What if they find out I'm pregnant by the man who kidnapped me and it disgusts them?"

"No matter what happens you'll always have a home wherever I am, Sam, but I know in my heart they won't care about that."

"And if they want to take me away?" Sam whispered. "I don't want to leave you, Sean. I don't want to leave Tara and Vicky. You are my family."

"We'll always be your family, Sam, but there are people out there who have wondered for years if you're alive or dead. If you don't want to go with them, we'll find a way for you to stay."

Sam wrapped her arms around her belly. "I know this baby wasn't made out of love, but I love him and I won't lose him."

"I will never let that happen," Declan interjected, having come out while the two of them were lost in their talk. Sean gave Declan a thankful look. Declan approached the swing and crouched down to look up at Sam. He placed one hand on her knee. "Your baby is part of this streak, Sam. You are a part of this streak. No one will take your child from you."

Sam sniffled and nodded. "Thanks, Alpha Declan."

Declan smiled at her and lightly squeezed her knee. "We are heading over to talk to Clarissa, the streak's teacher. I think it would be good if you and the others started lessons with Sean."

Brightening, Sam said, "Really?"

"Of course. I also think it would be good if the four of you started seeing our therapist."

Sean frowned. "What's a therapist?"

"A head shrink who listens to you and tells you what to feel," Sam grunted.

"They shrink your head?" Sean asked, horrified. He raised both hands to grip said body part. "Why would they do that?"

Sam grinned, but Declan huffed at her and she dropped the smile while Declan turned toward Sean and took hold of his hands, returning them to Sean's lap. "They don't really shrink your head, Sean. Sam was being funny."

"Oh."

"A therapist is a doctor of the mind and soul. They help heal you mentally while a doctor like Cameron heals you physically. I think it's important for you all to talk to someone who can help you deal with what you've been through and how to live with those events. You've all been through something horrifying and beyond understanding for many of us. Especially you, gorgeous. You've spent years being the punching bag for someone, taking care of so many others while struggling to survive, and seen death more than any child should."

Sam snorted. "Like they're going to understand any of it themselves?"

Declan gave Sam a look and she sighed. "I'm sorry, Alpha. I don't mean any disrespect, but I doubt anyone can begin to know what we've all gone through except each other."

"You're right, Sam. No one can ever truly know what happened to you and it may even be good for you all to have sessions together as well as apart. To talk about the things that you experienced in a safe space. Will you both consider it? Please? Speak with Tara as well."

Sam studied Declan for a silent moment and then nodded. "All right."

"Sean?"

Sean didn't really want to talk about and relive the last seventeen years of his life. He wanted to forget about them and just be happy he was out of that basement, but Declan seemed to really want him to see the therapist. "Okay."

Declan smiled and reached out to brush a strand of hair away from Sean's cheek. "Thank you, gorgeous. I think today we should see about getting this hair trimmed, too."

"On that note, I'm going to go find Tara and Vicky," Sam said and started to leverage herself to her feet. Declan stood and took both her hands, helping her upright. "Thank you, Alpha."

"Call me Declan or Dec, please."

"I'll try," Sam said, wrinkling her pert nose at him.

Once Sam had wandered into the house, Declan turned to Sean and held out his hand. "Let's go see Clarissa."

Sean laid his palm in Declan's and allowed him to lead him down the porch steps and through the compound. The walk didn't take more than a few minutes and they approached a brick one-story building with white trim. When they stepped inside Sean saw a small room with a couch, several chairs, and a T.V. on the wall. The wall was a cheery yellow with a plethora of pictures, drawings and photographs. There was a corridor that led further into the building and Declan encouraged Sean to head down it. There were four more doors as well as bathrooms at the end.

They stopped in front of an open door where a pretty blonde woman stood at a white board on the wall, a marker in her hand. Sean peeked in and saw there were rows of small tables with kids ranging in ages around them. Ronnie sat at one of those tables, but when he saw Sean, he gave a small shout of greeting and darted out of his chair to throw himself at Sean.

"Ronnie," Declan grunted. "Were you allowed to get up before asking?"

Ronnie backed away from Sean and flushed, looking at the ground. "No, Uncle Dec."

"I think you should apologize to Ms. Clarissa."

"Yes, Uncle Dec." Ronnie turned to look at the blonde woman. "Sorry, Ms. Clarissa."

She smiled and came over to where they stood. "Go have a seat, Ronnie. I know you were excited to see the Alpha and Alpha-mate, so I won't have you stay after to help clean up today, but please remember in the future to ask before leaving your seat."

"Yes, Ms. Clarissa." Ronnie rushed back to his chair and sat, but didn't take his eyes off Sean or Declan.

"I apologize for interrupting class, Clarissa," Declan said. "I wanted to know if we can have a moment of your time?"

"Of course, Alpha." Clarissa turned to face the children. "Class, please remain seated and take a few moments to review what we've already gone over this morning. I'll be right back. Megan, please take names of anyone who gets out of their seat."

A dark-haired girl who looked around the same age as Tara nodded with a serious expression. "Yes, Ms. Clarissa."

The three of them stepped out of the room and Clarissa closed the door until there was just a small crack remaining. "How can I help you, Alpha?"

Declan wrapped an around Sean's waist. "Clarissa, I'd like you to meet Sean. Sean, this is Clarissa. She's been teaching the streak's children for twenty years now."

Sean gaped. The woman didn't look a day over twenty-five. "You're really pretty!" he blurted then blushed.

Clarissa laughed and held out her hand. Sean accepted it and she gave his hand a light squeeze. "You're sweet, Sean. I'm glad I finally get the chance to meet the Alpha-mate.

Everyone has been abuzz with the news of our alpha having finally found his mate."

"Clarissa, I'd like you to start private sessions with Sean, the little girl Vicky, and the two teenage girls Sam and Tara. It's been a number of years since they were in classes and Sean has never attended school at all."

"Of course, Alpha! It would be my honor to teach them!" Clarissa looked at Sean. "Would it be all right if I ask you some questions?"

Sean nodded.

"Are you able to read?"

Sean shook his head.

"Do you know what the alphabet is?"

"Yes," Sean murmured.

"What about numbers? Have you learned anything about math?"

Biting his lips and leaning further into Declan's side, who tightened his hold a fraction, Sean shook his head. "Sam and Tara tried to teach me some, but I wasn't that good at it."

"Okay, so we will start with reading. When would you like to begin?"

Sean shrugged.

"It's already almost Friday, Clarissa. Why don't we start fresh on Monday?" Declan suggested.

Clarissa nodded. "That sounds great. It will give me some time to draw up some lesson plans. Would I be able to meet the girls? I'd like to ascertain what their levels are as well."

"Why don't you come by the house for dinner this evening? It'll give you a chance to speak with Vicky, Sam and Tara and also get to know Sean a little better as well. Just so you are aware, Vicky does not speak right now."

"That's quite all right. We can make up our own way to communicate," Clarissa said, smiling brightly. "I look forward to meeting the others. I am sure there are things I can arrange for Vicky as well."

"We'll see you tonight then," Declan said.

Clarissa bid them both goodbye and went back into her classroom. Sean could hear the kids giggling and Clarissa asking them to quiet down. Declan released Sean, but snagged his hand, entwining their fingers. "Let's go see about having your hair trimmed, hmm? Rose should be able to even out the ends."

Sean quietly followed Declan out of the school. There were several pride members working in their yards and they all waved at Declan and smiled at Sean. He didn't know how to respond so just smiled back as best he could. When they reached the house, they found Rose prepping vegetables for the evening meal.

"Hey, sis," Declan greeted, walking up to her and giving her a kiss on the cheek.

"Where'd you two get off to?" she asked, slicing a carrot with expert strokes.

Sean watched in awe. He'd probably cut his finger off, probably more than one! The knife just flew across the cutting board at lightning speed.

"Sean and the girls are going to start sessions with Clarissa next week."

"Oh, that's good to hear. I'm sure they will love it! And Clarissa is such a sweetheart! Ronnie adores her."

"I was hoping you'd have a little bit of time before dinner to trim Sean's hair." Declan grabbed a bottle of water from the fridge and cracked it open before handing it to Sean.

Sean took it, but didn't drink from it. He set the bottle on the nearby table instead.

"Oh, sure! Let me just finish up the rest of these carrots. Why don't you have a seat, Sean? Dec, would you grab my kit from the downstairs bathroom?"

Sean sat gingerly in one of the chairs at the table while Declan left to retrieve whatever she needed. Rose hummed under her breath while finishing the carrots and he continued to observe the way she chopped them. Declan returned a moment later and set a black bag, a spray bottle, and a white towel on the table near Sean. After washing her hands and drying them, Rose came to the table and opened the bag. She pulled out a comb and a pair of scissors and set them on the table.

"How much do we want off?" Rose asked while picking up the towel and draping it over Sean's shoulders.

"Just clean up the ends and even it out. I like it that length."

Rose leaned down and looked at Sean. "Is that what you want?"

Sean shrugged. "I don't really know. It's always kind of been this long. Sam and Tara tried to cut it when they could, but I don't really remember it any other way."

"You have no idea how much you break my heart," Rose mumbled and picked up the comb.

"I'm sorry," Sean whispered.

Suddenly Rose hugged him from behind, her arms wrapping tight around his shoulders and her cheek pressed to his. "You have nothing to be sorry for, Sean. I wish we'd found you all sooner is all."

Rose cleared her throat and released him. She grabbed the spray bottle and started spritzing his hair while combing. Sean closed his eyes when a few droplets dripped, tickling his eyelashes. He heard the snick of the scissors several times. "You have such beautiful hair, Sean. I'm jealous. I can never do anything with mine."

She kept up a string of chatter while cutting his hair and it couldn't have been more than ten minutes when she stepped back. "There. So much better, right?"

Declan held up a mirror to Sean. Both sides were now even and the ends were no longer ragged. "Thank you, Rose," Sean said.

She smiled while removing the towel. "Of course, sweetie. I help Declan keep his mane tamed, too."

She bustled around sweeping up the bits that had fallen to the floor. Victor came into the house then and Sean noticed Declan tense. Declan stood when the two men shared a glance and Victor headed toward Declan's office. "I need to speak to Victor, baby. You'll be okay if I leave you here with Rose?"

"Yeah."

Declan kissed him quickly and then strode from the room. Sean couldn't help his curiosity, but didn't feel he had the right to ask what was going on. It must be something important because Declan had seemed upset.

Sean folded his arms on the table and laid his head on top of them. So many things in his life had changed in such a short time. He hadn't really allowed himself to hope he could shift, but he could admit to himself he really did want to shift. What kind of animal was he? The one thing he'd always wondered was why had he never shifted before Carl placed the collar on his neck. Then again he couldn't remember much before his life in the basement. Maybe he had, but his other half just hadn't been able to break through the magic enough for him to know.

Of course, that caused his thoughts to turn to wondering if Carl really hadn't been his father. If so, where were his parents? Did they still think about him? Did they miss him? Had they had more children and didn't need him anymore? His chest tightened at the idea of them forgetting about him. Even though he didn't know for certain they were out there it still caused a slight pall over the happiness he'd started to feel.

Then he started to wonder about Declan's family. Rose had Ronnie, but he'd yet to meet Ronnie's dad and what about Declan and Rose's parents? "Rose?" Sean said, sitting straight in the chair again.

She glanced at him. "What's up, hun?"

"Where's Ronnie's dad?"

Rose started, the hand with the knife halted, and he saw her take a deep breath before turning to face him. Sean saw such a deep sadness in her eyes. He immediately guessed. "I'm sorry," he murmured.

She gave him a wobbly smile. "It's all right, Sean. He's been gone for a year now, but I still miss him. Ronnie... he remembers him, of course, but Declan has really helped by spending time with him and kind of standing in as his dad in most ways."

"What about your parents?" Sean queried.

Setting the knife down, she wiped her hands on a towel and came to sit by him. "Our dad was in a really bad accident and since our parents were life mates, Mom followed not long after him. She couldn't really live without him."

Sean gasped. "I'm so sorry."

Rose nodded. "It's okay. I think if it weren't for Ronnie I may have gone the same way after losing David. But I have to be here for him. He deserves at least one parent in his life and I can't imagine leaving him behind like that."

"Would that happen to... to Declan if I..."

"It's most likely, sweetie. You see, life mates, when they bond, they share a part of their souls with one another. It's all very mystical, I guess. When one of the pair passes, it tears something in the other and they end up living a half-life."

He covered his mouth with his hand. "Is that how you feel?"

She shrugged one slender shoulder. "Sometimes. Ronnie helps. More than he knows."

Before he could ask any further questions, Sam and Tara wandered into the room, Vicky between them. "Hey, Sean," Tara greeted. "Rose, we thought we'd come help you prepare dinner."

"That sounds wonderful. I would never turn down help, especially from a cutie like you," Rose chirp, gently tapping Vicky on the nose with one finger.

Vicky giggled and lifted her arms for Rose to pick her up. Rose didn't hesitate and Sean could see Vicky had come so far out of her shell in such a short time. He hoped one day she'd feel safe enough to talk again. "Ronnie mentioned something about a movie night?" Sean asked while Rose ended Vicky's hug and set her back down.

"Oh, now that is a great idea," Rose said. "Let's see how much time we have after dinner tonight."

Sean nodded eagerly, excited at the prospect of watching an actual movie. "I've never seen a movie in full. What can we watch?"

Rose closed her eyes for a split second and he saw her take a breath before she replied, "Anything you want, Sean. You choose."

"But I don't know what there is," Sean said.

While prepping dinner, she started to list off movies and explaining what each one was. He couldn't wait to see every single one she mentioned.

18

DECLAN

eclan followed a somber Victor into his office where Victor waited for Declan to close the door before relaying his news. "We've finished exhuming the remains, Alpha."

"Have all of the clans been identified?"

Victor shook his head. "Three are still yet undetermined. Cameron has started documenting the cause of deaths and validating the ages based on what the Alpha-mate has given us."

Declan growled low. "Are the others from either of the clans coming in two days?"

"No, Alpha. The rest so far are either from packs further out or packs we hold strong alliances with."

"Put together a list of the clans and the associated names and shifters for each child. I will request their presence on the same day. It may prevent escalation. I also don't want this information leaked until we are ready with answers."

"Yes, Alpha." Victor hesitated and then asked, "What of Mr. Hunter's contact?"

"Kyle has left to retrieve the witch responsible for that

abomination around Sean's neck." Declan could hardly wait to incinerate the damn thing. Such a contraption should never exist!

"Does he require assistance?"

"No, I don't think so."

"I will inform you as soon as Mr. Hunter arrives with the package."

"Thank you, Victor. Also, please inform the streak I would like them to attend a meeting this evening. I apologize for the late notice, but with the clan members arriving tomorrow I need to make everyone aware there will be others in the compound and why."

Victor grimaced. "Yes, Alpha."

Declan sighed. "Please call me Declan, Victor."

Tipping his head in acknowledgment, Victor said, "Yes, Alpha."

Declan knew Victor wouldn't ever change his ways. The man had been around since his father's time as alpha and he'd rarely ever seen Victor even angry or happy. He didn't know why Victor seemed to keep himself closed off, but Declan appreciated the man more than anything for everything he'd done for him and his family for several decades. "Thank you, Victor. That'll be all."

Victor nodded once and left the office. Declan paced to the window and stood there, arms crossed over his chest, while staring out at the streak's land. He knew the next few days would not be pleasant ones. His streak needed to know the true details of what lay ahead to prepare for any potential backlash. There was nothing else to do except wait for the chips to fall where they may.

He moved back to his desk and took a few moments to comb through his emails. There were several which needed to be answered, but they could hold until the next day. Declan saw another from Nicole and Arthur Bianca. They were heading back home the following week. He shot off a quick reply to wish them a safe trip and he would see them when they arrived. After, he rejoined the others in the dining room and tried to push the weight on his shoulders away for at least a couple of hours.

Dinner was the usual loud affair and Declan couldn't be happier when he saw the way Sam, Tara, and Sean opened up to Clarissa. They seemed excited at the prospect of taking lessons with her. Vicky still hadn't spoken, but she watched Clarissa with wide eyes and she even climbed up on Clarissa's lap to play with Clarissa's long blonde hair. Declan wondered if she reminded Vicky of her own mother.

When everyone had finished dinner, Declan instructed everyone to meet outside in a half an hour as he needed to address the entire pride. He saw Rose glance at him, curiosity in her eyes, but she didn't ask him any questions. She ushered Vicky and Ronnie from the room to clean up before the gathering. Declan hadn't eaten much, his stomach too twisted in knots to be very hungry.

"Is everything okay?" Sean asked him when they were alone.

"Of course, baby."

"You didn't eat much for dinner."

Declan gathered Sean into his arms and rested his cheek atop Sean's head. "Just a lot on my mind."

"Is it because of what you asked me? About the gr- graves?"

He remained silent for a moment, but he didn't want to lie to Sean and it would be better if Sean were prepared when he revealed everything to the pride. Declan breathed in deep and leaned back far enough to look Sean in the eye. "Victor came to tell me they finished removing the remains from the graves."

Sorrow darkened Sean's blue irises to an even deeper sapphire. "Oh."

"Almost all of them have been linked to their home clan and several individuals from those clans will be arriving in two days. The pride needs to be made aware of the situation in case there is any backlash to what has gone on so close to our compound."

"You think they'll be mad at everyone here?" Sean asked, a frown wrinkling his brow.

Declan lifted a hand to smooth the lines of Sean's forehead. "I'm not sure what their reaction will be, but we must be prepared for all outcomes."

He could see Sean didn't understand why they would be angry at the Royal Taiga Streak. The innocence Sean still retained after everything he'd gone through amazed Declan. Cupping Sean's cheek, Declan leaned in and kissed him gently, his heart aching for his sweet mate. Breaking the kiss, he rested his forehead against Sean's. "Sometimes things don't always make sense in the world we live in, Sean. There are people who are full of hatred for things they don't understand or things that scare them. Some can't see reason when they're close to something because they're blinded by their own feelings toward it."

Sean didn't respond, but Declan could see the light of awareness enter Sean's gaze. The sound of footsteps on the stairs forced Declan to step back, but he took hold of Sean's hand in his. "If you think you are up for it, I'd like to introduce you to the entire streak tonight."

Wariness wiped away the light and Sean bit his lip, appearing to think about Declan's question, then gave a small nod. "You don't have to if you don't feel ready."

"I'm okay," Sean murmured, squeezing Declan's hand lightly.

A smile spread over Declan's lips. "I am beyond proud to call you mine, baby."

Red dusted Sean's cheeks and he ducked his head, but Declan caught an answering smile on Sean's lips. He yanked Sean close again to whisper in his ear, "You keep looking like that and we won't make it out the door."

Sean flushed even further and buried his face against Declan's bicep, a small giggle breaking free. Declan grinned in delight at the sound of happiness. Rose and the others entered the room then, stopping any further action Declan may have taken. He could also hear his streak members out front, talking amongst themselves about why they were called to a meeting. "Let's do this," Declan said.

They all filed out onto the porch with Rose and the others going down to join the rest of the pride. Sean would have followed them, but Declan wrapped his arm around Sean's shoulders. "Your place is at my side, Sean."

The din of voices faded away and they waited to hear what Declan had to say. "I know the news of me finding my mate and the abducted shifter children has been spreading like wildfire throughout the pride. I asked you all here tonight to confirm the rumors. I did find my life mate."

Declan turned his head to look at Sean. "My friends and family, please welcome Sean, your Alpha-mate, and one of the children taken many years ago."

Murmurs rose from the crowd, but were quickly extinguished when Declan swept his gaze back over them. "I expect you to treat him with the respect due him as such. Sean and the others have been through something none of us can even begin to imagine the horrors of. Yes, it is true, there was a human male living on the outskirts of our territory abducting shifter children."

A sob came from Becky and Declan gave her a sympathetic glance. "As you have most likely heard, Becky's own daughter Gina was one of those children. Over the years this sick individual kidnapped many, but few were rescued. There were fourteen others laid to rest by my mate in the very backyard of the house they were kept in.

"Cameron as well as a select few have spent the last twenty-four to thirty-six hours exhuming the remains so we may reunite them with their families. Many of them have been identified and this is the primary reason I have requested your presence tonight. Three of the cubs were found to belong to the Koda Sleuth, the Cast Clan, and the Clan of the Claw."

Declan's announcement was met with tension and cries of shock. Many of the members were very aware of the strained relationship the Royal Taiga Streak had with those three in particular. "Representatives from each of them will be arriving in two days' time. They have not been informed of the children or that they were kept so close to our compound. I need each and every one of you to remain on alert while they are here. But, I also need you all to know this could not only fracture our ties with these three clans, but sever them entirely, potentially leading to a war between us."

The murmurs began again and grew louder with dread and anxiety. Declan let forth a loud roar, effectively silencing them. "My enforcers and I will handle this as delicately as possible to try and circumvent retaliation from any of the clans. I ask you to please not allow your fear to control your actions. If there is any backlash, we will deal with it as a clan."

Tanzie came forth. "How do you intend to do that, Alpha? Our numbers are few compared to those clans. Even if all of us were to fight, we surely would lose."

Declan gave them all a determined look. "If it is absolutely necessary, I will issue the Alpha Challenge."

A collective gasp went up from the pride. The Alpha

Challenge was a well-known shifter law where the alpha of a clan may demand a fight to the death to defend their people. The one still standing at the end could either absorb the pack or pride members left behind into their own or leave them to the risk of another taking over or destroying the remnants of the clan. Declan did not make the decision lightly. If he lost, Sean would perish with him, but he would not lose. He couldn't, because he would never allow anything to happen to Sean.

"We will stand strong as we face this together. I take full responsibility for this tragedy. I never should have been so lax about patrols not being assigned to the edge of our land. My father pulled them back in to protect the streak, but we have grown in numbers since then and there is no excuse for my lapse."

Matthew came forward and stopped beside Tanzie. "None of us could have known, Alpha. There isn't even a way to be certain we would have discovered anything if we had patrolled so far out. Your father moved us inward to ensure there couldn't possibly be another loss like we suffered then. They can't blame the pride for something we had no hand in."

"We may not have had a hand in the events which unfolded in that house, but we should have known. The other clans will not see reason when it comes to one of their own being abducted and murdered."

When Matthew would have gone to argue again, Declan shook his head. "Stop. We can debate this all night, but it won't change the facts. Several clan alphas or representatives of those clans will arrive the day after tomorrow and we must stay alert to the dangers they may pose."

The pride members nodded and several whispered amongst themselves. Declan knew the slightest imbalance could offset everything. He prayed to their ancestors to help them through the next several days. Everyone disbanded and wandered off, either to their homes or to gather in groups and talk amongst each other. The only ones who stayed behind were the parents of Fredrick and Tomas.

Brigette, a statuesque brunette, came forward. A slightly shorter, but stocky man followed on her heels. "Alpha, if I may, I'd like to thank Sean for what he did for my Fredrick and Tomas."

"Of course, Brigette. Sean, this is Fredrick and Tomas's mother and father. Brigette and Jean-Paul."

Sean was swept into a tight hug by Brigette. "Thank you so much for what you did for my boys. Because of you they came home to us."

Jean-Paul grabbed hold of Sean's hand when Brigette released him and gave it several hard shakes. "Yes, thank you so much, Alpha-mate. You've given us our world back!"

A flush traveled over Sean's cheeks. "I didn't do that much."

"Nonsense!" Brigette exclaimed. "They've told us all that you did for them while that awful man held them in cages like beasts! Filthy monster!"

"You must let us thank you by having you and the others over for dinner, Alpha-mate," Jean-Paul added.

"Oh, that's not necessary!" Sean protested.

"It is totally necessary," Brigette scoffed. "We owe you a debt and a dinner is the least we can do. Next week, I will find you and we can settle on a night."

Sean didn't get a chance to say anything else before the two bid them goodnight and left. "They really don't have to do that," Sean murmured.

"They are grateful for everything you did for their boys. Turning them down would be more of an insult," Declan said.

"Oh, I wouldn't want to do that."

Declan led Sean to the porch swing and sat, guiding Sean to sit beside him. Exhaustion hit him then and he couldn't suppress a sigh. Sean leaned his head on Declan's shoulder causing Declan to smile slightly. "Maybe if I tell them all what happened," Sean whispered into the darkness.

"No," Declan said.

"But maybe I could help them to understand," Sean replied, his voice stronger now. "Carl made sure none of them left the house. I was the only one allowed outside. It would have been impossible to know about the others."

Declan didn't want Sean reliving the pain he'd suffered through all those years, especially in front of a bunch of strangers. "I appreciate the offer, baby, but I can't let you do that."

Sean pulled away to look at him. "After everything you've done for me, I want to!"

Declan shifted around until he faced Sean. "You don't owe me or the pride anything, Sean, and what you're asking of me, to allow you to hurt like that to help others is more than I can bear. What you don't understand is when you are in pain, I am in pain."

"But how?" Sean exclaimed.

"Because you are the other half of my soul and it kills me you had to live through what you did. The idea of you going through it all over again even if just by words and memories crushes me." Declan took Sean's hand in his and raised it to his lips where he brushed a kiss over Sean's knuckles. "There's still a lot you don't understand or know about being life mates, especially being the chosen for an alpha. We are predisposed to preventing our mates from being hurt and for alphas that urge is ten times stronger."

"But I really want to do this for you and for the streak," Sean replied. "I want them to know how you couldn't possibly have known the truth of what was happening with my father. I mean Carl."

Smiling, Declan held Sean's hand to his chest. "And it makes me proud how willing you are to stand up for us. You are the perfect Alpha-mate. But we will handle it as a streak, together."

"If I'm a part of the streak then why can't I do whatever I can to help?" Sean challenged.

Declan could see the fire kindling in Sean's bright sapphire eyes and he'd thought he couldn't be prouder of Sean until right then. Despite everything Sean had gone through, his spirit hadn't been crushed. There were things that would take work and effort to get through, but Sean's true being would come through someday. He didn't want to brush off Sean's offer or make it seem trivial in anyway. Those actions may well dampen the passion Sean exhibited. "What if we make a compromise?"

Sean frowned. "Compromise?"

"It means we make a decision together to settle a disagreement."

"How would we do that?"

"Even though I loathe to see you even a little bit in pain, if it comes to a point where telling your story may diffuse the situation then I won't try to stop you."

He could see Sean thinking hard on what he'd said and he squeezed Sean's hand. He didn't want to stunt Sean's choices or stand in the way of what Sean wanted to do with his life. The idea of others seeing the pain in Sean over the children and knowing he only showed his pain to stop them from blaming Declan or the others in the Royal Taiga streak chafed at him hard.

"So if these people get mad, I can try to help?" Sean finally asked.

"Yes." Declan prayed it wouldn't come down to it though.

A brilliant smile spread over Sean's features and a heady sense of satisfaction filled Declan. He could practically touch the feeling of happiness coming through their connection. "Come here," Declan growled and yanked Sean into his lap until he straddled Declan's lap, uncaring of the little squeak Sean released at the abrupt move.

He ravaged Sean's mouth with his, extremely turned on by the joy Sean felt. Sean melted beneath his kiss, his hands gripping his shoulders to steady himself as the swing shifted under their weight. Declan knew even if they had a hundred years together it would never be enough for him. The taste of Sean's lips, the smell of his soft skin, and the little noises Sean let forth were ambrosia to Declan's senses. He circled Sean's slim waist with him hands, rocking him forward against the hard bulge in his jeans. Sean gasped into Declan's mouth and Declan swallowed the sound while using the momentum of the porch swing to his advantage.

Shudders wracked Sean's thin frame when Declan pressed him downward gently while thrusting his hips upward. "Declan," Sean whimpered, wrapping his arms around Declan's neck.

Declan reached between them to cup Sean's cock through his pants causing Sean to cry out. He wanted nothing more than to strip Sean bare and take him right where they sat, but he snarled at the idea of anyone witnessing Sean in the throes of lust or seeing Sean without clothing. So, he stood, taking Sean with him and slammed into the house, still holding Sean in his arms. The sound of the others in the dining room barely registered as he took the stairs two at a time. He needed to be buried inside of Sean and nothing would stand in his way.

"But we were going to have a movie night," Sean said breathlessly.

"Another night, sexy. I need you."

Sean relented with a giggle and buried his face against Declan's shoulder. When they reached the bedroom, he managed to get the door open and then kicked it shut with his foot. The moment they were alone Declan set Sean on his feet and impatiently said, "Take off your clothes," while removing his own clothing.

Sean pulled his shirt over his head and began to undo his pants. Declan allowed his gaze to feast along Sean's pale skin and the light brown nubs on Sean's chest. "You are so fucking beautiful," he said, his voice trashed from the desire rushing through him.

A flush trickled over Sean's cheeks and along his throat, but Sean never stopped in his efforts to divulge himself of his clothing. And the moment he stood bare before him, Declan stalked him toward the bed, his own cock hard and stiff, pointing like an arrow toward Sean. Declan followed Sean down to the mattress, covering Sean's body with his, and captured his lips once more.

He slid his palm down Sean's chest, loving the feel of his smooth skin beneath his hand. Using his thumb, he flicked one of Sean's nipples lightly causing him to tremble. "Do you like that?" Declan murmured.

Sean didn't answer him, merely continued to let forth small, breathy gasps. Declan plucked at the nub this time and a mewl issued from Sean along with the quiver of his body. "De-Declan," Sean stuttered.

The flush of longing invading Sean's cheeks and his half-lidded eyes shining from behind thick lashes was the most beautiful thing Declan had ever seen. He leaned over to grab the lube from the nightstand drawer, needing more than anything to feel Sean wrapped around his cock. The snap of the cap sounded loud in the silence surrounding them and Declan watched Sean's face as he spilled some of the slick fluid onto his fingers. Tossing the tube onto the nightstand without care, Declan slid his hand between Sean's thighs, never once breaking eye contact with him.

A moan rattled in Sean's chest when Declan probed the entrance to Sean's body. Sean closed his eyes completely, but Declan growled, "Look at me."

Sean reopened his eyes, his bottom lip clenched between his teeth. Declan leaned down and coaxed him to release the bruised flesh with his mouth and tongue. He sank his index finger slowly into Sean and broke away the hold on Sean's lips to watch the red blush deepen. Declan's patience felt ready to snap, but he wouldn't hurt Sean for the world by being rough and callous.

Declan worked Sean's channel, thrusting a single digit in and out until Sean had relaxed enough to allow a second. A purr rumbled through Declan when Sean clenched around his fingers. "Does it feel good?" Declan asked.

Instead of answering him, Sean raised a hand to cover his eyes. Declan negated it immediately. "Don't hide from me, Sean. Never hide from me."

The moment Sean's gaze met his again, Declan speared his fingers deeper, grazing the small gland many labeled a "sweet spot". Sean cried out and arched a fraction from the bed. Declan leaned in to nip Sean's earlobe before murmuring, "I need you to tell me when something feels good and when it doesn't. I never want to do anything which causes you fear or pain. Does this make you feel good?"

Declan stroked over Sean's prostate once more causing Sean to grip at the sheets. "Yes," Sean moaned.

19

SEAN

Embarrassment and ecstasy raged within Sean. He felt vulnerable and exposed when looking at Declan while he touched him in such an intimate way. The only thing he wanted to do was cover his face and hide the way Declan made him feel. Yet Declan wouldn't let him. He demanded Sean to focus on him, to see him, and to tell him if what he did caused Sean pleasure or pain.

He couldn't contain the shudder that went through him when Declan stretched him further with a third finger. Declan claimed his lips in a deep kiss before levering himself over Sean, his hips slotting between Sean's parted thighs easily. The snick of the bottle of slick barely registered over the sensation of Declan pulling his fingers free of Sean's body. "Are you ready for me, baby?" Declan asked, his voice harsh with strain.

Sean knew what Declan meant, but he didn't know how to tell Declan yes so he locked gazes with Declan and gave a small nod. Declan didn't seem to think the nod was enough though. "Words, sexy, use your words."

"I-I'm ready," Sean managed to stammer, his hands reaching to grip at Declan's biceps.

Never breaking eye contact with Sean, Declan began to sink into him, becoming a part of Sean. The sheets rustled as Declan started to move, the sound mixing with their raspy breathing and the soft gasps Sean couldn't stifle. Sean dug his fingernails into Declan's arms, attempting to hold on in the wave threatening to drag him under. He couldn't figure out which way was up or down. Nothing in his life could have prepared him for the sensations of what it felt like to be joined with someone else in such an intimate way.

When Declan retreated, Sean tried to stop him by wrapping his legs around Declan's waist. He didn't want them to end, but when Declan rolled his hips forward, plunging back inside him, Sean couldn't stop a scream from exploding from his lips. Declan never once fully pulled free, splitting him wide again and again.

"De-Declan," Sean whimpered, his eyelids slamming closed once more. Declan did not allow Sean even a second to hide from the sensations inundating his being.

"No," Declan growled. "Eyes open, baby. I want to see you fly apart beneath me."

It took immense effort for Sean to comply, but when he did he could see Declan's tiger shimmering beneath the surface of Declan's gaze. Sean lifted a shaking hand to touch Declan's cheek, his fingers sliding up and through Declan's hair. "Declan," Sean murmured.

Sweat built along their skin, their breathing grew harsher the closer they grew to the precipice waiting for them, and Declan chose that moment to roll them, placing Sean on top. "Ride me, Sean. Take your pleasure from me."

Sean sat there, surprised at the abrupt movement, until Declan gripped his hips and encouraged him without words to undulate forward slightly and then back. The new position allowed Declan to hit further depths inside of him and Sean took his cue from Declan, beginning to rock faster. He braced himself on Declan's chest, his fingers splayed over the hard muscles.

A shudder rippled down his spine when he found the quicker he moved, the better it felt. Declan wrapped one large hand around Sean's aching prick and gave a light tug, matching Sean's movements with his own. A tingly sensation built in Sean's groin and he knew the band inside of him would snap soon. Declan started to push upward into Sean to meet Sean's movements. "Close, my mate?" Declan rumbled.

"Clo-close to what?" Sean gasped.

Declan caught Sean by surprise when he jackknifed and suddenly wrapped his arms around Sean, trapping Sean's cock between them. The friction between them teased the head of Sean's prick causing Sean to moan and clutch Declan's shoulders. "Ready to come apart in my arms," Declan growled huskily.

With an almost vicious motion Declan began to jerk Sean down onto his cock while thrusting hard into him. Sean gripped Declan tighter, unable to stop his head from lolling backward as he cried out at the uncompromising invasion of his being. It didn't take long for Sean to hit the crest of his orgasm, spilling between them, but a second climax rolled through him the instant Declan sank his fangs into Sean's shoulder. White light clouded Sean's vision and he heard a muted roar and then the pulse of Declan's shaft inside of him. He fell into oblivion, his body unable to handle the overload of sensations and they dragged him under.

When he finally became aware, he found himself lying amongst the sheets and Declan curled around him, one hand idly stroking the outside of Sean's thigh. The only light in the room came from the moonlight shining between the curtains. "Okay, baby?"

Sean turned his head so he could see Declan. A sated look covered Declan's features. "Yeah," he mumbled, gazing back at the nearby window.

Declan nuzzled at the scar on Sean's shoulder then pressed a kiss to Sean's cheek. At some point, Declan must have cleaned them both up because Sean didn't feel sticky anywhere. "Declan?"

A small hum met his query.

"Do you... do you think I'll be able to shift?"

Declan brought his arm around Sean's waist and pulled him tighter against him. "I know you will, gorgeous. Soon."

Sean nodded a bit, but he didn't know if he could believe Declan's faith in him. He covered the top of Declan's hand resting on his belly and entwined their fingers. Declan made him feel safe, loved, and like everything would be okay. Yet he couldn't ignore the voice in his head telling him he'd never be enough for Declan. The words of the man he'd thought to be his father calling him vile names and how he should have been aborted from his mother.

"Tell me a good memory, Sean," Declan murmured close to his ear, interrupting the awful thoughts running through his mind. "A light in the darkness of your past."

Sean didn't know of many. After all, there weren't many days which went by without a beating or having to clean up Sam or Tara when Carl had finished with them or even having to dig a grave for another of his victims. "I can't think of anything," he whispered.

"Nothing?" Declan sounded sad and Sean didn't want him to feel anything but happiness.

He took a moment to think and then gave a small smile. "There is one year when we had our own Christmas. Carl passed out by eight on Christmas Eve and I managed to sneak an extra can of Spaghettios downstairs for all of us. We made each other hats out of old newspapers and Sam and Tara made up a small play to put on for the little ones. They even were able to get the younger kids to laugh. It was the best day of our lives… until you saved us."

"God," Declan said hoarsely, his arm tightening to an almost painful grip around Sean's waist.

Sean felt a drop of water hit his cheek. He reached up to touch it and frowned. Another splashed down and rolled across his lips. He instinctively flicked his tongue out and tasted salt. His eyes widened when he realized Declan was crying. "Declan?"

He tried to turn to look at Declan, but Declan buried his face against Sean's hair. "Why?" A shudder wracked Declan's large frame. "Dec? Please don't cry."

When Declan finally managed to speak, his voice sounded scratchy and Sean could hear the strain behind Declan's words. "I swear to you until the day I die, baby, I will do everything in my power to give you memories so happy you'll never be able to choose just one."

"But you already have," Sean replied.

Another tremor raced through Declan and then Declan rolled Sean to face him. Tracks of dampness on Declan's cheeks shone in the moonlight shining in the window and he didn't even have the chance to reach out and wipe at them before Declan stole his breath with an intense kiss. "Every single minute," Declan said between kisses, "of every single day," another kiss, this one softer, "you will never have cause to cry or be unhappy.

"I swear it."

Sean heard the absolute certainty in Declan's tone. He knew Declan meant it, but he also wasn't naïve enough to believe he'd never have a reason to cry again. "I'm already happy," he said, smiling crookedly.

Trailing the tips of his fingers over Sean's throat and over the collar, Declan said, "When all of this mess with the clans is over and you can finally shift, I want to take you on a vacation, Sean. Take you to see the world, to see the beauty of the mountains and the vastness of the ocean. I want to bathe with you in the waters of Japan and make love to you under the lights of the Aurora Borealis."

Sean had no idea what an Aurora Borealis was, but everything Declan said sounded beautiful. "I want that too, so much."

"We will and there will be nothing but happy memories in our future."

Sean burrowed closer to Declan, closing his eyes and allowing the promises of a brighter life lull him to sleep. His dreams were of running with Declan in his true form, rolling together in the grasses of the forest surrounding them, and seeing Sam holding her baby while Tara sat with Vicky on her lap. Vicky was finally talking and happy.

When he started to awaken from his dream, he found he didn't want to. He wanted to hold onto those moments and never let go, but a hand on his arm pulled him free. "Baby?"

He opened his eyes to see Declan seated on the bed beside him, fully dressed. Sunlight filled the room and Sean knew he'd slept quite late into the day. A tray sat on the bed next to him with food on it and Sean smiled, rearranging himself until his back rested against the ornate headboard. Declan placed the tray over Sean's lap and moved to Sean's other side.

There were scrambled eggs, toast, bacon, and orange juice. "You're going to spoil me," Sean murmured while taking hold of the fork.

Declan shrugged. "It's my right as your mate and you deserve it. I want to spoil you."

The food tasted amazing even being simple fare. Declan

fed Sean several bites despite Sean's protests of being able to feed himself. He also made sure Sean took the vitamins Cameron had prescribed.

Sean could sense a tension in Declan, but didn't ask. He figured Declan had a lot of things on his mind after hearing about the other prides and packs. But it was only when the plates were empty and Sean had finished the orange juice that Declan dropped the bomb in Sean's lap.

"Kyle is back."

Those words caused Sean to stiffen and he dropped the glass onto the tray hard, wincing at the noise it made. Excitement warred with fear and anxiety. He wanted the collar removed, but knowing the pain and uncertainty that awaited the moment he was free of the circle of leather scared him. No, the idea terrified him, almost as much as the sound of Carl's boots on the stairs of the basement. "Did… did he find the witch?"

"Yes. Maximus is with Kyle. I've already spoken to him."

"Did he tell you anything?"

Declan seemed hesitant, but finally answered, "The collar didn't work on its own."

"What do you mean?"

"The injections, the ones you mentioned, they contained a powerful serum Maximus said worked in tandem with the collar to suppress your ability to shift."

Sean's breath caught in his throat and the remembered agony of those shots twice a year, every single year, caused him to start to hyperventilate. He barely noticed Declan remove the tray. All he knew was Declan straddled his lap much as the tray had and held Sean's face between his palms. "Breathe in slower. Slower. Now let it out."

Time passed at a crawl for Sean and he tried to follow the instructions Declan gave him. Finally, he felt the anxiety and panic begin to wane. "What does that mean?" Sean whispered.

"It means, depending on the last time you were injected, that you can shift as soon as the collar is removed." Declan released Sean's face and lowered his hands to his thighs.

With how painful they were, Sean could never forget when they were administered. His father would hold him down with a knee on his chest and jam the needle into the side of his neck. Sean closed his eyes and worked to keep from going into a frantic panic attack again. "H-he gave me the shot three months before w-we were rescued."

"We'll need to let the witch know that and see what his answer is before we can fully know what will happen. Are you ready for this, baby? We can wait if you aren't."

Sean ran a shaky hand through his hair. Was he ready? What if he really couldn't shift? Declan cupped Sean's cheek stirring him from his thoughts. "No matter what happens, Sean, if you can or can't shift, you *are* my mate and I love you."

Surprise brought Sean's gaze immediately to Declan's. It had been a while since Declan said it the first time. Declan smiled. "Don't worry, gorgeous. I don't expect you to say it back. I'll go grab you some water while you get dressed."

"Okay," Sean said and waited until Declan left the room, taking the tray of dishes with him, to leave the bed. Excitement warred with fear inside of him. He wanted to shift, but at the same time he didn't. What if Cameron was wrong and he couldn't shift? What if because he'd never shifted as a child it meant he could never as an adult?

He pulled on some blue jeans, a red t-shirt, and the sneakers he'd been wearing the last few days before heading into the bathroom to brush his teeth, use the toilet, and comb his hair. Declan stood near the window when he exited the bathroom, a bottle of water dangled from one hand. He turned to Sean and handed him the bottle. "Why don't you take a few sips and when you're ready we'll head down to meet with Kyle?"

Sean took the water, cracked open the cap, and take a small drink to appease Declan, but he really didn't want to drink anything. The breakfast he'd eaten already sat like a rock in his belly and the water only added to his nausea. He placed the cap back on it and looked at Declan. "I'm ready."

Declan took Sean's hand in his and they went out of the room and downstairs together. When they entered Declan's office, Sean couldn't bring himself to walk any further than the doorway. The man with the light brown hair who'd helped his father imprison him sat tied to a chair, several bruises on his face and a split lip, but Sean still recognized him. Familiar purple eyes turned his way and Sean stepped back. But when he saw the fear, pain, and guilt shining at him from the witch's gaze, he couldn't help except move closer. He felt almost drawn to the man.

Sean took a tissue from the box on Declan's desk and perched on the chair beside Maximus. When he went to dab at the blood gathered at the corner of his mouth, Maximus flinched, but when Sean did nothing more than clean his wound, Maximus appeared surprised. "Why?" Maximus asked.

"Because no one deserves to be hurt," Sean replied simply.

Tears welled in Maximus's eyes, spilling over and down his cheeks. "I'm so sorry, Sean. I didn't want to do it. I had no choice. Your father had my talisman. He threatened to destroy it if I didn't help him. I never wanted to hurt you."

Sean shook his head. "It's okay."

Declan growled, "It's not okay!"

Maximus winced and dropped his chin to his chest. "He's right, Sean. It doesn't make it right what I did to you and that I never tried to stop him."

"What is your tal-," Sean struggled to remember the right word, "talisman?"

Misery flooded Maximus's features. "It's the primary source of a witch's power. Without having it in our possession, we can only perform basic magics, small glamours, tracking spells, and without the talisman, we never feel whole. If he smashed it he would have drained my magic from me."

"And that's okay at the expense of Sean's life?" Declan roared. "Your magic is a pittance compared to the life of a *child*! He could have suffered spirit rot! Do you even know what that does to a shifter?"

Maximus jerked and more tears fell. "I am my magic just as your spirit is your animal."

Sean felt sad for Maximus. He laid his hand on Maximus's knee. "I understand."

Maximus lifted his head, his mouth trembling. "I'm sorry," he whispered. "I'm so fucking sorry. I knew what he was doing was wrong, but I didn't know how to stop it."

"Telling someone would have been a god damn good start," Kyle grunted. Sean had almost forgotten Kyle was in the room as he'd been so quiet up to then.

"And what about the other children?" Declan demanded, rounding the desk and leaning down into Maximus's face. "How could you let that happen?"

Confusion chased away the pain and guilt. "Other children? What other children? I only ever saw Sean."

"You didn't know?" Sean asked.

Maximus shook his head. "No. There was only ever Sean." He paled. "There were others? What happened to them?"

"Carl kept them in the basement."

If it were possible, Maximus paled even further. "What?"

"In fucking cages, like animals!" Declan snarled.

Sean touched Declan's forearm. "He didn't know, Declan. And I don't blame him."

"How can you not blame him for the years of pain and abuse you went through?" Declan asked, incredulous. "If he'd only told someone you would have been rescued! Even reunited with your family!"

Sean gave a small smile and took Declan's hand in his. "You told me our animal halves are an integral part of our being. The same must apply to Maximus and his magic."

Declan crouched beside Sean. "You continue to surprise me every day, mate," he murmured, the rage gone for those moments. "After everything you've suffered through to have such a beautiful, caring heart is humbling to me."

Heat flooded Sean's face, but he focused on Maximus again. "What did your talisman look like?"

Hope warred with uncertainty in Maximus's face. "Flat, like a coin. One side had the image of a Celtic wolf and the other is the Celtic Goddess Morrighan."

Kyle snorted from his position where he leaned against the wall close to the window. "Celtic Goddess of death and war. Not exactly helping your case, are you?"

"She was not just a goddess of death and war!" Maximus snapped. "She was also a wolf goddess. The image that appears on the opposite side of the coin tells us who our life mates will be. They're forged when we're born and only once we come fully into our powers do the coins reveal the other half of our soul."

"I remember that. Carl wore it around his neck and he never took it off," Sean interjected, frowning. "But I don't know what happened to it."

Declan scowled. "Most likely burned with what was left of his carcass when I was through with him."

"No!" Maximus cried, struggling at his bonds. "No! Please tell me you didn't burn it!"

Sean gave a pleading glance at Declan and Declan sighed. "I will have Victor check the house for it."

"Thank you!" Maximus sobbed.

"Enough of this! Tell us how to remove the infernal collar around my mate's throat or you'll never live long enough to see the talisman again," Declan demanded.

Maximus shrank as far into the chair he sat in as possible. "I can't."

"Why not?" Declan growled.

"I need the talisman!" Maximus whimpered. "I-I can't remove the collar without it."

Sean saw Declan glance at Kyle who shrugged. "How do we know you aren't lying?"

"Why would I lie?" Maximus choked. "You'd just kill me if I was."

"Smart little witch," Declan shot out. "You're damn right I'll kill you if you try anything stupid or you hurt Sean any further."

The violence of the situation, the rage emanating from Declan, and the obvious telltale signs of abuse on Maximus's face caused Sean to flashback to a similar moment in the basement. His father stood over one of the younger children, his hands fisted at his side, eyes wild with rage. Bruises and blood, screams of agony and distress, the smell of urine when the boy had messed himself, all raged through Sean. A whimper stuck in his throat and he found he couldn't move, couldn't look away from the horrible scene before him. *"Daddy, no! Please stop! Don't hurt him!"*

But Carl never listened to him, never stopped, his fury too great. It wasn't until the cub lay lifeless and broken did Carl stop. A scream welled up in Sean's throat and it was too great to hold back.

DECLAN

The only thing Declan focused on was finding a way to force the witch who'd placed the collar on his mate to remove the fucking vile thing. He didn't notice at first the terror and panic beginning to build on Sean's face or the way he went as white as a sheet. It wasn't until a whimper caught his attention did he tear his attention away from Maximus. Before he could even act, Sean began to emit this terrible scream. His ear drums almost burst with the volume.

"Sean!" Declan reached out to grip Sean's shoulders and the scream grew louder, if that were even possible. Sean struggled against Declan's hold, lashing out and catching Declan in his stomach. Declan hadn't been ready for the reaction and it took him by surprise. Sean knocked Declan's hands away from him and stumbled into the far corner where he crouched down and covered his head, the same scream still practically rattling the glass windows.

"Jesus!" Kyle shouted, holding his hands over his ears. "What the fuck is wrong with him?"

Declan didn't know how to get Sean to stop. The idea of

slapping his mate to snap him out of whatever awful place he'd gone to in his head brought acidic bile rushing to the back of his throat.

"Do something!" Kyle yelled.

Moving to where Sean crouched, Declan dropped to his knees in front of him. He grabbed hold of Sean and yanked him to his chest, wincing as his ears protested the decibel. "Sean! Baby, stop! You're going to make yourself sick!"

Declan ran his hand down Sean's back, trying to soothe him the best way he knew how. But it didn't seem to sink in and the scream continued. "Sean!" he said sharply. "Concentrate on my voice, baby."

The sound grew a little less sharp, but Sean kept screaming. "Listen to my voice, sexy. I've got you. That's it." Declan ran the palm of his hand the length of Sean's spine. "Come back to me, Sean. I can't go wherever you went."

Sean shuddered in his arms and the god-awful cry began to fade until the only sound was Sean's ragged breathing. "There you go, sweetheart. Just breathe. Deep breath in and then out. Good. Like that."

Guilt bit Declan hard. He'd been so focused on his anger and disgust with Maximus he hadn't once thought of how his mate would respond to his emotions. Damn it! He should have known because of Sean's previous reactions to anger or raised voices. His fury at Maximus turned inward and Declan laid his cheek atop the crown of Sean's head, holding him tight against his chest. "I'm so sorry, Sean. I didn't think. I'm an insensitive ass."

Another tremble wracked Sean's thin frame and Sean shook his head. "It's not your fault," he croaked, his voice trashed.

"I should never have gotten angry while you were in the room with us. I should have spoken to the witch alone."

Sean moved until he could meet Declan's gaze. Declan's

heart clenched at the exhaustion evident on his face. "I wanted to be here. I needed to know why he helped my father... I mean Carl."

Declan knew it would take time for Sean to disconnect from the man he'd believed was his father for so long. He really needed to call Amanda to set up the appointment for Sean and the others. The last several moments cemented just how much pain and horror Sean held inside him.

"I think you need to go upstairs and rest until we are able to retrieve the witch's talisman."

What worried him was how easily Sean agreed with a small nod of his head. He'd seen the fire and the stubbornness inside Sean many times in the short period he'd known him. For Sean to cave without a word of protest indicated just how wrung out the situation had made him. He cupped Sean's cheek in one hand and slid his thumb over the high cheekbone. Sean leaned into the touch, eyelids going to half-mast.

Leaning down, Declan placed his lips over Sean's in a gentle kiss. He meant it to be nothing but an attempt at comforting his mate, but it quickly escalated. Declan felt Sean's response and deepened the kiss. He flicked his tongue along Sean's bottom lip, coaxing Sean's tongue to come out and play with his. Lust flooded his loins and Declan could feel his cock harden, pushing insistently at the front of his fly. He slid one hand into the black locks at the back of Sean's head, holding him steady for the onslaught. Everything else faded around them and Declan hungrily slipped his other hand down to grip Sean's ass, dragging him tighter against him. He almost took Sean to the ground, forgetting there was anyone else in the room, but the sound of a throat clearing broke the heated fog he found himself encaged in.

"As much as I am sure we'd love the floor show, I don't think you'll be happy about us seeing it, Dec," Kyle said dryly.

Fuck! He'd almost lost his head and taken his mate in front of others. Not to mention how exhausted Sean was! Shame clawed at his belly at letting his cock allow him to forget what Sean just went through.

Declan growled when Sean attempted to move away from him. He didn't want anyone else seeing the hard bulge he could feel against his thigh. Instead of releasing Sean, he levered to his feet and carried him around to the other side of his desk where he placed him in his seat, ensuring the surface blocked Sean's groin. "I will send Victor to the house to locate the talisman if it is even still there."

Maximus gave a sigh of relief and Kyle nodded. "I'll go with him."

"No. You stay here and make sure *he* doesn't go anywhere," Declan said. "I am going to take my mate upstairs for now."

Kyle nodded and resumed his casual leaning stance against the wall. Declan looked at Sean. "Do you feel up to walking?"

Sean nodded. "I'm fine."

Declan held out his hand. "Then let's go."

They left Declan's office and headed to their bedroom. Declan encouraged Sean to sit on the bed so he could remove his shoes, but Sean stopped him. "I want to go back down there as soon as they get back with the talisman."

Declan didn't argue with Sean. He moved to sit beside Sean on the edge of the bed and looked at Sean. "What happened downstairs, Sean? I know my being angry at the witch scared you, but you must know by now I would never hurt you."

He didn't answer right away and Declan would call Amanda the moment he could. He didn't have any idea how he'd managed to get Sean to calm down, only relying on instincts to comfort Sean. Sean and the others wouldn't be the only ones attending the sessions either. If something like that were to happen again, he wanted to be more prepared in the future on what to do because he'd rather cut off his own arm than to cause Sean more harm.

"When y-you got angry," Sean began, "and seeing the br-bruises and blood on Maximus, it reminded me so much of what he used to do to us, to me. I felt like I was back there and he was there, hur-hurting one of the cubs. I beg-begged him to stop, but he wouldn't listen. And he-he kil-killed him."

Declan swore and gathered Sean close. "I'm so sorry, Sean. I didn't even think. What you must think of me. I never should have brought you in there."

Sean leaned into Declan. "It's not your fault and I wanted to be there. I know I never went to school, but I'm not dumb and I'm not a kid either."

"I know you aren't," Declan replied. "I don't think of you as a kid and I know you aren't dumb. You've had to grow up so fast and witness things most people would have lost their mind over years ago. You're brave and smart and your heart is so amazingly big even after everything. But there are times when you shouldn't have to see things. Especially if it triggers the attack you had."

Sean lifted his head enough to see Declan's face. "I didn't know I would do that."

"Sometimes we can't control our reactions to things. A mind can be fragile and the smallest situation can cause ours to act out. Tomorrow I will arrange your first session with Amanda. She is a human, but she is the mate of one of my streak members."

Declan rubbed Sean's shoulder. "Why don't you lay down and try to rest? It will probably be at least an hour before they get back from looking around the house."

"You won't forget to wake me, will you?" Sean asked.

"I promise I'll come get you. Now, let's get you into bed." Declan helped Sean remove his shoes and then pulled the covers back, holding them up as Sean climbed beneath them. He laid the blanket over Sean, kissed Sean on his forehead and brushed a strand of hair back from his cheek. "I won't be far, baby."

Sean nodded and curled onto his side, closing his eyes. Declan left the bedroom and paced the hallway for several long moments before taking out his cell. The first call he made was to Victor where he instructed him to search the house for the talisman. He instructed Victor to take Michael with him. Then he called Amanda Binson.

"Hey, Declan. How are you?" she answered on the second ring.

Declan smiled. She was a very kind-hearted human. One of the best he'd ever met in his life. "Hey, Amanda. I'm good. How's things with Dirk and the cubs?"

Amanda was married and mated to Dirk, a pride beta whose family had been in the Royal Taiga Streak since the early eighteen-hundreds. "Dirk is great. Sherry has a minor cold and George is not far behind her."

"Sorry to hear that. Did you have Cameron or Dr. West take a look at them?"

Westley Friedman or Dr. West as many of the streak called him was the second-in-command at the clinic with Cameron.

"Dr. West saw them. Cameron was busy with exhuming the bodies with the help of my mate and Victor."

Declan winced at the disappointment in her tone. He hadn't brought her in yet to talk to any of the children recovered and he knew she wouldn't be happy about it. "That's actually why I'm calling. I wanted to set up appointments for each of them to meet with you. I wanted to give them a chance to settle in and rest, kind of heal a little before throwing more at them. They've been through a lot."

"I know, Dec, and I completely understand. I am just sad you didn't involve me sooner and I had to hear everything second hand from Dirk and the gossipers in the streak."

"I'm sorry, Amanda. I didn't purposefully leave you in the dark. As I am sure you heard last night, I found my mate and my sole attention has been on him and his recovery."

"I am so happy for you. I know you've wanted to find your mate for quite some time. I'm sorry the circumstances are so grim. I can clear my schedule for them to meet with me tomorrow and to make it less stressful on them, I think it would be best if I met them at your home for the first time. As a group first and then individually."

Declan agreed. "Would you be able to come by this evening? I would say tomorrow is fine, but the clans will be arriving and with how precarious the situation may become, I don't know if tomorrow will be an option."

Amanda hummed. "Okay. Let me see what I have on my schedule and see if I can move any of my appointments to next week."

"Thanks, Amanda."

They hung up and Declan headed downstairs to his office. Kyle sat with one ankle on top of his other knee while Maximus sat slumped in the chair with a defeated air, eyes closed. Declan moved forward and crouched in front of the witch. Maximus opened his eyes and they widened a fraction when he saw Declan. Fear entered the violet orbs and Declan felt guilt tug at his gut. He knew they'd been rough on the guy, but he still couldn't see past the fury he held in his heart about the years of pain and torture his mate had endured.

"Why didn't you come to the streak, witch? You could have told me what was happening. About the talisman and the threats he made."

Maximus raised his head a fraction, his features sad. "What would you do if you could lose your entire identity? The very thing that makes you who you are? I didn't know he abused Sean. I only thought he just didn't want Sean shifting. If I'd known…" he trailed off.

"You'd have said something then?" Declan challenged, gritting his teeth. "Or you would have just looked the other way still?"

"I don't know," Maximus whispered. "I knew what he had me do was wrong, but I didn't know how to stop it. I didn't know you or your streak. I had no idea if you would even want to help me or if you would even care about what that bastard was doing."

Scowling, Declan stood up straight and leaned his hip against the desk, crossing his arms over his chest. "You could have tried!"

Maximus shook his head. "I know what many shifters believe of witches. How we only use our power for evil and it's never enough for your kind that some of us don't adhere to the labels you've given all of us. The war in 1920 showed all of us just how much shifters hate witches. Before and after, shifters condemned witches and painted us all with the same tarred brush."

Declan knew of the war. He'd still been a young cub and not involved in the discussions or fighting. His father had tried to keep the Royal Taiga Streak away from the epicenter of the battle, but when the unrest came to the edges of their land, there'd been no choice except to get involved. Several of the streak members had been lost during the war. Declan held no ill will toward witches and he'd even found it rather distasteful that shifter kind had nearly wiped them off the face of the planet. Though now he had to wonder if they hadn't had the right idea after seeing what one of them had allowed to happen to innocent children.

"I never thought the same as the others," Declan replied stiffly.

Maximus gave him a look of disbelief. "Yet here I sit, tied up like a common criminal, beaten and threatened with death."

Declan managed to fight back the cringe he instinctively wanted to give. Maximus wasn't wrong. "You helped a sick human keep a shifter child hostage for almost twenty years! What could you possibly have expected? Tea and biscuits while we met for a chat? Kyle had to bring you here by force in the first place."

"Because I didn't know he was dead!" Maximus shouted, eyes wild with defiance and anger.

Declan looked at Kyle who shrugged again. He knew of Kyle's less than stellar conversational skills. The guy spent a lot of time alone in his line of work and witnessed some of the most heinous things in the shifter and human world. He didn't know the true extent of Kyle's life or history, but he'd be willing to bet they were horrors Declan would suffer nightmares from. "Okay, say I buy you'd have come willingly if Kyle had told you Carl McNeely was dead. What are you going to do about it now?"

Maximus tilted his head, studying Declan for several seconds of silence. "I'm going to remove the collar."

"Good answer." He watched Maximus for a moment then asked, "If I untie you, are you going to try and run?"

"No," Maximus replied, head high. "I want to undo what I did."

Declan motioned to Kyle who stoically came forward and started to remove the ropes. "If the serum was administered three months ago, how long will it be before Sean can shift once the collar is removed?"

Maximus rubbed at his wrists once they were free. "I don't know. Sean built up a tolerance over time to the serum.

Maybe it was his shifter half fighting it, I can't say for sure. This isn't an exact science. When Sean hit maturity at the age of thirteen, he partially shifted. He probably doesn't remember it, but the collar stopped him from the full shift. Carl had me come back to reinforce the spell on the collar and to wipe the memory of the incident out of Sean's mind."

It took every ounce of Declan's willpower not to deck the fucker. He walked around to the other side of his desk to put something between them just in case he lost control. "Did you ever ask him why?"

Maximus sighed. "I asked McNeely when he first demanded the spell, but the only thing he said was something about 'the bitch deserves it', and that was it. I never understood it. I knew he couldn't be talking about Sean so I could only hazard a guess it had something to do with his mother."

Declan's cell rang before he could pursue Maximus for more information. He answered it. "Did you find it, Victor?"

"We're on our way back now, Alpha. I believe I have the object of which you spoke of."

"That's great news, Victor. We'll see you in a few minutes."

Maximus gave him a hopeful look. Declan said, "They believe they found it."

Relief blossomed over Maximus's face. "Thank the goddess," Maximus whispered.

"You just better hope nothing happens to Sean," Declan growled. He didn't like the idea of just returning the talisman to the witch. He may not be a complete bastard, but he also wasn't naïve enough to think Maximus was a good person. "If he dies, I will gut you."

Wincing, Maximus lifted a shaky hand gingerly touch the corner of his mouth. "I'm not stupid and I also don't want anything to happen to him."

A knock came not long after. "Enter," Declan bid.

Victor came in with Michael close behind. "Alpha."

Michael remained by the door, arms crossed over his chest. Declan could see the loathing in Michael's gaze when he looked at Maximus, but Declan couldn't deal with that right now. It would only become an issue if Michael made a move toward the witch. "Where is it?"

Victor opened his hand and held it out palm upright. "We found it in the dirt on the basement floor. The chain was broken."

A small silver disc sat in the center of Victor's hand. Declan reached out to take it, but Maximus beat him to it, moving before he even knew Maximus had moved. Michael snarled and went to intercept, but Declan stopped him with one hand raised. "It's all right, Michael."

Maximus held it tight in his hand against his chest, head bent. "Thank you," he gasped, his voice rough.

"Don't forget your promise, witch," Declan snapped. "I'll bring Sean down now."

"I won't leave him like that," Maximus swore, raising his gaze to Declan's.

He saw the guilt and anguish in Maximus's eyes and wondered if maybe the witch really did regret what he'd done. It still didn't change the past and Declan wasn't sure he could find it in him to forgive Maximus for helping to hold his mate prisoner, but he also didn't feel like strangling the little prick anymore either.

Declan looked at Victor. "Call Cameron. I want him here."

Victor nodded and took out his cell immediately.

Declan headed out of his office and took the stairs two at a time. Sean lay curled up on his side when Declan entered the bedroom and he approached slowly, smiling at the lax expression on Sean's face. Perching on the bed as he had earlier that morning, Declan reached out to touch Sean's cheek. "Sean."

A little sigh slipped from Sean, but he didn't wake and Declan slid the pad of his thumb of Sean's cheekbone. "Baby, it's time to wake up."

Lips pulling into a frown, Sean's eyes squinted tighter as though he were fighting to stay asleep. Declan moved his hand to card his fingers through Sean's hair. "Come on, sexy, it's time to become who you are."

SEAN

Sean heard the deep rumble of a voice, but he didn't want to let go of the peacefulness he'd found in his dreams. Pouting, he attempted to hold on to sleep tighter, but the feeling of a hand in his hair woke him. The deep woodsy scent of Declan washed over him and Sean smiled, eyes still closed. When he blinked them open, he found Declan sitting beside him with a look Sean could only describe as affectionate. At least he thought so based on having seen the same look on the face of someone in a movie his father had been watching one day while Sean cleaned the living room of the mess his father had made.

"Hi," Sean murmured.

A smile tipped the corners of Declan's mouth upward. "Hi."

"Is it time?"

"It is."

Nervousness instantly swamped him and Sean sat up with his back to the headboard. His fingers trembled when he tried to straighten the comforter a little. Declan set his hand on top of Sean's. "I will be there with you every single step of the way, baby. You don't have to be afraid."

He met Declan's gaze. "I'm scared."

"I know, but you don't have to be. We're going to get this collar off and you're going to shift and we'll be running together before you know it."

"You think so?"

"I know so."

Licking his lips, Sean asked, "How can you be sure?"

"Because I know it deep in my heart you're going to be okay and besides," he gave a cocky grin, "I'm the alpha and I won't have it any other way."

Sean managed a small chuckle at Declan's words. He pushed the blanket back and Declan stood, holding out his hand to Sean. "Let's go do this."

He decided to try and stay positive. His fear mixed with the excitement of finally being able to shift. What he wouldn't give to know what he could change into. Declan led the way down the stairs to the office. Sean saw Maximus stood by the desk, no longer tied to a chair. Maximus motioned Sean toward him and he moved until only a foot or so separated them. Declan never left his side.

The only others in the room were Cameron, Victor, and Kyle. Cameron appeared tense and Sean wondered if maybe he anticipated something going wrong. Before he could begin to worry again, Maximus said, "Sean, I need you to sit, please."

Sean sat in the chair Maximus had been in a short time ago and stared at him. "What now?"

Declan placed his hands on Sean's shoulders from behind. Maximus reached out and touched the collar with one hand, closed his eyes, and started to murmur something under his breath. Sean watched in fascination, only to jerk in surprise when the collar began to grow hot beneath Maximus's hand. "What's going on?" Sean whispered.

Maximus didn't answer and didn't stop his chanting. The feeling of electrical surges began to pulse through Sean's entire body and Sean started to sweat. He curled his fingers around the arms of the chair, his breathing deepening. The surges became uncomfortable and Sean started to fidget. He felt Declan's hands tighten on his shoulders in a comforting gesture. Just as Sean would have spoken again, a pain unlike anything Sean had ever experienced struck through him and he couldn't contain the scream wrenched from his very soul. He clamped his eyes shut and struggled to get away from the object causing him such agony.

"Hold him still," Maximus grunted. Sean barely heard it, but he knew those words meant the pain would continue.

"No more," Sean cried, tears running down his cheeks. "Please!"

"Maybe we should stop," Declan growled.

"We can't stop. It's too late."

Another jolt of pure excruciating torture struck through Sean and he scream again, his body bowing from the chair. Then Maximus was gone, the familiar weight of the collar around his throat disappeared, and Sean slid to the floor, his arms wrapped around his belly as something clawed at his insides. "It hurts," he sobbed.

Declan knelt beside him, gathering him close to his chest. "I know, baby. Just let it take over. It'll be over soon."

There was nothing in the world, no words of any kind, that could describe the pure fire eating at Sean's body. He could never describe the way every bone inside of him all seemed to break at once, pops and crackles echoing throughout the office. Maybe if he'd been able to, he'd have laughed at the nauseated expression on Maximus's face, but all he could do was writhe in Declan's hold, pleading for them to make it stop.

"Jesus! You never said it would be this bad, Cam!" Declan roared.

"I didn't know! There's no way to know how he would react. This is something we've never seen before," Cameron protested. A low yowl came from Kyle's direction, at least Sean figured it had to be Kyle since he'd been the only one standing near the far wall of the office. "No one could have predicted this. Not even me."

The sensation of his fingernails being pried out all at once caused Sean to lose all coherency and he blacked out. He had no idea how long he was unconscious for, but when he did return to his senses, the room was quiet. No one made a sound and Sean lifted his head only to blink in shock. The majority of the colors were gone, replaced by varying shades of gray and white. All except for blues, greens, and yellows. He blinked again, wondering if maybe he just needed to clear his vision. Only the colors remained the same. He tried to speak, but only a low yowl came out.

Surprise brought Sean stumbling to his… paws? Wonder and excitement danced through him and Sean looked down to see paws instead of feet. They were covered in white fur with what appeared to be dark stripes. He glanced up at Declan and gave another yowl. Declan's eyes were wide and Sean thought maybe something was wrong. He tilted his head, trying to understand.

"You're beautiful, mate," Declan breathed and then suddenly his arms wrapped around Sean's very wide neck.

Then Sean remembered his ability to speak with Declan through his mind. *What am I?*

Declan pulled back and smiled. *Exactly what I thought you'd be. Only so much better.*

"Bring me a mirror," Declan demanded of the others around them without looking away from Sean.

Sean rubbed against Declan, butting his head at the broad chest. Declan laughed, a husky sound which went straight to Sean's groin. He would have frowned at the odd feeling, but wasn't sure how to do that in whatever form he'd shifted into.

"Here, Alpha."

Declan stood and took the large mirror from Victor. He slowly turned the surface around until Sean saw a huge white cat staring back. He could see the bright blue of his eyes, the white of his fur, and the dark stripes covering his entire body. He looked just like Declan only white. *I'm a tiger! Like you!*

"You are, baby, and so amazingly beautiful."

Sean turned his body enough to see his side. In this form, he was at least three times his usual size.

"What does this mean, Alpha?" Cameron asked.

Declan glanced at Cameron and shook his head. "I have my suspicions, Cam, but I don't know for sure yet."

Sean flicked his tail and giggled inside his mind. He dropped into a crouch, growled, and then tried to pounce his tail, spinning in a circle until he crashed into the chair he'd been sitting in before. Declan and Maximus laughed while the others just continued to stare. *Can we run outside?* Sean asked excitedly.

"Of course." Declan moved to the double glass doors on the opposite side of his office. "Wait for me."

Sean barely acknowledged Declan's command as he moved out into the sunlight. The warmth seeped into his fur and Sean tossed his large body to the ground and began to roll around in the grass on his back. A low rumble brought his head up enough to see Declan's orange tiger exiting the same doors. Sean returned the sound, surprised at how quickly he'd begun to adapt.

Declan approached him in a slow stalk, his head lowered with his large eyes trained on Sean. Some instinct in Sean told him not to let Declan catch him so easily and he rolled, leapt to his feet, flicked his tail in Declan's face, and bolted. He didn't know the compound as well as Declan, but he'd caught sight of the forest on more than one of the walks through. He veered into the tall trees, crashing through underbrush, and scaring away birds.

A warm laugh tickled Sean's mind and he'd only made it a few hundred yards into the forest before Declan tackled him, tumbling him down into a pile of dead leaves at the base of a tree. Only Declan didn't remain there, he danced away from Sean, preening and teasing him. Sean regained his footing, shook his body, and darted in the other direction, once again causing the birds to scatter from nearby bushes and tree branches.

"Someday I'll teach you the art of stealth, love."

The entire time they spent playing a tiger's version of tag, Sean found himself distracted by smells and sounds, even sights, he'd never witnessed from the eyes of his tiger. He could barely believe how freeing and wonderful it all was. Why would Carl hate something so magnificent? He even found himself rooting through the grass whenever a small field mouse caught his attention, though he never caught one.

"I don't understand why he hated shifters," Sean murmured over their connection.

"I don't know, baby. Sometimes we can never truly understand why a person does the things they do or says the things they say. But you're free of him, of that life, and you never have to go back."

Sean skidded to a stop near a bush, his ears perking forward. He heard the slight rustle of leaves. Then a bundle of fur came leaping out of the greenery and Sean launched himself toward it, barely missing what he thought was a rabbit. The creature disappeared into a hole and Sean sat down on his haunches and huffed. Another chuckle slithered through his mind and then Declan dropped down from overhead, landing beside Sean. *"Stalking is a form of art, sexy. Let me show you. Stay quiet and don't move."*

Declan climbed the tree to the overhead branch again and Sean attempted to follow, sliding down several times before he successfully managed using his claws to hoist himself up to join Declan on the branch. They waited and waited and finally another crackle of leaves caught their attention. For just a moment, Sean wanted to give into the instincts and the urging of his tiger and jump down to give chase. Only he held himself in check. Suddenly Declan launched himself off the branch and landed on whatever prey burrowed through the grasses below them.

Sean eyed the ground, wondering if he should jump or not, but figured if Declan could do it, why not him? So he leapt off the branch only he misjudged the distance and bowled into Declan. Declan gave a surprised chuff and rolled with Sean, losing the hold he had on a rabbit. Sean couldn't contain the giggles in his head and lay there, his tiger panting with his laughter.

"Think that was funny, do you?" Declan challenged, rising up to stand over Sean.

He nodded his head, unable to force any words between them. Declan flopped partly down on top of Sean, surprising him. His laughter died off, but not out of fear. He could never be afraid of Declan.

"Shift, gorgeous."

"How?"

"Picture your human self and push the thought to the front of your mind."

Sean thought over the last time he'd seen himself in the mirror and closed his eyes. He tensed expecting pain, but this time, the shift was so flawless he barely registered the change until a light breeze wafted over his bare skin. "It didn't hurt," he murmured.

Then he became aware of a very human, very naked Declan lying on him. "It's not supposed to hurt, love. It's supposed to be freeing, a part of who you are, and you were robbed of that when you should have been embracing it. There will be no more pain."

Tears stung Sean's eyes. The man he'd known as his father for almost his entire life had stolen something so wondrous and amazing from him. "Hey, now. No more tears," Declan said, brushing away the tears at the bottom of Sean's eyelids.

Declan leaned down and kissed him, gently, but it didn't take long before the kiss became more. Hot, hungry, and deep in a way which caused Sean's cock to harden. Sean slid his arms around Declan's back, eagerly opening for Declan, his tongue meeting Declan's in a dance he was still attempting to learn.

He wanted Declan, wanted to feel him inside of him, connected to the one man who'd quickly become his everything. He didn't know the words to express his emotions, but he could use his body to show his desire for Declan. Sean moved until he could wrap his legs behind Declan's hips, arching to create friction on their stiff lengths. "Declan," Sean whimpered.

"We don't have anything out here for me to prep you, baby," Declan growled.

Sean shook his head. "I don't care."

"I do," Declan replied, his voice strained.

Pushing upward, Sean struggled to retain the sensations he could never seem to get enough of. "Please, Dec."

"Fuck," Declan swore and then Sean suddenly found himself on his stomach, his ass jutting into the air.

"Oh, God!" Sean keened when he felt the swipe of Declan's tongue over his hole. His eyes widened as he stared unseeing into the forest around them. He hadn't even had a chance to feel embarrassed over what Declan was doing to him with his lips and tongue. His cock wept profusely beneath him, dribbling clear liquid to the grass and leaves under him.

When Declan added a finger to his movements, Sean gave a small cry which quickly faded to an incoherent moan. Then Declan stiffened his tongue and pushed inside, soaking his entrance with saliva over and over. He clenched his hands into the grass and undulated backwards, trying to increase the pleasure he felt. Declan pushed and pulled his finger in and out of Sean's hole and eventually added a second and third digit to the first. When he began spreading those fingers, Sean groaned, enjoying the slight burn of the stretch by then.

Then, Declan moved from lapping at and fingering Sean's channel to wrapping a hand around Sean's cock and maneuvering the shaft enough to engulf as much as he could. Sean cried out, the sound so loud, two birds in a nearby tree took flight, scared by the noise. He couldn't stop the tingle rushing down his spine to gather in his balls and then he spilled into Declan's mouth. A hum from Declan caused Sean to jerk with the added sensation on his cock.

But Declan didn't swallow his release. It took a moment for Sean to realize, but Declan actually spat it back into his hand and began stroking his hard shaft with the slick fluid. Sean panted where he lay, his ass still in the air, his cheek pressed to the ground. He gave a fine shiver when Declan pressed the head of his cock to his hole.

Nothing could come close to describing the feeling of

being stretched open as Declan inched inside of him, slow yet steady. But none of it could compare to when Declan fully claimed his body, the way each retreat pulled at the sensitive flesh of his hole, or the complete invasion on every thrust deep into him. Sean clung to the earth beneath him while Declan held tight to his hips, never changing pace, always slow and steady.

Sean was pretty sure his own cock hadn't gone soft even after coming in Declan's mouth and when Declan changed angles just a slight bit, it sent blood pulsing through his shaft causing him to gasp. Dots of color raced behind his closed eyelids and Sean knew he'd release again soon. Their skin slapped together in such a naughty, delicious way causing Sean's lust to ratchet even higher.

"De-Declan," Sean groaned.

"Does that feel good, baby?" Declan rasped.

"Yes," Sean hissed.

A purr rumbled from Declan's chest and this time Sean's inner cat answered, sending vibrations through him. "Fuck, that's so fucking sexy," Declan growled, giving a sharp rut of his cock into Sean in response.

Sean felt Declan's hands move to spread his ass wider, exposing where they were connected further. He opened his eyes and looked over his shoulder at Declan whose gaze never strayed from where his cock slid in and out of him. The knowledge he lay bare before Declan in such an intimate way didn't frighten him or shame him, but only flamed his desire for Declan higher. He wanted to make Declan feel good, wanted to show Declan how much he trusted the older shifter.

Then Declan slipped one hand underneath Sean, grasping hold of Sean's bouncing prick and began to stroke him in time with the measured thrusts into Sean. Sean dropped his cheek back to the grass and clenched his eyes closed, the dual sensation making his head spin. "I-I-"

"That's it, sexy. Come for me," Declan bid, his voice strained, and Sean could sense Declan wasn't going to last much longer either.

With a shout, Sean let go, a second orgasm washing over him and he shuddered as he came. He was so lost in his own release he almost didn't hear the strangled cry Declan gave or sense the feeling of Declan filling him with his warmth. They collapsed to the ground, Declan beside him, but Declan remained buried inside of him for several moments until he'd softened and slipped free. Sean could feel several droplets trickling from his well-loved hole and down his thigh to the forest floor.

Declan kissed his shoulder, one large hand caressing along Sean's chest. "I will never get enough of you."

Sean smiled into the growing dimness around them. The sunlight no longer filtered through the trees overhead, but he still found he could see as though it were still full daylight outside. Declan nuzzled at his shoulder blade, holding Sean tighter. "The more your tiger comes to the surface, the more of his abilities you'll gain. Including better eyesight and strength."

"Why was everyone surprised by what my animal turned out to be?" Sean asked finally. He'd seen the shock and wonder on their faces, but he'd been too preoccupied to ask until now.

Declan encouraged Sean to lie on his back so he could lean on his elbow and look at Sean's face. "White tiger shifters are rare, Sean. So rare that there are only a handful of them left in the world."

The implication of what Declan was saying sank in and Sean's eyes widened. "Does that mean..."

"It means I think I may know who your parents are, baby."

Sean sat up, ignoring the soreness in his ass from their recent activities. Eagerness enveloped him. "Who are they?"

Declan moved to a sitting position as well. "I don't know for certain, Sean, so please don't get your hopes up until we are completely positive."

Sean had no idea how he'd be able to do that. "I'll try."

"There's a family who is part of our streak."

His breath caught in his throat. Had he been so close to his parents and not even known it? "I haven't seen many in their animal forms. Which ones are they?"

Declan shook his head. "They're out of the country right now. They went to visit family members in Russia."

"Oh," Sean whispered, his hopes crashing.

"They'll be back next week."

Sean brightened. "Tell me about them! Please, Declan."

Chuckling, Declan reached out and pulled Sean into his lap, uncaring of their nudity. Sean listened with rapt attention while Declan told him about the family named Bianca. Their names were Arthur and Nicole and they had a son named Austin. If they were his family, he'd have a brother! Austin was seventeen and wanted to be a musician. Arthur, the man who could be his real father, worked as an accountant for the streak and Nicole, the woman who Sean wanted to be his mother so badly, was a seamstress and helped repair clothing, blankets, and anything else the streak needed.

"They sound wonderful! Do you have pictures of them?" Sean asked leaning his head against Declan's shoulder.

"I do, back in my office. Do you want to see them?"

"Yes!" Sean replied enthusiastically, pulling away to stare at Declan with a pleading expression. "I really do. Will you show them to me?"

"It's almost dinner time. Let's head back and I'll show you them before we eat, okay?"

Sean nodded eagerly and the two of them shifted. Declan led the return to the main house. A few members of the streak waved at the two of them on their way past, several staring in surprise and Sean thought even awe. Sam and Tara waited on the steps when they arrived and he saw both of their eyes widen. Then Sam and Tara were down the steps, throwing their arms around Sean's neck and hugging him tightly. "You did it, Sean! Oh, you're so amazingly gorgeous!"

"Wait until Vicky sees you!" Tara exclaimed. "She's going to adore you even more!"

DECLAN

eclan allowed the girls a few moments to fawn over Sean before chuffing and nudging his mate into the house. He didn't want anyone seeing Sean naked and, since he'd pretty much shredded the clothing he wore during his first shift, he needed to get the two of them to their bedroom. Sam opened the door for them and Declan padded into the house and up the stairs. Sean followed behind him.

Once they were in the bedroom, Declan shifted and closed the door. "Come on, sexy. Change back and we'll go see those pictures."

It took a moment or two for Sean to fully shift, but he could already see Sean doing so much better already. The blue of his eyes fairly glowed with his animal spirit. Declan wanted to forget about dinner, forget about the pictures of Sean's possible family, and throw his mate down on the nearby mattress, but he kept a tight rein on his urges. Especially since he knew Sean was beyond eager to see the pictures.

He also thought about the therapy session he'd requested

for Sean that evening, but he could already see exhaustion on Sean's features after everything he'd gone through for the day. It wouldn't hurt to wait until after his meetings with the clans. Especially if it came down to Sean having to recount the details of his life in the basement of Carl McNeely's home. He sent off a quick text to Amanda to postpone the session until tomorrow night.

Sean didn't take long to throw on a pair of sweat pants and a t-shirt similar to the ones Declan pulled on. "Do you think they'll know me?" Sean asked, his face flushed with his excitement. "Do you think they'll remember me?"

"No one could ever forget you," Declan said, holding his hand out to Sean, who immediately took it. Every day was another step toward Sean fully emerging from his shell, learning to live, and experiencing so many of the things he'd missed out on. Sean trailed after him on their way to Declan's office, almost bouncing on his feet. Affection warmed Declan's heart. If he hadn't already fallen in love with Sean, he would have right then and there.

He booted up his computer, urging Sean to sit in the desk chair. He opened his last correspondence they'd sent a picture in and opened the attachment. Sean leaned in so close to the screen he almost fell out of his seat. Unable to stifle a laugh, Declan gripped Sean by his shoulder. "Easy, Sean. You can't climb through the screen."

Sean stared at the image, eyes wide, and he reached out to touch Nicole's features. "She's beautiful."

Declan could see the resemblance right then and he knew without a doubt they were Sean's family. He couldn't believe he hadn't noticed it sooner really. Knowing his mate would have been in the streak regardless of the situation blew Declan's mind. He'd been right there, right under Declan's nose, and he hadn't even known it.

"I knew they'd lost a child, many years ago, but I never

made the connection because I didn't know what type of shifter you were. I sensed cat, but since you'd never shifted, we couldn't know for sure."

"So, I really could be their son?" Sean murmured, never taking his eyes off the picture.

"Yes, baby, I think you are."

Sean finally ripped his gaze away from the monitor. "I have a family. I have a brother! Declan!"

"You have a family no matter what, Sean," Declan said.

The excitement in Sean's eyes dimmed. "Do you… Do you think they'll want me?"

"Oh, baby, I know they will." Declan yanked Sean from the chair and crushed him to his chest. "They'd be crazy not to."

Sean shuddered and burrowed closer to Declan, his fingers tangling in the hem of the shirt he wore.

"Come on, we should eat. Shifting burns a lot of calories. You need to make sure to stay hydrated, too. Let's join the others."

They left the office and headed to the dining room. When Sean halted abruptly in the doorway, Declan glanced past him and saw Maximus sitting at the dining table beside Rose. "What is he doing here?" Declan snarled, nudging Sean behind him.

Rose spoke first. "I invited him to join us for dinner. It's the least we can do after you all beat him to a pulp."

"He's still able to walk and he isn't that badly injured," Declan scoffed.

"It's okay," Sean murmured.

"One wrong look and I'll-"

"Enough, Declan," Rose snapped. "We get it. You don't have to like him, but I am serving him dinner along with everyone else."

Declan glared at Rose, but didn't pursue the topic. He

guided Sean to the seat beside his usual, helped him pull into the table, and sat. Kyle was nowhere to be seen so Declan figured the bounty hunter had taken off once his job was finished. He'd have to direct deposit the money into Kyle's account later. He definitely owed him a big, fat bonus for helping find the witch and bringing him there.

Maximus didn't speak the entire time everyone ate, merely quietly passed whatever dish he was asked for. Declan barely took his eyes off Maximus even while everyone exclaimed over Sean being able to shift, asking how his first shift went, and if he loved it. A smile hovered on his lips listening to Sean exclaim over everything he'd experienced, noticeably leaving out their lovemaking in the forest. Declan knew the other streak enforcers on patrol had steered clear of where they were, but weren't far enough away that they wouldn't have been there to help if something had happened. They'd most likely heard quite a bit as Sean didn't seem to be able to remain quiet or stifle his expressions of pleasure. Not that Declan was complaining. He enjoyed every noise, every cry, and every moan Sean let out.

After dinner was finished, Declan stood and gave a hard look at Maximus. Before he could demand the witch leave, Rose offered him a room to stay in for the night. "Absolutely not!" he growled.

Rose ignored him and Declan ground his teeth together. "Rose."

She glanced at him; her expression full of false innocence. "It only makes sense for him to not have to travel at this time of night. I highly doubt he's going to kill us all in our sleep. He looks like a feather could knock him over right about now."

Declan turned his attention to Maximus. "If you so much as put a toe out of line you won't have a second to utter a single word before I rip your throat out."

Maximus swallowed noticeably and just nodded, eyes wide. Declan ignored the stab of guilt at how harsh he'd been. If anything were to happen to anyone in his streak because of the witch, Maximus would wish he'd never been born.

Sean yawned, wide enough to where his jaw popped. Embarrassment flooded Sean's features. "I'm sorry."

"You've been through a lot today. I'd be surprised if you weren't falling asleep on your feet." Declan slid an arm around Sean's waist. "Let's get you into bed."

Sean preceded Declan upstairs to their room. He got Sean settled into bed, stripped down to his skin, and slid into bed beside him, immediately pulling him close. "I'm so proud of you, baby."

"For what?" Sean mumbled, clearly already in the process of falling asleep.

"Just for being you," Declan murmured before pressing a kiss to Sean's temple.

Sean merely hummed and in seconds a small snore came out. Declan grinned and closed his eyes. He knew today could have gone a completely different direction, but Sean had accepted everything in stride. And seeing how Sean came into his own while in his tiger form made Declan so fucking proud of his mate. He couldn't wait for the Bianca family to arrive home to meet their long-lost son, knowing in his heart they'd accept him with open arms.

The next day, Declan needed to prep for the arrival of the other clans so after a quick breakfast, he left instructions for Victor to not leave Sean's side and to keep an eye on Maximus to make sure the witch left as soon as he was able. He didn't want his mate alone while the others were on streak land. They would be arriving mid-day and Declan wanted to prepare what he intended to say to them, what he needed to reveal to them, and he also contacted Cameron because he would be the one to take them to collect the remains.

Cameron sounded tired when he answered the phone. "Dr. Green."

"Cam, it's Dec. I wanted to talk to you about today."

"Declan. Yes, of course."

He heard the rustle of blankets and frowned. "Did I wake you?"

"No, not at all. Just having a late morning."

Something seemed off about Cameron, but Declan couldn't worry about that at the moment. "I'm going to meet with the clan representatives a couple at a time. Once I've explained what has happened and how we've recovered the remains, I'd like you to take them to claim them, do whatever validation they need to know it is one of their own, and assist with preparations for transportation."

"I will take care of it," Cameron promised. "What time will they be arriving?"

"I've instructed them an hour or so apart in order to keep the possibility of someone else telling the other clans before I can explain the situation to them. The first will arrive at noon."

"I'll be at the main house at eleven-thirty."

"Perfect. Thank you, Cam. You sound as though you had a late night. Why don't you get some more rest until then?"

Cameron gave an almost choked laugh, but then said, "I'll be all right. Thanks, Dec."

"I think we owe our thanks to you, Cam. You made sure those spirits were disturbed as little as possible and could be reunited with their families."

"Thanks, Dec. See you soon."

Declan hung up and spent the remainder of the morning

debating on the way to break the news to the other shifter clans. How did you tell someone their missing children were dead? He sighed and leaned back in his chair, running a hand down his face. A knock at the door caused him to drop his hands to his lap. "Come in."

Michael entered the room, trailed by a person that brought Declan to his feet immediately. "Alpha Declan, Alpha Luthor Ashford from Clan of the Claw."

"You're early," Declan said.

Luthor shrugged carelessly and walked forward, holding out his hand for Declan to shake. "I figured it must be something important or you would never have asked to meet."

The alpha of the Clan of the Claw was comparable in height and body to Declan's own frame, but he could sense a steel core beneath the surface despite the unconcerned air Luthor attempted to give. A strong jawline, full firm lips, a tapered nose, and blond hair shorn in a neat style only cemented that Declan should not under estimate the man before him.

"Have a seat, please. Can we get you anything to drink?"

"No, that's quite all right, but my assistant and brother would possibly appreciate it."

Declan looked at Michael. "Would you please offer them a drink and show them into the living room?"

Michael nodded and left. Declan returned to his seat across from Luthor. He didn't know Luthor as well as he'd known the alpha's father. "I heard you'd taken over instead of your older brother."

Luthor studied Declan for a moment. "You were surprised."

It wasn't a question. "I will admit it's typically the oldest son who takes over as alpha, though Victor did inform me your brother is a seer."

"He is. Our mother thought it prudent I take over since he

does not possess the traits of an alpha. Now, I would very much like to know why I'm here and what all of the secrecy is about."

Declan kept his gaze steady when he relayed everything about the situation concerning the kidnapped cubs and how they came to find them. The only insight to Luthor's thoughts came in the spark of fire in his dark hazel eyes. Anger burned bright in the depths of Luthor's gaze. When Declan reached the part about the graves, Luthor snarled and stood, pacing the room. "You had no idea this was happening? Not even on the edge of your own lands?"

Holding his temper in check, Declan knew the panther shifter in front of him had every right to be pissed off. "Our patrols never traveled to the outskirts. That has been rectified, but unfortunately it is a little too late."

Luthor stalked toward Declan's desk, but Declan stayed calm and in his seat. He never took his eyes off of Luthor, watching for any signs the man intended to attack him. "Where are the remains?"

"Our streak's doctor has them at his clinic. He's already identified the children and the clans they belong to. When you are ready, he will take you to claim those of your people."

The fury in Luthor never died. "Your streak is as much to blame for this as that *human*."

Declan knew there would be some, if not all, who blamed them. "I understand your anger. My own mate was amongst the ones who were being kept in such filthy conditions. But the human is dead and there is nothing any of us can do to change the past."

"I expect restitution!" Luthor spat.

Tension tightened Declan's shoulders. He'd been expecting Luthor to want further reparations. "What exactly are you anticipating?"

Luthor stood straight, his shoulders back. "I demand the

life of one of your own in exchange for the life that was stolen from my clan."

Declan raised a brow. "I think that's a little extreme considering the person responsible for this travesty is not a part of my streak nor were we aware of his existence until my own nephew was kidnapped."

"None of that matters. Your streak did not do their job protecting their lands and because of this lapse in judgment, our children suffered for it. If restitution cannot be met then I claim the right to call for an Alpha Challenge."

Standing finally, Declan glared at Luthor. He'd known there would be push back, but he hadn't truly thought any of the other alphas would call for the challenge. "You dare to disrespect my home and my streak?"

Luthor sneered. "We deserve justice!"

"Justice was served by ripping the fucker's throat out!" Declan roared.

"It should have been my clan who meted out justice!"

Before Declan could respond, a knock at his office door interrupted their argument. "Enter!"

Cameron stepped inside, hesitantly glancing between Declan and Luthor. "Everything is ready, Alpha Declan."

"Cameron, this is Alpha Luthor of the Clan of the Claw."

Cameron made a small dip of his head in acknowledgment and patiently entwined his hands in front of him.

"Luthor, please allow Dr. Green to escort you to the clinic."

Luthor glared at Declan. "This isn't over."

"I didn't assume it was." Declan watched Luthor follow Cameron out of his office and leaned heavily on his desk, sighing. He rubbed the back of his neck, attempting to loosen the muscles. There were still several more clans that he would need to go through the same with. He didn't look forward to telling them about their cubs.

He, of course, was right in his assumption that many of the leaders would be enraged. Though some were more peaceful than others about it, merely quietly accepting the remains and leaving the compound. Luthor was the only one who demanded blood for blood while the alpha of the Koda Sleuth declared all ties with the Royal Taiga Streak broken. He swore if he caught any of Declan's members on his lands they'd be put to death swiftly and immediately.

It was only Luthor who remained in the compound once all of the others had taken their leave. Declan hadn't expected anything else.

"The others may have accepted your pathetic excuses," Luthor spat, "but I do not. Perhaps your streak deserves a better alpha."

Exhaustion, anger, sadness, and his own fears Sean would be injured further brought everything to a head and Declan pushed into Luthor's space. "Are you issuing a formal challenge, Luthor?"

Luthor sneered at Declan. "As you've already taken away the right to claim justice for our clan members, it is only fitting you should stand in his stead!"

"When?" Declan snarled.

A glimmer of uncertainty flitted through the hazel eyes staring back at Declan. "Tonight. Moonrise."

Before Declan could agree, a soft voice interjected, "Luthor. You mustn't do this."

Declan started and turned his head a fraction to glimpse a slender, brown-haired young man standing in the doorway of his office. He could see the family resemblance and knew the man must be Luthor's brother. The eyes were a deep green though and his build definitely wasn't the definition of an alpha's.

"Casey, go back to the other room," Luthor growled.

Casey shook his head and stepped in further. "No,

Luthor. I've seen the outcome to this fight and you will not win."

Luthor trembled with rage. "Our clan deserves justice!"

"Alpha Declan was not at fault, Luthor. It was always meant to be this way."

The sneer on Luthor's face faded away and he jerked his head toward Casey. "What have you seen?"

Casey flushed under the intense scrutiny Declan leveled his way. He wrung his hands in front of him, and worried his bottom lip with his teeth. "There's a far bigger danger coming for the clans, brother."

Luthor stepped away from Declan, turning to face Casey. "Tell me."

"It's too uncertain now, Luthor, you know my visions don't show me everything. One tiny change, one tiny misdirection and they can change completely. But I saw a black shadow, a malevolent being, coming toward us. I can feel the evil, the hatred." Casey's voice trembled with emotion. "It intends to destroy us all."

Declan frowned. "Do your visions always come true?"

Casey looked at Declan. "Almost always, one outcome or another."

"Are you able to see who or what is coming?" Declan asked.

"No. The images are still too hazy and unclear."

Swearing beneath his breath, Declan called out for Michael, knowing his enforcer wasn't far. Michael entered the office, his eyes flicking over the other two occupants beside Declan. "Did you need something, Alpha?"

He quickly reiterated Casey's words to Michael. "We need to reinforce the patrols. Keep everyone on alert."

"Yes, Alpha."

Luthor had pulled Casey over to the opposite side of Declan's office. Declan politely tuned out their whispered conversation and patiently waited for Luthor's attention to turn to him again. He saw Luthor's shoulders tense and his hands ball into fists at his side. "Are you certain?"

"Yes, Luthor," Casey murmured.

Finally, Luthor turned to Declan. "It would seem we must return home straightaway, but we will continue this *discussion* at another time."

"Any time," Declan growled. Then he glanced at Casey. "But if there is some force coming for all of us, Luthor, I believe it would be best if we worked together."

Luthor sniffed in disdain. "As Casey said, it is not for certain, and I am sure my clan will not require help from the likes of you."

Gritting his teeth, Declan replied, "If this evil is as big and bad as your brother has implied, you may not have a choice."

"There is always a choice," Luthor snarled. He took Casey by the wrist and pulled him toward the office door. "We'll see ourselves out."

Declan watched the two panthers leave and called out to Michael once again, informing him to have one of the patrols ensure they were off their lands. *"Sean."*

SEAN

Sean sat in the dining room with Sam, Tara, and Vicky, Victor practically glued to his side, when the first clan members arrived. The front door opened and he heard a deep voice announce Alpha Luthor of the Clan of the Claw, and then he heard Declan's enforcer Michael request all but the alpha wait in the living room. Curiosity got the better of him and Sean got up and peered around the corner of the dining room across to the living room. A young man with light brown hair settled into a chair near the window while a taller, scarier looking male stood sentry next to his chair.

Sean couldn't contain a small intake of air when bright green eyes met his. He swallowed hard and then the young man smiled gently at him. The stranger stood and, with the scarier man trailing him, approached Sean. "Hello, I'm Casey."

"Hi," Sean whispered.

"You're the Alpha-mate," Casey said.

Victor snarled and stepped forward, his hand coming to

rest on Sean's shoulder. "How do you know of our Alpha-mate?"

Casey looked at Victor. "I have seen him."

Sean frowned. "I've never seen you before."

Another smile tilted Casey's lips up at the corners and warmth radiated at Sean from his gaze. "I am a Seer, Alpha-mate. My visions tell me things."

Sean tilted his head to the side, confused. "I don't understand."

Casey patiently explained how he could see the future and the past, the paths their lives could take, and how they intertwined with one another. "I've seen you at Alpha Declan's side. Your tiger is absolutely beautiful."

He tried hard to understand, but he still couldn't shake his confusion off. Casey held out his hand. "May I?"

Sean looked at Victor and Victor gave an infinitesimal nod. He set his hand in Casey's and watched Casey closely. Casey closed his eyes and seemed to be lost in thought. Surprise, pain, and horror chased each other across Casey's features. It was only when his eyes flew open again did Casey speak. "I am so sorry, Alpha-mate," Casey croaked, tears glittering in the bright emerald gaze. "The inexplicable things you've experienced and witnessed should never be something inflicted upon a child."

Flinching, Sean bit his lip and curled his arms around his waist. "I don't know what you mean."

Casey shook where he stood and the frightening, silent shifter with him wrapped an arm around Casey's shoulders. He flicked a quick grateful glance to the man before turning back to Sean. "My brother won't understand, but I do. I will try to make him see he's wrong."

"I don't understand," Sean said, eyebrows furrowing. "What is he wrong about?"

"My brother is very much controlled by his emotions. He

will feel the need to demand justice for our lost brethren and will demand your alpha provide him with it."

Victor stiffened next to Sean, but didn't speak. Sean leaned a little closer to Victor without realizing his attempt to soothe the older man Declan seemed to trust wholeheartedly. "What will he ask for?"

"Either for the man who hurt our clansman or for blood in return from your streak."

"He's dead," Sean whispered.

Casey gave Sean a sympathetic look. "I know."

"What does blood in return from our streak mean?" Sean asked. "He'll want someone else to take my father's place?"

Casey gave a small nod. Sean gasped and trembled. "But it wasn't their fault!"

"Luthor will not see it that way."

"I have to tell him! I have to tell your brother it's not their fault," Sean said, trying to pull away from Victor and run to Declan's office.

Victor tightened his hold. "You must remain here, little one. Alpha Declan will be able to handle this."

Sean looked at Victor, feeling helpless. "But Carl was the one who ki-killed the others. They have to understand that."

Victor shook his head. "Trust in Declan. It'll be all right."

Closing his eyes, Sean leaned into Victor's side, soaking up the strength pouring from the other shifter. "It's not their fault," he whispered again.

Someone touched the back of his hand and Sean opened his eyes. Casey smiled encouragingly. "He is right, Alpha-mate. Everything will be all right."

Sean nibbled at his bottom lip then nodded. "Okay."

"Would you please introduce me to your family?" Casey asked, glancing over Sean's shoulder to where Sam and the others sat.

He cleared his throat and turned. "This is Sam, Tara, and the little one is Vicky."

Sam eyed Casey warily. "Who are you?"

Casey glanced at Victor for a split second and then ventured further into the room. His bodyguard never left his side, much as Victor did not leave Sean. "My name is Casey Ashford. My brother is Luthor Ashford, alpha of the Clan of the Claw. We are here at the request of your alpha."

"If you're a seer, why weren't you able to see what that bastard was doing to your brethren?" Tara demanded.

"Tara!" Sean reprimanded her for being so blunt and for the language she'd used, especially in front of Vicky. She raised her brow at Sean, but didn't say anything else.

"It is okay, Alpha-mate. She is just curious." Casey turned to face her. "My visions are… tentative, Ms. Tara. I can't call them at will. I have to touch someone or something the person has touched in order to see anything. Many of my visions aren't clear, they lack the finer details and only reveal the broadest of information sometimes.

"A seer does not mature into their visions until they reach puberty and even when they come into their abilities there is no certainty how long it will take to master them. When Yuri was taken, I was a toddler and by the time I reached puberty, the energies that cling to an object had faded. I couldn't have known what happened to him or any of you."

The front door opened and Sean spotted Cameron entering the house and heading toward Declan's office. He wanted nothing more than to follow the kind doctor, but he had to remember Declan's promise. If he needed Sean there, he would call for him. He refocused his attention on Casey. "Will your brother try to hurt Declan?"

"Not outside of the laws of the clan."

"What does that mean?" Sam asked.

"Luthor would not risk his right to justice by attempting

to attack Declan without issuing a challenge."

"What kind of challenge?"

"The most likely choice, an Alpha's Challenge. They will fight to the death in front of both clans. The alpha still standing at the end will have the choice to either take control of the other's clan or leave them without an alpha."

Sean sucked in a breath at the thought of Declan being hurt. He couldn't lose Declan. "Is there any way to stop it?"

Before Casey could answer, they heard Declan's office door open and then Cameron and Luthor appeared there. "Casey," Luthor snapped. "Let's go."

Casey flinched, but schooled his features quickly. Sean gave him a sad look. He knew what it was like to live under someone who controlled you. "Forgive me, Alpha-mate. I must go."

Sean nodded and watched the four shifters leave. He dropped into a seat beside Sam. "Is Declan going to be okay?" Sean rasped, fear for Declan nearly paralyzing his vocal cords.

Victor settled into the seat next to him. "He will be all right, Sean. He would never allow anything to happen to you."

He gave a weak smile to Victor. Worry and anxiety tangled his stomach into knots. Sean had already begun to suspect his feelings for Declan went deeper than that of the man who'd saved him and his family. He loved Sam, Tara, and Vicky, but he knew the love he held for Declan was different. When he thought of the girls, he didn't have the same warm feelings in his heart or the way a single smile from Declan made his belly flutter as if it held butterflies in there. He wouldn't let anyone harm Declan. Not when he loved him more than anything.

Over the next few hours, many strangers came and went. Much shouting could be heard from down the hallway to

Declan's office, and Sean had chewed his thumbnail down to the quick, beyond nervous. But during all of it, Declan never once requested him to come in to explain the past, and as selfish as that may make him, he couldn't have breathed a deeper sigh of relief mentally when the last one left. Luthor and Casey still remained behind, Luthor once again disappearing into Declan's office while Casey returned to the dining room where they all sat.

Casey told them about their lands, how beautiful it was where they lived, and the way the clan helped one another through good times and bad. Sean really liked Casey. Somehow, he knew Casey was a good person, someone he could see being friends with. The almost quiet happiness Sean sensed from everyone, despite the somber reason for the gathering, caused his tiger to stretch languidly in his mind. It was one of the strangest things Sean had ever experienced, but it also had him grinning because he could finally sense his animal half.

The seemingly pleasant air to their small group shifted dramatically when Casey touched Victor to gain his attention. Casey's eyes widened and his features paled. He trembled and then wrenched away from Victor. "I need to see Luthor. Now."

None of them knew what was happening and Casey ignored any questions thrown his way as he rushed to Declan's office. Sean followed, but stopped just outside the doorway. He heard everything Casey said; about the dark shadow aiming for them, how Luthor wouldn't win whatever it was he thought he could, and he heard the snarled words between them.

Luthor brushed past him when he left Declan's office, ignoring him, while Casey gave him a strange sympathetic glance and a quick squeeze of his hand. "We will meet again, Alpha-mate."

Unsettled at Casey's words, Sean watched them leave then heard Declan call for him through their connection. He turned and entered Declan's office, rushing to Declan when he held out his arms to Sean. The worry and fear faded the moment Declan wrapped him in a tight embrace, resting his chin atop Sean's head. Sean closed his eyes and breathed in the deep scent he knew so well.

"I need you to promise me you won't leave the house without Victor or myself at your side," Declan said.

Sean heard something in Declan's voice, a tension he'd never heard before, and he leaned back enough to peer into Declan's eyes. "What's coming?"

Declan stiffened. "You heard?"

A blush stole over Sean's cheeks. "I was outside the office."

"Where was Victor? He shouldn't have left your side." Declan scowled.

"He didn't," Sean hurried to say. "He never let me out of his sight."

His reassurance seemed to settle Declan. "We don't know what is going on yet, but until we know of whatever force Casey spoke of, I don't want you alone. Please promise me."

"I promise," Sean murmured.

"Thank you," Declan whispered then kissed him. Sean immediately opened to Declan's seeking tongue. When Declan broke the kiss, he leaned his forehead against Sean's. "I've had many days where things weren't what you call easy, but today tops the list of the worst ones."

"It's not your fault," Sean protested. "No one could have known what was happening."

Declan sighed. "One thing you'll learn the longer you're around people, when they think with their heart, emotions tend to skew someone's idea of right and wrong."

Sean frowned. "So having emotions is bad?"

"No. Not at all, baby. I just mean sometimes our emotions blind us to seeing the truth."

"I still don't understand."

"You know how you feel about Sam and Tara, right?"

He nodded.

"What if someone were to harm them again?"

Sean growled, anger rising quickly at the thought of one them being hurt. "They've been through too much already."

Declan placed his hand over Sean's heart. "That anger you have right now, it's what the clans feel for their lost children. Now think of someone harming Sam, but you know nothing about it until someone tells you."

Sean furrowed his brow, struggling to truly grasp what Declan said. "But it wouldn't be that person's fault."

"No, but what if they could have stopped it? Like Maximus?"

"But I don't blame Max!" Sean protested.

Declan smiled affectionately. "Your heart is so pure, my love. The purest I've ever known. You know my anger toward Max?"

"Yes."

"Do you understand why I am mad at him?"

Sean tilted his head a fraction. "Because he didn't tell anyone about us being held there?"

"Yes."

Finally, Sean understood what Declan meant. "I can see how you would be angry at him. Even though it wasn't him hurting us, he didn't do anything to help us either."

"That's how the other clans feel."

"But you didn't know about us. It still doesn't seem to be the same thing."

"Their feelings blind them to the truth of your words, baby."

Sean still struggled to fully grasp why anyone would be

blinded by how they felt about someone or something, but he did sort of understand after Declan's explanation.

"After dinner, Dr. Binson is coming over to introduce herself and start her sessions with you."

"Okay," Sean replied, figuring Dr. Binson was the one Declan had mentioned the other day. "What do we talk about?"

Declan moved to the nearby couch, pulling Sean along with him. He sat and gently urged Sean onto his lap. "She is going to help you deal with the things you feel and the experiences you've had."

"Can we go for another run soon?" Sean asked.

"Any time you want, baby. What about tomorrow morning?" Declan asked.

Sean nodded eagerly. "It was fun."

"It certainly was, sexy. I loved being able to run with you at my side." Declan cupped Sean's cheek and brushed his thumb over Sean's lower lip. "Especially what happened afterward," he growled low.

Sean blushed, but whispered, "So did I."

He'd never known there could be such pleasure from another person touching him. "Do-Does it always feel that way?" Sean asked, dropping his gaze to stare at the base of Declan's throat.

"If two people agree to it, yes, it should. There are many things I have yet to teach you, my love, but we have time to explore."

Biting his lip, Sean looked at Declan from beneath his lashes. He wanted to try some of the same things on Declan. He'd seen how much Declan enjoyed using his mouth on him and he couldn't help his curiosity in wondering why. "Can I..." he stumbled to a stop, nervous about asking.

"Can you?" Declan nudged, moving both hands to encircle Sean's slender waist.

"I want to touch you the same way you touch me," Sean rushed through. "Um… with um… your mouth."

Sean saw Declan's eyes widen a fraction and he heard Declan's breath stutter a bit. "Are you sure, Sean? I don't expect anything from you."

He nodded and met Declan's gaze fully. "I want to try."

"I would never say no if it's something you truly want to do," Declan replied.

"I want to make you feel good, too," Sean murmured, lowering his gaze once more to study the interesting design of the shirt Declan wore.

Declan used his index finger to tilt Sean's head back until their eyes met again. "Never, ever feel as though you owe me anything, Sean. I would love for you to find the confidence in yourself to do whatever *you* want to do, not what you think anyone else wants you to do. Including me. Understand?"

"But I do want to," Sean said.

A low rumble vibrated in Declan's chest and Sean watched an almost wicked smile curve the corners of his mouth. "Close and lock the door, sexy."

Sean climbed from Declan's lap and went over to do as he bid. When he turned back, his heart leapt into his throat. Declan had removed his shirt and now slouched casually against the sofa. He held out his hand to him, and Sean swallowed hard as he walked back to Declan. When he reached the couch, Declan helped settle him onto his knees between his spread legs.

Through their connection, Sean could feel Declan's arousal, but also saw the obvious bulge beneath Declan's jeans. He licked his lips and tentatively reached to open Declan's zipper.

2 4

DECLAN

When Sean had offered to give him a blowjob, Declan immediately suspected he only wanted to do it out of gratitude or a sense of obligation. But the certainty in Sean's gaze and the sense he'd gotten from their bond convinced him otherwise. His cock pulsed at the idea of feeling Sean's lips on him. He saw the hesitation in Sean's movements and knew his mate was nervous.

"Open my jeans, baby," Declan rasped, tucking one of the strands of hair behind Sean's ear.

Sean pinched the zipper between his index and thumb and slowly pulled it down, the sound harsh in the silence. A shudder wound through Declan when the backs of Sean's fingers brushed over his already hard cock. Sean separated the fabric carefully, revealing the black briefs Declan wore underneath. Wetness already dampened them from his excitement.

"Take it out," Declan murmured, his breathing already choppy.

A flush worked its way over Sean's cheeks, but he

followed the instruction, releasing Declan's stiff prick to the cool air in the room. He couldn't contain a small moan when Sean wrapped his fingers around him. Heavy-lidded, Declan watched Sean study him, the way he lightly squeezed and stroked his hand up and down the shaft. If he weren't careful, it wouldn't take much to make him come. "Lick the tip," Declan instructed.

Sean leaned in closer and the pink of his tongue flashed out and over the head of Declan's cock. This time Declan hissed, his stomach muscles clenching. Sean backed off instantly, fear on his face. "Did I hurt you?"

God, this would probably kill him before the impromptu lesson on giving head was over. "No, baby. It felt so fucking good."

"Oh," Sean murmured and he bent down again, repeating the swipe of his tongue over the knob. This time he gathered the small dob of liquid that seeped from the slit. "It tastes… sort of sweet but sour at the same time."

For several breaths Sean continued to use his tongue over the sensitive end, but eventually Declan demanded, "Take the tip into your mouth."

Declan almost lost it when he saw and felt those sexy lips wrap around the head. Sean used his tongue while slowly sliding his mouth down the shaft. He only reached halfway when he gagged and pulled off, coughing. But that didn't seem to deter Sean because once he'd regained his breath, he engulfed Declan's cock again. This time he added pressure by suckling on each traverse back to the tip.

"That's it, sexy, suck it just like that," Declan groaned, threading the fingers of one hand through Sean's hair. His words seemed to encourage Sean to go a little faster and increase the strength of his suction. Using his other hand, Declan expertly freed his balls, fondling them in combination with Sean's sucking. "Fuck," Declan almost howled when he felt Sean's throat tighten around the end of his cock.

The soft wet sounds Sean made only inflamed Declan's arousal higher. He tried to think of very unsexy things to hold back the impending orgasm. Though he'd never admit it to his mate, he'd had more experienced blowjobs which had never once threatened to send him over the brink so quickly. Knowing he was the only one who'd ever and would ever feel Sean's mouth on them brought forth a sort of caveman satisfaction.

When Sean let out a small moan, Declan realized Sean had freed his own cock and was stroking himself in time with his mouth on Declan. The small vibrations on his dick went straight to his balls and Declan knew he wouldn't last much longer. "Harder, baby, oh, fuck yeah. Just like that."

Declan felt the telltale tingle in his sac and the way they drew tighter to his body. The scent of semen tickling his nose and the slight slowing of Sean's movements told Declan Sean had come. The knowledge tripped him over into oblivion and he gave a loud shout, his fingers tightening a fraction in Sean's hair, as he flooded Sean's throat and mouth. What surprised him was Sean never once let up, even with some of his semen spilling from the corners of his mouth.

The sight caused his cock to pulse a final spurt before Declan loosened his hold on Sean's hair. A growl tore from him when Sean pulled free and licked at his lips to gather what he'd missed. Desire sparkled at him from Sean's sapphire eyes and Declan reached down to yank Sean into his lap to kiss him. The bitter taste of his own release stung his tastebuds, but he only deepened the kiss further.

"That was so fucking amazing, baby," Declan snarled against Sean's mouth.

Delight trickled through their bond and Declan chuckled

huskily, pulling back a fraction. "You're very satisfied with yourself, aren't you?"

Sean smiled, an obvious 'cat-got-the-canary' look on his face. "Can we do that again?"

The small chuckle turned into a booming laugh and Declan hugged Sean tighter. "Baby, anytime you want to do that, you are more than welcome."

After they'd straightened their clothing, Declan ignored the responsibility of dealing with any further fallout relating to the other clans and just cuddled with his mate. He only released Sean when it was time for dinner which was the usual boisterous affair with Rose, Ronnie, the girls, and a couple of pack members who'd helped prepare dinner.

Declan wanted to shield Sean from ever reliving the horrible things he'd experienced at the hands of the monster Carl McNeely, but he knew Sean needed to talk with a therapist. Seeing the way Sean broke down in the face of violence solidified just how deep the trauma ran in his young mate. When Dr. Binson arrived after dinner, Declan couldn't help except notice the way Sean tensed during their introduction.

"Sean, this is Amanda Binson. She's the wife of Theo Binson and a certified psychologist. She's going to talk with you and the others. Help you understand and deal with what happened."

"Okay," Sean whispered, eyeing Amanda with distrust.

"Why don't you use my office?" Declan suggested to Amanda.

Amanda smiled and nodded. "That would be wonderful, Alpha Declan."

She looked at Sean. "I promise I'm not here to hurt you, Sean. I just want to get acquainted with you. Will you show me to Declan's office?"

Declan knew he wouldn't be able to relax while Sean was with her, but he watched Sean lead her down the hallway. He hated feeling helpless to do something, anything, for Sean. Yet he knew in his heart he didn't have the ability to help him fight the ghosts none of them could see except Sean.

Rose came to his side. "He'll be all right, Dec. I know it. He's already come out of his shell so much in the short time he's been here."

"It's just that me and my tiger hate how there is nothing for us to rip to pieces to protect him."

"I know, big brother, but sometimes we can't always fight the battles for our loved ones, no matter how much we want to."

Declan sighed. "How are the girls doing?"

"They're well. Vicky still hasn't spoken a word."

"They given any information on how to find their clans?"

"Sam and Tara are truly afraid their families will make them leave Sean. They don't want to tell me anything to help."

"I'll have Victor look through the records of missing children around the time we think they were taken. Maybe there will be something in there."

She hummed and then tugged him into the dining room and urged him to sit down. "Let me get you some coffee and we can chat."

Declan nodded, still lost in thought about the volume of things to still deal with. Then he thought back to what Casey had said. God only knew what malevolent being was coming. "Alpha?" Victor interrupted his musings.

"Yes, Victor?"

Victor came into the room and sat in the chair next to his. "The patrols confirmed all clans have left our lands. They've also reported Maximus is gone as well."

"Good. I need you to look into any missing children from eight or so years ago, Victor. Two girls, look for pictures of them. Also for any girls taken in the last three years, any which would be Vicky's age by now. I know they wish to remain with Sean, but their families deserve to know what happened to them."

"Whatever you need, Alpha." Victor went to stand, but Declan stopped him.

"Also, use your contacts, find out if anyone has caught wind of any threats against shifters or any potential dangers we may face."

Victor nodded. "I'll report as soon as I have information."

He left the dining room and Rose returned. She carried two mugs, one of which she set in front of Declan. Rose chatted about streak news, the last results of Sam and Tara's exam by Cameron, and how Sean had already put on several much-needed pounds. Declan grunted or one word answered her throughout the time they waited for Amanda to finish with Sean. The girls would start their own sessions the following day, already booked for their own hour each.

To keep a tight rein on his tiger and his own need to be at Sean's side, Declan closed off their bond, knowing any negative feelings Sean had would send him rushing for his office. As it was, Declan nearly bolted from his chair the moment he heard the door open. He entered the hallway and saw Sean's face ravaged by tears. A growl rumbled in his throat and Amanda glanced his way. She frowned at him, but didn't say anything. "I think we should definitely have more frequent visits for a while, Sean. What do you say to three times a week?"

Sean shrugged, his arms wrapped around his middle. Declan waited until they were beside him before he embraced Sean, tightening his arms around his mate protectively. "Three times a week sounds good, Amanda."

"I think we made good progress today, Sean. I look forward to talking to you again. Tomorrow I'll bring the notebook we talked about when I come to see Sam, Tara, and

Vicky. Sometimes writing down our thoughts is very therapeutic and I believe it'll help you work through a lot of what we'll talk about during our sessions."

Declan pressed a kiss to Sean's temple. "Thank you so much, Amanda."

She smiled warmly. "We'll take it one step at a time."

Sean remained quiet the entire time of bidding Amanda a good night and then heading upstairs to prepare for bed. Declan didn't want to crowd Sean, but it tore at him to see the pain on Sean's face. He led Sean into the bathroom, turned on the shower, and then helped Sean remove his clothing. He tenderly washed away the tear tracks and sweat build up from the day's activities. Still nothing was said until they lay in the dark, Sean draped over his chest.

"Declan?" Sean murmured.

"Talk to me, sexy," Declan said, running a hand down Sean's spine.

"Why do you think Carl chose me?"

"I don't think anyone can answer that question, Sean. Sometimes monsters like him make decisions for reasons we can't fathom. He may have had a messed-up childhood or maybe he hated shifters because he wanted to be one. Whatever his reasons, they aren't your fault."

Sean sniffled and Declan tightened his arm around Sean. "I th-thought I wa-was go-going to di-die in that ba-basement."

Declan's heart broke even further for his mate. "But you didn't. You're here with me, with Sam, Tara, Vicky and everyone else. I found you and I'm never going to let anyone hurt you like that ever again."

Sean sobbed quietly while Declan just held him, knowing Sean needed to get everything out. He'd known the sessions with Amanda wouldn't be easy, in fact he'd anticipated Sean breaking down. What he hadn't anticipated was his own eyes watering at just how much Sean had suffered. Nor did he expect the words Sean uttered when he'd finally calmed down. "I love you, Declan."

He'd never admit to anyone how choked up he became at hearing Sean say those words, but he did roll them both over until he rested atop Sean and captured Sean's mouth with his. If the kiss tasted slightly salty, he'd insist it was from Sean's crying jag. Alphas don't cry.

When Declan broke the kiss, he rested his forehead against Sean's. "I love you, too, baby, so fucking much."

Sean smiled, wrapped his arms around Declan's neck and tugged him down to kiss him once more. The kiss quickly turned heated and it didn't take long for Declan to claim Sean all over again. He ravished Sean well into the night until they both collapsed from exhaustion, covered in sweat and cum.

Τhe sessions with the girls went the same as with Sean, just a different outcome at the end of the day. Declan would have done anything to remove their past, for it to never have happened, but there was no way to change it. The only thing everyone could do was focus on moving forward, one day at a time.

Declan treated everyone to a trip into the nearby city and allowed them to buy whatever they wanted from Harley's bakery before heading to the nearby mall. He tasked Victor and Michael to stick with Rose and the girls when they made a beeline for the girl's section in Macy's while he, Sean and Ronnie wandered to the men's. Declan picked out several warm jackets and shirts for Sean, knowing the winter months were heading in soon. They didn't get a ton of snow, but the nights did get bitterly cold sometimes.

Sean protested the number of items Declan placed over

his arm, but Declan brushed him off. "You need warmer clothing. The clothes already ordered for you aren't meant for the colder days coming soon."

Grumbling, Sean stopped trying to prevent Declan from spoiling him and just followed along behind. Declan was tempted to go with Sean into the changing room, but he couldn't leave Ronnie alone so he instructed Sean to try on everything and whatever didn't fit toss back out of the room. When they were done, Declan held at least three bags in each hand. "Let's go see how the girls faired."

Ronnie barely looked up from his handheld game and Declan shook his head. It always amazed him how Ronnie could do that without walking into a wall or something else. "I'm hungry," Ronnie said when they joined the others.

"There's a food court here in the mall," Rose said. "Let's go there. Lots of different choices so there's something for everyone."

Declan stopped Victor and asked him to take the bags to the SUV and then rejoin them. He grabbed Sean's hand the moment his was free, uncaring of some of the other patrons giving them dirty looks. He knew many in the human world judged same sex couples, but he didn't live by their rules. Shifters didn't care about straight, gay, bisexual or polka dots. When a shifter found their mate it was a life changing event and it didn't matter if they were the same sex or not. Of course, it usually worked out to where their mate would match their orientation. Declan had never seen otherwise, but he supposed the fates wouldn't have it happen any other way.

Sean dragged him toward an ice cream stand and Declan laughed softly. "After we eat actual food, baby. I'll buy you all the ice cream you want."

A pout formed on Sean's face and Declan knew Sean

would eventually figure out he had Declan wrapped around his little finger. "All right. Let's get some ice cream."

Smiling brilliantly, Sean rushed to the glass and stared at the various flavors. "What kind do you want?" Declan asked.

"I don't know. There's so many," Sean whispered.

Declan saw eight containers in there. "Give me a scoop of each."

The attendant raised a brow, but didn't say anything. It took three bowls to hold all eight flavors and Declan had to help Sean take them to their table. Rose chuckled and shook her head at Declan. "You're spoiling him."

He lifted one shoulder in a shrug. Sean deserved everything he wanted. He watched as Sean happily ate each and every flavor. Of course, he wasn't feeling too good afterward. Declan helped him out of the mall and into the SUV where Sean collapsed against him, falling asleep fairly quickly. Sam and Tara squeezed into the middle next to him and Sean while Michael drove with Victor in the far back beside Rose and Ronnie.

"Declan?" Tara said.

"Everything okay, Tara?" Declan asked.

"Thank you for making him happy." Tara gave him a smile from the other side of Sam.

"No thanks necessary. I'd do anything in my power to make him happy."

"I know," Tara replied, a satisfied glint in her eye.

Declan pulled Sean into his lap, who barely even snuffled at the movement, to give the two of them more room. He would have wanted to do it anyway just to hold Sean though. When they reached the house, he carried Sean upstairs and carefully put him in bed before grabbing some chewable Pepto and a glass of water from the bathroom. He knew his mate would have a seriously upset stomach by the time he woke.

After, he went downstairs to his office to focus on some of the streak business. An email from Nicole Bianca came in while he was reviewing an application for streak funds to repair a roof. They'd be home by the late afternoon on Tuesday. Declan breathed a sigh of relief when it appeared no one had told her about his mate or the fact he could shift into a white tiger. In truth, he found it rather surprising someone from the clan hadn't emailed either of the Biancas with the information. Maybe most didn't remember the lost cub and hadn't put two and two together. He shot off a quick reply to travel safe and they'd see them then.

The remainder of the weekend went by fairly quickly and uneventfully. Declan took Sean for a run with Tara and Ronnie, giving them the chance to roughhouse together. He'd never seen Tara's wolf before then and found it surprising that despite her being so slender and short as a human, her wolf half almost gave Sean and Declan a run for their money in their tiger forms. It sparked a memory of meeting a similar white wolf at one of the annual shifter gatherings. If he wasn't mistaken, they were about a couple hundred miles north of them. He brought up his theory to Victor when they returned to the house and it wasn't long before Victor located what he already knew.

"Their name is The Farkas Pack. The alpha is Andras Veres." Victor handed a picture of a little girl to Declan. The one in the picture looked just like Tara, only younger. "Do you wish me to contact them?"

"Not yet," Declan said. "Let me speak with Tara."

Victor dipped his head in acknowledgment. "Also, your mate... he is very kindhearted, Alpha, yet I can sense the strength in him."

"More than he will ever see in himself, Victor. His ability to survive all those years shows just how strong he is."

"Casey Asher, the brother of Alpha Luthor, he is a Seer."

Declan nodded. "You heard the same as Sean did."

Victor had the grace to appear guilty. "I did, Alpha. Are there any ideas on what or who we should be prepared for?"

Sighing, Declan ran a hand over his face. "I don't really know yet. I've heard nothing from the other shifter clans. No rumors or gossip. The only thing we can do until they or it shows their hand is stay vigilant. Sean is to go nowhere without you or me. No one should go anywhere alone either."

"Can we afford to keep the patrols further out right now?" Victor asked, reminding Declan of his recent changes because of Sean and the others.

"For now, we'll continue with the patrols to the outskirts until we find out more information about this force Casey mentioned."

"As you wish." Victor left the office then leaving Declan to his thoughts.

Declan only remained downstairs for a short while later before heading up to bed where he pulled Sean close. Thoughts of what evil could be coming chased one another round and round in his head. Whatever happened, he'd protect Sean and the streak at all costs. But in order to keep Sean safe, he'd also have to stay safe. He wouldn't let anything happen to his mate. It took another couple of hours until he actually fell asleep.

SEAN

When Sean woke on Monday, he found himself rather looking forward to attending school with the others and learning. Declan escorted him and the three girls to the same building they'd gone to last week. "Don't leave here unless Victor or myself are here to pick you up," Declan instructed them.

"Why?" Sam asked with a frown. Sean hadn't told her or Tara about the conversation he'd overheard. He didn't want to upset them in case nothing actually happened.

"Until you're more comfortable with getting around, I'd rather you let one of us guide you."

Sean saw Declan glance at him and give him a very minute shake of his head. He didn't want them knowing about the potential danger yet either. They entered the building and Clarissa met them all in the front room this time. She smiled brightly and greeted all of them. "I've brought in another streak member to assist with my regular classes until we can assess where you're at and what needs to be our primary focus. Why don't you all follow me?"

Declan caught Sean's hand before he could trail behind

the others and tugged him into a firm embrace. Sean hugged him back tightly before pulling away. "I'll see you later," Declan said before turning and stalking out the door.

Sighing, Sean turned and spotted Clarissa waiting for him at a door further down the hallway. He hurried forward and she gestured for him to precede him into the room. "Sit wherever you'd like, please."

Sam and Tara helped Vicky to a small table with chairs nearby and sat on the floor next to her. Sean chose to sit near them. He felt uncomfortable because he really couldn't read. Sam and Tara would have taught him, but if Sean tried to ferret a newspaper downstairs and Carl spotted it, none of them would have been left unscathed.

Clarissa gave the girls a couple of pieces of paper and a pencil. "I'd like the two of you to answer whatever you can. It doesn't matter if it's right or wrong. I am only trying to ascertain what your knowledge is of the subjects."

Sam and Tara started to do as she instructed while Clarissa handed Vicky another piece of paper and another pencil. She knelt next to Vicky with a smile. "Hi, sweetie. I know you don't speak right now, but do you know how to add numbers together?"

Vicky nodded slowly, her face showing her wariness of Clarissa. Sean's heart ached for her. "Why don't you do the ones you can, okay? It doesn't matter if they're right or wrong. Just add the ones you think you can answer. I'll check back with you in a few minutes."

Sean watched Vicky while Clarissa went to her desk and grabbed a small box. She sat in front of Sean. "Today we're going to start with the basics of recognizing letters, ok?"

He nodded, nervous and slightly ashamed at just how little he knew about anything. But Clarissa put him at ease quickly with minimal effort and they made it through half of the cards she had with characters on them before she stopped. "Why don't you take the ones we've done so far and practice saying the letters on your own? I'm going to check in with the girls."

The rest of the day pretty much followed the same pattern. Sean's head throbbed a bit by the time they were ready to go home and he didn't join them in the dining room for lunch. Instead he headed upstairs to the room he shared with Declan where he collapsed across the bed, pulling a pillow over his eyes.

He heard the door open a couple minutes later then the bed dipped near him. A warm hand came to rest on his chest. "You okay, sexy?"

Declan's voice flowed over him and Sean sighed at how just hearing Declan's tenor caused a calmness to fill him. He rolled closer to Declan, dislodging the pillow, and squinted up at his mate. "My head hurts a little bit."

Before he knew Declan's intention, he'd moved both of them to where Sean's head rested in his lap and he started gently massaging Sean's temples. "Lot to learn?"

Sean closed his eyes and hummed, his body relaxing at Declan's touch. Declan didn't speak again for several long moments and Sean found himself starting to drift. But Declan's next words roused him from the beginnings of sleep. "I have some good news for you, Sean."

"Hmm?" he managed to push out.

"The Biancas are arriving tomorrow."

Sean opened his eyes and he sat up, dislodging Declan's hands. "Really?"

Declan smiled and nodded. "Their flight lands around midday and they will be back on streak lands by the afternoon."

Excitement and anxiety battled their way through Sean. "Do you think they'll know me?" Sean asked. "What if they don't remember me? Or they don't want me?"

"They couldn't possibly forget you or not want you," Declan replied, taking Sean's hand in his. "I promise you, baby, they will love you."

The knowledge that he would possibly be meeting his family for the first time tomorrow had him restless the remainder of the day. He could barely sit still or eat at dinnertime and more than once the others had to call his name to get his attention. After dinner Sam and Tara demanded to know what was wrong with him. Of course, they were happy for him, but there was still that one tiny seed of doubt in his heart. What if they really weren't his family? What if they had moved on and didn't want him disrupting their life? He hadn't been in it since he was a baby so maybe they had moved on and didn't want him upsetting the balance they had.

By bedtime, his bottom lip had been practically chewed raw and he couldn't lie still. He sat with his back against the headboard while Declan was in the bathroom brushing his teeth and preparing for bed. Would their son, his brother, even want to be his brother? What if they were disgusted by what his father had made him do? He started biting at his lip again and pulled both knees to his chest, wrapping his arms around them.

He barely registered Declan walking out of the bathroom strikingly naked or the movement of the mattress when Declan sat down beside him. It was only when Declan pulled him into his arms did Sean jerk back to awareness. "Ah, baby, you have to stop worrying so much," Declan murmured while using his thumb to dislodge Sean's lip from between his teeth.

"I can't," Sean whispered.

"You have nothing to worry about. I've known Nicole and Arthur almost my entire life and I have known Austin since he was a baby. They are good people and I am more than certain they will love you as much as I love you."

Sean sighed leaned into Declan, soaking in his warmth. "What's Nicole like?"

"She's warm and caring with a great sense of humor. But she's also strong on the inside. Like you. I'm pretty confident she's where you got your strength from."

"But I'm not strong," Sean protested.

"You are. You're the strongest person I've ever met and I will tell you that until the day we die. In order to survive the things you have, you'd have to be." Declan nuzzled at Sean's temple. "Try to get some sleep. Everything will be fine. I swear it."

They shifted around until they lay flat, Declan never letting Sean go. Declan's words made sense and he knew he'd always have Sam, Tara, and Vicky, but he couldn't shake the fear in him of being found wanting by his real parents. Declan passed out before him, leaving Sean to lie there staring at the ceiling, his mind still going in circles. It was late when he finally let sleep pull him under, no longer able to fight his drooping eyelids.

The following morning, Sean and the others were delivered to the school building once more. Only this time Sean found it beyond impossible to concentrate. Clarissa asked him more than once if he were all right. They'd barely accomplished anything by the time their classes with Clarissa were finished. Clarissa stopped him at the door after the girls had already headed toward the front. "Are you sure you're okay, Sean?"

He gave her a tremulous smile. "I'm fine, Ms. Clarissa. Just... I may be meeting my parents for the first time today and I can't help but worry they'll be disappointed in me."

"Oh, Sean." Clarissa wrapped him in a tight embrace. "No one could ever be disappointed in you. You're such a bright, amazing, strong individual. I've never known anyone I admire as much as I do you."

Sean gave her an incredulous look. "Admire?"

"How anyone could survive what you did for so long is something I can't imagine. I know I would never have been able to withstand it. And to care for the others as you have and still do. It's beyond humbling, Sean. You can't even see just how kind and sweet you are. They're going to love you and if I know anything about how a mother feels about their child, she is going to adore you."

Her words made him blush. "Thanks, Ms. Clarissa."

"Now go on before Declan comes searching for you." She gently nudged him out of the classroom, following behind him and closing the door. "Good luck today, but I don't think you'll need it."

Sean thought over everything she'd said on the walk back to the main house. While it helped settle him a fraction, it wasn't enough to curb his anxiety. He went straight to Declan's office instead of stopping in the dining room for lunch. He couldn't have eaten a stitch even if he'd wanted to.

Knocking, he heard Declan call out to come in and opened the door. Declan sat at his desk, staring at the computer screen. Sean waited until he looked up and then Declan smiled. "Hey, gorgeous. How was your day?"

The benign question almost made Sean snort, but he shrugged. "Couldn't really pay attention."

"Come here," Declan said, pushing back from the desk a bit. Sean walked over to him and Declan pulled him down into his lap. "Not much longer and then you can laugh at yourself later for being so worried. Until then, why don't you stay here with me and we can make out."

Sean eyed Declan. "Make out?"

Declan grinned and leaned in to kiss him, cupping Sean's cheek in one hand. "Making out means kissing you until you can't think straight," Declan said and captured Sean's lips again.

Of course, it worked. Within minutes he couldn't think past the feel of Declan's mouth on his or the evidence of Declan's desire against his bottom. Sean had grown to understand some of the things he could do to make Declan moan or growl. He especially liked when Declan purred and he could feel the vibrations in his own chest. They went straight to his lower region and dampened his underwear quite a bit. Opening his mouth, Sean sucked Declan's tongue into his, enjoying the rumble deep in Declan's throat.

Declan broke the kiss, panting, and rested his forehead against Sean's. "Damn, baby, you've certainly learned very quickly how to make me forget anything but the need to throw you over my desk and fuck you until we both can't walk straight."

Sean squeaked in embarrassment, his cheeks heating. "Declan!"

A husky laugh tumbled from Declan. "I love it when you blush."

"It's not nice to tease me," Sean reprimanded without heat.

"I'm sorry," Declan replied, still smirking. Sean rolled his eyes as he'd seen Sam do so often. He opened his mouth to say something back, but Declan captured his lips in another deep kiss.

Both of them were gasping for air and their lips swollen when Declan ended it the next time around. Sean sensed Declan's tiger just beneath the surface as he had many times since they'd mated. Usually it was only when Declan was either really angry or really turned on. This time though, he could actually feel his own tiger pacing in response, wanting nothing more than to let their mate dominate them, make them come apart as he always did. "Declan," Sean murmured.

"I can feel it too, sexy," Declan rasped. "But we don't have time for what I'd love to do to you right now."

Sean snickered and laid his head on Declan's shoulder. "Would it make me seem bad if I said I don't care?"

Declan kissed the side of Sean's neck. "Not at all. I would love nothing more than to say to hell with it. But I know you wouldn't want to have that scent on you when you meet the people who are most likely your parents for the first time."

Sean sat back on Declan's lap to look at him. His words reminding him of the soon-to-change-his-life event happening in the next hour or so. "You're right. Thank you."

"You don't need to thank me. You're my mate and I only want to make you happy."

Frowning, Sean said, "But I have no idea how to make you happy in return."

Declan's expression softened. "Baby, don't you understand how you just being in my life makes me happy? Nothing else matters."

"But-" Declan placed a finger over Sean's lips. "Nothing else matters."

Peace flowed over Sean and he nodded. Declan smiled. "Now, want to play a game of solitaire until they get here?"

"Okay."

Declan kept Sean on his lap the entire time, helping point out when Sean got stuck on what card to move. He found himself enjoying the game even more than last time and it even distracted him from his worries. Until a knock came at the office door. "Come in," Declan called.

Victor entered. "Alpha, the Biancas are here."

Sean stiffened and Declan ran his hand down Sean's back. "It's okay, Sean. Just try to relax." Looking at Victor, Declan said, "Can you have Rose bring them something to drink and seat them in the living room?"

"Of course, Alpha." Victor left.

Turning Sean enough to face him, Declan said, "Do you want me to go out there first and explain things to them?"

Did he? But Sean knew he couldn't hide. He needed to know if they were his family or not. So he shook his head. "No. I'll go with you."

Declan smiled. "So strong, gorgeous."

Sean rolled his eyes again, huffing, but he couldn't stop his lips from curling at the corners in answer. "Let's go."

They stood and Sean preceded Declan out of the office and down the hall. He stopped at the entrance to the living room, just out of eyesight, and took a deep breath. His heart pounded fiercely at his ribcage and his palms grew sweaty. Declan rested his hand on Sean's shoulder in comfort, but didn't say anything. Sean closed his eyes and breathed in once more. Then he stepped forward, coming to a halt in the doorway at the sight of a beautiful, dark-haired woman seated on one of the sofas.

A man, equally handsome as the woman was beautiful, sat next to her while a teenager, around Tara's age, slouched in one of the straight-backed chairs. It was the woman who glanced up first and she gasped, staring at Sean. Her hand rose to her chest and Sean felt as though he were staring into a mirror. Her eyes were the same sapphire blue as his own. They had the same long, slender nose resting above full light red lips.

"Nicky?" the man said, brows furrowing, and then he followed her gaze to Sean. His eyes widened and he stood immediately. "Alpha, who is this?"

Declan nudged Sean a little further into the room. "Arthur, Nicole. I'd like you to meet Sean, my mate."

They both remained where they were, but Sean could see

they were confused. The teenage boy looked up from his phone then and Sean realized he was looking at Austin. His possible brother. "Congratulations on finding your mate, Alpha," Arthur murmured, still staring at Sean.

"I don't understand," Nicole whispered. "Who is he?"

Sean almost jumped when Declan took his hand to lead him to the sofa. He'd been so focused on them, trying to gauge their feelings, their thoughts. Declan helped guide him to sit and then Declan began the long explanation of how he'd found Sean.

DECLAN

Tears ran down Nicole and Arthur's cheeks almost the entire time Declan talked about Ronnie being abducted, Sean helping him escape, and even the exhumed bodies now home with their families. "If we hadn't arrived when we did, Sean wouldn't be here with us," Declan said.

"What was the man's name?" Nicole asked, her voice quiet.

Sean clasped Declan's hand and took a deep breath. "Carl McNeely."

Nicole gasped while Arthur turned the air blue from curses. Sean flinched and burrowed closer to Declan. "It's all right, Sean," Declan murmured.

Arthur immediately stopped swearing and gave Sean an apologetic look.

"Why does it seem you know that name?" Declan asked.

Nicole swiped at her cheeks and gave a bitter smile. "Before I met Arthur, I dated Carl. He discovered I'm a shifter, but he didn't care. He swore to keep my secret. The year we were to be married, I met Arthur, my life mate. I couldn't marry Carl and I broke it off. When you find your life mate, it takes precedence over everything else."

Declan nodded.

"Carl grew angry and he threatened Arthur's life, my life, and he told me he'd find a way to make me pay. After Arthur and I mated, we never heard from him again. It wasn't long after that we were expecting our first child. Things were perfect and we were so excited to have a baby. I completely forgot the threat from Carl by the time the baby was born and it never once crossed my mind he would still be holding a grudge."

Nicole looked at Sean, tears welling in her eyes again. "A few years later, when I went to town to the mall for new clothing for our child, I turned my back for just a moment and when I looked back he was gone."

Declan passed Nicole a box of tissues from the side table. She gave him a tremulous smile in thank you. Taking one out and dabbing at her eyes, Nicole continued, "We looked everywhere. No one had even seen who took him. I still had hope he was okay, that he was alive, and whoever had taken him would care for him like I would have."

She never stopped watching Sean while she spoke. "I loved our son before I even held him in my arms for the first time."

Sean nibbled at his bottom lip, a habit Declan recognized as nervousness. He pressed a kiss to Sean's temple. "Do you think I-I'm your son?" Sean whispered.

Nicole stood up and moved to sit beside him. She took his hands in hers and gave him a watery smile and a small nod. "You look so much like Arthur, but you have my eyes."

"Is my name really Sean?" he asked. It had never occurred to Declan to doubt Sean's real name, but it made sense to think McNeely would have changed it or not known it.

She nodded again. "You were named after my grandfather. Sean Vasiliev."

Tears welled in Sean's eyes and they spilled down his cheeks. Nicole pulled Sean into a fierce hug, her eyes closing as she started crying again. "My baby. I've missed you so much."

Silent sobs shook Sean's slender frame and Declan's heart ached for everything his mate had lost and filled with hope for the future for all of them. He ran his hand over Sean's leg in a comforting gesture.

Arthur came forward and perched on the edge of the coffee table in front of the three of them. He didn't say anything before wrapping the both of them in a hard hug. "Welcome home, son," Arthur murmured.

Austin, who'd been quiet until then, said, "Does this mean I have to share my room?"

Nicole chuckled. "I think Alpha Declan plans on keeping Sean here, sweetie, since they're mates."

"Oh, okay. Cool." Austin shrugged and returned to the game on his phone.

Declan considered cuffing Austin on the back of the head for being so standoffish, but he could understand how it would be hard to relate to suddenly having a brother appear out of nowhere. It would probably take the teenager some time to adjust. "Would you like to stay for dinner?" Declan asked.

Nicole nodded, never once releasing her hold on Sean. She pulled away from him enough to see his face. "You must tell me everything. I want to know my son."

Sean frowned. "There isn't much to tell."

"There's a lot for you to tell me. What does your tiger half look like? Are you all white with black stripes or a shade of orange?"

"He's all white with black stripes. It's how I had the idea he may well be your missing child," Declan said.

"I'm so pleased!" Nicole replied.

"Are you both tigers?" Sean asked.

"We are. Your father is a white tiger while I am only half tiger, half lion. My father was a lion while my mother was a tiger. I'm what they call a liger nowadays. Though the term didn't exist when I was first born."

Declan excused himself to go alert Rose to the addition of three more to dinner. Satisfaction and love trickled through him when he heard Sean losing some of his reticence and begin asking questions. He knew Sean had been worried, fearful they would reject him. Their bond allowed him to feel many of Sean's emotions. The only way Sean would be reassured had been to meet them. Declan had known Nicole for most of his life and he'd seen how devastated she'd been after Sean had been abducted.

Rose was in the kitchen with Sam and Tara helping her prep some of the ingredients for the evening meal. "We'll have three more for dinner," Declan told her when he reached the counter. Snagging a piece of tomato, he tossed it into his mouth and leaned against the counter by Rose. "The Biancas are staying."

"Who are they?" Tara asked, her brow furrowed.

Declan debated on letting Sean tell them, but he didn't want to lie either. "They're Sean's parents."

Sam dropped the knife she held while Tara's eyes widened. "His parents?" Sam whispered.

Declan sensed the fear and agitation from the two of them. He approached Sam and rested a hand on her shoulder. "It'll be all right. Remember, he's mated to me so he'll be staying here."

Sam swallowed hard and nodded, but Declan could see she still wasn't reassured. "They're a part of the streak, Sam.

Even if he were to move in with them, they wouldn't be going far."

"Oh, that's good," Sam mumbled.

"Would you like to meet them?"

Tara and Sam shook their heads. "Not yet," Tara replied.

Uncertainty still shone on both of their faces. Declan looked at Tara. "Can we talk for a few moments?"

The uncertainty grew on Tara's features and Declan said, "It's nothing bad."

Tara looked at Sam who didn't say anything. "Can Sam be there?"

"Whatever makes you most comfortable, Tara."

Declan led them to the dining room table and gestured for them to sit. He sat in front of Tara and never allowed his gaze to waiver. "We believe we've found your pack."

Tara paled. "No," she whispered.

"We haven't contacted them yet, but I really do believe they should know you're alive."

"But I don't want to leave Sean or Sam or Vicky!" Tara exclaimed.

"I won't force you to leave or to contact them if you really don't want to, but Tara, put yourself in their shoes. Your baby is here with you, in your belly, but what if he or she were already born and someone took them from you. Wouldn't you want to know what happened to them? Were they being taken care of? Were they being loved?"

Tara fidgeted in her seat and wrapped a protective arm around her protruding abdomen. It wouldn't be long now before she gave birth. "What if they try to take me away?"

"I won't allow it to happen, Tara. I promise. They can come here to visit you and really it's only about a three-hour drive to their pack lands."

"Tara, you can't seriously be thinking about this, can you?" Sam demanded.

"Alpha Declan is right, though," she whispered. "I can't imagine not being able to hold my child after she's born. What if someone took her from me?"

"No one is taking your baby!" Sam growled. Impressive for a lynx.

"But what if someone did?" Tara replied. She looked at Declan, the steel core he knew she possessed evident in her gaze. "I'll do it."

Declan took her hand in his. "It'll be all right."

"Tara, you can't!" Sam exclaimed. "You can't leave us!"

"I'm not leaving," Tara said. "But Declan is right. I have to at least let them know I'm alive."

Sam scowled and crossed her arms over her chest. "If they take you away from here, Tara, I'm going to kick your butt."

Declan bit back a chuckle while Tara sighed. "I'm not going to leave, Sam."

He knew Sam's anger was merely a front to hide her fear and worry. The things they'd witnessed together, the things they'd experienced together, had bonded them more as a family than if they were actually blood. "I'll have Victor reach out to them today."

"What's the name of the pack?" Tara asked.

"The Farkas Pack. The alpha is named Andras Veres." Declan noticed her tense and some of the color in her cheeks leeched as she paled. "Do you know him?"

"Th-That's my last name," Tara rasped. "Veres."

Declan grimaced. If Tara was indeed related to the alpha, it would be difficult to keep her with them. He didn't remember much about Andras. In fact, he couldn't even be sure the man had been at the last gathering they'd had. The white wolf he'd run with had definitely been female. Perhaps Andras had a mate and Tara was their daughter? "We'll find out what we can before worrying," Declan said. "Okay?"

"I don't want to go back to them," Tara said. "I want to stay with you, Sean, Vicky, Tara, and everyone!"

Until he'd known of Tara's possible relation to the alpha, he'd thought for certain it wouldn't be an issue for her to remain on streak lands if she wished it. But knowing her blood relatives started with the alpha, if they wanted her back with them, Declan wasn't sure how he'd stop them from retrieving her. Yet despite Tara's concerns about being taken away, he knew he couldn't not inform them now that they knew the truth. He already had enough disgruntled clans on his hands. One of which wanted his head on a pike.

Standing, he walked to her side, placed his hand on her shoulder and gave a gentle squeeze. "Whatever happens, everything will work out as it's meant to."

He went to Victor who still stood near the entrance of the living room and requested he reach out to the Farkas Pack to extend the alpha and his family an invite. Victor gave a silent nod and left while Declan joined Sean and the Biancas. Arthur had moved to sit next to Sean on the couch so Declan chose a nearby chair.

Austin sat up straighter in the chair across from Declan and started scenting the air. He frowned. "What's that smell?"

"What smell?" Declan asked, sniffing also to see what Austin referred to. He caught Nicole, Arthur, and Sean, but didn't find anything out of the ordinary.

"It's like... chocolate with..." He breathed in again, nose higher this time. "Ginger."

Nicole looked at Austin. "I don't smell anything, sweetie."

Austin stood and started wandering through the living room to the front entrance. Declan decided to follow, curious if his current thought was right. "I've never scented anything like it," Austin murmured, moving further toward the dining room.

A light laugh came from the kitchen and Austin turned to

follow the sound. He stopped in the doorway of the kitchen and Declan remained just behind him. Tara turned to look their way where she stood arguing with Sam over her sneaking several pieces of whatever she was cutting up. He saw Tara's eyes widen and she dropped the knife she held. Austin froze, staring at her.

"What's going on?" Sam asked, frowning.

"I believe young Austin here has found his mate," Declan replied.

Sam's mouth dropped open and she glanced between Tara and Austin. Austin moved closer to Tara, only stopping once he stood in front of her. "Hi," Austin murmured.

Tara flushed and managed a rough, "hi," in return.

Declan smirked before returning to the living room. No matter what the alpha of the Farkas pack thought, now Tara had ties to the Royal Taiga streak. He sat in the chair he'd left previously. When Nicole asked him about what just happened, he merely replied, "A mate finding a mate."

The remainder of the evening went by with everyone clamoring to get to know one another. Sean introduced his parents to Sam and Tara where Austin wouldn't let her hand go through most of dinner. Nicole welcomed Tara to the family, but requested they wait until they were older to bond. Declan couldn't have been happier for Tara. He knew she'd been scared of being taken away from the only family she'd ever known, but now they would have no choice except to let her stay if she wished it.

Tara's secrets had been pulled into the light, but now they still needed to locate Sam and Vicky's clans. Something Declan was certain wouldn't be easy. But nothing could be resolved in a day. They'd already accomplished so much in the time since finding them. Declan figured it wouldn't hurt to wait a little longer.

They followed the Biancas out onto the front porch

where Nicole reluctantly hugged Sean goodnight and promised to return the following day after his lessons with Clarissa. Sean watched them leave, his emotions plainly felt through their connection. Declan wrapped an arm around Sean's shoulders and pulled him into his side tightly. "They'll still be here tomorrow."

"I know. I just… I can't believe how much things have changed. I always believed I'd die in that basement and one of the others would be forced to bury me. But you saved me, saved them, and you've given me everything I have ever dreamed about. I can't even begin to think of a way to repay you for everything."

Declan turned Sean to face him, tilting his head back until their eyes met. "You've given me more than enough, my love. You've given me three new sisters, a new brother, and a new mother and father. You've given me your heart and your soul. There is nothing more I could ever wish for."

Sean closed the scant inches separating them and kissed him, his hands coming to rest on Declan's pectorals. Declan slipped his arms around Sean's waist, tugging him closer. When they broke apart, Declan boosted Sean onto the porch railing, nudging his way between Sean's thighs. "The only other thing you can give to me is to always be happy. Do the things in this life you want. Just take me with you and never leave my side."

A loving smile broke over Sean's lips and Sean said, "I wouldn't want to go anywhere without you, Declan. I love you."

"I love you, too, sexy," Declan growled and leaned in to kiss him once again.

Life wasn't perfect. There was no guarantee in life that they'd always be blissful, but Declan sure as hell planned on trying for Sean. The threat of something dark lurking, waiting for the chance to strike, worried Declan. He didn't know exactly what was coming, but whatever it was, he'd protect Sean and his streak until his dying breath. Though if he died, Sean would follow, but he didn't regret sharing his soul with Sean. He could never regret saving the one destined to be his. Now his only fear would be keeping both of them safe because of the choice he'd made the night he saved Sean's life.

Sean broke their kiss long enough to say, "I think it's time for bed."

Declan chuckled huskily. "I think you may be right, mate."

He lifted Sean from the railing, but didn't set him on his feet, instead he urged Sean to wrap his legs around his waist. The night had grown cool around them and the only lights were those of the streak members who lived closest to the main house and the moonlight overhead. A strange noise brought Declan around and he saw someone stumbling toward the front porch, a hand to their stomach. He quickly set Sean down by the door and demanded, "Go inside and get Victor. Don't leave the house."

Sean tried to protest, but Declan gave him a harsh look. "Go."

The seriousness in Declan's tone must have worked because Sean wrenched open the door and rushed inside while Declan spun to face the individual. Declan's breath caught when he realized the person coming toward him was Kyle. The bounty hunter looked beat to hell with blood covering him almost everywhere. Declan darted forward to catch Kyle before he could crash to the ground. "Kyle, who did this?"

Victor exited the house then and Declan barked, "Go get Cameron!"

Declan could see cuts from claw or knife all over Kyle's arms, legs, and even a deep wound on his belly. It took a lot to kill a shifter, but blood loss would do it every time. The shirt Kyle wore was soaked to the bone with the sticky life essence and he'd grown pale. His eyes were closed, his breathing thready at best. "Kyle, can you hear me?" Declan asked.

A low moan escaped Kyle's lips, but Declan couldn't get anything else from him. He felt for a pulse and heaved a sigh when he found one, slow but there. Cameron and Victor arrived moments later. Cameron, a man of poise and elegance, blanched and swore up a storm when he saw Kyle lying there. "What happened?" Cameron demanded.

"He arrived like this. I couldn't get anything from him before he fell unconscious."

"We need to get him to my clinic. Fast. He's going to need blood with how much he's lost already. Hurry!"

Declan and Victor supported Kyle between them as they followed Cameron across the compound to the clinic. Cameron led them straight into an exam room where he indicated for them to lay Kyle on the bed. "Declan, I need you to go into the supply room across the hall. Get me the kit with the scissors, thread, and suture needle. Victor, I need you to cut his clothes off."

They hurried to do what Cameron instructed while Cameron began slipping on gloves and arranging the supplies needed to begin the blood transfusion. Declan came back into the room to find Cameron already sliding a small tube into Kyle's arm. He moved quickly and efficiently. "I need to suture his wounds before I start the transfusion or he'll just lose what I put in him. Declan, give me the kit."

Declan handed him the small plastic box. Cameron expertly prepped the needle. He began working on the largest wound, the one in Kyle's stomach, stitching it fast and clean. Once done, he examined the other wounds, but found them to be superficial at best. "Until he is conscious enough to shift, he won't start the healing process. I'm going to give him enough blood to replenish him, but when he wakes, we need him to shift."

Nodding, Declan and Victor stood aside while Cameron set up the bag of blood. Kyle hadn't awakened once and Declan prayed the man would make it. He also wanted to know who'd done this to him because he fully intended on making them pay. Kyle may be transient, but he'd always come home. Declan considered him a member of his streak and no one fucked with his family.

"Is he going to make it, Cam?" Declan asked.

Cameron appeared stoic, unaffected by the state Kyle was in, but Declan knew him well enough to know it was all a façade. There was worry and fear in Cameron's eyes. "He better," Cameron growled.

They could only wait. Declan called Rose and gave her the rundown on what had happened. He asked her to make sure Sean got some rest. He had no idea how long he'd be there. After disconnecting the call, he paced the small hallway, anxious to be there when Kyle woke. He'd walked the same path dozens of times when Cameron finally called for him. "Alpha!"

Declan strode into the room and straight to Kyle's side. "Kyle? Can you hear me?"

"Th-They're co-coming," Kyle moaned. "Couldn't st-st-stop them."

"Who's coming, Kyle?" Declan demanded.

"The-They kn-know he's he-here," Kyle managed and then he shifted. A large black panther took his place.

Declan sighed and rubbed at his face. They wouldn't get any further answers out of him now.

"He'll sleep for quite some time, Alpha. If you'd like I will call you when he wakes," Cameron murmured, his hand reverently stroking down the panther's side.

"Thank you, Cam. For saving him."

Cameron nodded. "Just doing my job."

Declan knew something wasn't right between the two men, but he wasn't one to pry or stick his nose into their business unless it outright affected the streak. "Call me as soon as he wakes."

Thankfully Kyle would be all right now that he'd shifted. Declan caught a glimpse of the clock as he walked through the downstairs of his home. Just after one in the morning. He heaved a sigh of exhaustion on his way to his room. Sean was already asleep when he entered the bedroom so he quietly went in and closed the bathroom door to take a quick shower. He made short work of rinsing away Kyle's blood and sweat from the day's activities. Finished, he shut off the water, grabbed a towel, and dried off before tossing the towel over the shower rod to dry.

He slid into bed naked and immediately curled around Sean. Sean murmured in his sleep and snuggled closer to him. Smiling, he nuzzled at Sean's temple. They wouldn't know anything more from Kyle until he awoke again, but Kyle's words along with Casey Asher's warning sent a frisson of apprehension through Declan. The last time he could recall there being a force targeting their kind had been the witches, but their numbers had drastically dwindled in the century plus some odd years since the last war.

Declan decided to shelve all worries and doubts until they had more information. They could only prepare for the worst and hope for the best. Maybe Casey's visions had been wrong or maybe they could be changed if they could figure out what was threatening them. He wrapped around Sean even tighter. The only thing he knew for certain was he wouldn't let anything more happen to Sean or the others. They deserved a life of peace and freedom from fear.

Sean mumbled again. "Declan?"

"Shh, go back to sleep, baby."

"Is Kyle okay?" Sean whispered.

"He'll be fine."

"That's good," Sean murmured before drifting off again.

His heart swelled with pride over Sean's natural instincts to care for others and Declan knew his streak couldn't have a better Alpha-mate. Sean surely held Declan's and his tiger's hearts in his slender hands and once the entire streak grew to know him, he'd have theirs just as well. He closed his eyes, breathed in Sean's familiar scent deep, and drifted off dreaming of the places he intended on taking Sean to explore together. The rest of it could wait for another day to intrude upon the peace they'd found so far.

Love paranormal shifter stories? My True Mates series is perfect! Check out Book One Chasing Seth & Book Two Forgiving Thayne!

Thank you for reading Declan - Heart of a Tiger. If you enjoyed it, I would truly appreciate if you could let your friends know so they can also enjoy the relationship between Declan and Sean. If you leave a review for Declan - Heart of a Tiger on the site in which you purchased the book, Goodreads or your own blog, I would love to read it. Please email the link to jrloveless@gmail.com

Royal Taiga Streak Book Two coming 2021!

ABOUT THE AUTHOR

J.R. Loveless began her adventure in writing at the young age of twelve. Her foray into creating her own worlds and telling her characters' life stories was triggered by her own love of reading. She currently resides in South Florida with her dog and two cats, and by day works as a manager for a financial lending institute.

Her journey into gay romance began in 2005 when she began posting her original fiction on a forum for feedback and readers' pleasure. In 2010, a good friend urged her to submit to a publishing company, and the day she received the acceptance and contract was the best day of her life. Since then, she has been noted to be one of the most purchased audio books after Fifty Shades of Grey on Audiobook.com and received best gay romantic fiction for Touch Me Gently in the 2011 TLA Gaybies.

J.R. adores her fans and loves hearing from them.

Never miss out on an update or sale by subscribing to J.R.'s Website. As a thank you, you'll receive a free short novelette called White Rain about two friends who become lovers!

J.R.'s Blog

J.R.'s Facebook Reader Group